What should a proper lady do when she believes her days are numbered?

Step One: Take a Lover . . .

After being told she will not survive beyond the year's end, prim and lovely Marguerite Laurent intends to live what remains of her life to the very fullest. Though she may never know love, she *will* know passion—and she agrees to a whirlwind romance with a former admirer. But hours before embarking upon her grand adventure, Marguerite is abducted by an unscrupulous rogue who boldly announces his intentions to bed and *wed* her before the week is out!

Step Two: Live With No Regrets . . .

Ash Courtland pulled himself up from the gutter to become a successful man of business, and now he wants revenge on his one-time partner for betraying him. Still, his enemy's bewitching daughter is most certainly *not* about to surrender her innocence to the infuriating—if shockingly attractive—cad who took her captive. Yet with no more than a touch, Ash makes her tremble with desire . . . and resisting the heat of his passion could cost Marguerite her last, best chance for ecstasy.

By Sophie Jordan

WICKED NIGHTS WITH A LOVER
IN SCANDAL THEY WED
SINS OF A WICKED DUKE
SURRENDER TO ME
ONE NIGHT WITH YOU
TOO WICKED TO TAME
ONCE UPON A WEDDING NIGHT

Sophie Jordan

Wicked Nights With A Lover

AVON
An Imprint of HarperCollinsPublishers

This is a work of fiction. Names, characters, places, and incidents are products of the author's imagination or are used fictitiously and are not to be construed as real. Any resemblance to actual events, locales, organizations, or persons, living or dead, is entirely coincidental.

AVON BOOKS
An Imprint of HarperCollins*Publishers*
10 East 53rd Street
New York, New York 10022-5299

Copyright © 2010 by Sharie Kohler
ISBN 978-0-06-157923-3
www.avonromance.com

First Avon Books paperback printing: December 2010

Avon Trademark Reg. U.S. Pat. Off. and in Other Countries, Marca Registrada, Hecho en U.S.A.
HarperCollins® is a registered trademark of HarperCollins Publishers.

Printed in the U.S.A.

10 9 8 7 6 5 4 3 2 1

For Lindsay
with love for hours of laughter

Chapter 1

Marguerite Laurent was not given to emotional histrionics as so many females she had come across in the course of her five and twenty years. It was this, her lack of excitability, her utter constancy, that perfectly suited her for her particular vocation. Only now, on this particular occasion, did she find herself tested beyond custom.

"But I simply don't understand," Mrs. Danbury whined in shrill, petulant tones. "Why must you leave now? I am going to live! I should think you would be happy about that." The widow affected a great sniffle as she set about her morning regimen of toast and honey—at least her morning regimen when she had not been prostrate at death's door. She brandished a drippy spoon in the air, waving it like a weapon to be plied. "One would almost think you wished I had died."

"Don't be silly," Marguerite gently chided. "You are well. A fact, I promise you, that fills me with only the greatest relief."

Mrs. Danbury sniffed yet again, and repositioned her considerable girth in her chair as she took a crunchy bite.

Against all odds and the dire predictions of physicians, the widow Danbury had taken a turn for the *better*. Such the case, Marguerite counted herself unneeded and had already begun preparations to move on to her next assignment. Moistening her lips, she yet again went about the difficult task of explaining to her patroness that she only attended to the infirm and dying.

"You're going to live, Mrs. Danbury. While I couldn't be more pleased, I am a sick nurse." *I'm better with the dying*. Biting back that morbid thought, Marguerite stepped forward and cupped a linen beneath the dripping spoon before a dollop of honey landed on Mrs. Danbury's dressing robe.

The widow pursed her lips. "Well, you could be my *well* nurse."

Marguerite smiled, but could not help her niggle of discomfort. This was a wholly unique situation for her. By the time the agency referred her, her patients were quite beyond recovery. No one had ever recuperated before. She'd never had to beg an exit. Usually, the family was happy to be rid of the sight of her for all that she reminded them of their loved one's final days.

"I have another assignment waiting." Marguerite had received the note this very morning from Mrs. Driscoll at the agency that a position was available.

"You cannot go yet," Mrs. Danbury insisted with an unappealing pout of her honey-moist lips. "Not until we're sure I'm well and mended."

Marguerite blinked. "Why, you're a vision of health, Mrs. Danbury. You've been free of your bed well over a fortnight. Your physician vows you are cured. Yesterday you rode in the park and ate so many scones that I lost count."

"Posh! Meaningless all. I can't be certain until I've seen *her*. Only then can I know for certain. She'll be here any moment. Now excuse me while I dress." With a flick of her hand, the two maids lurking in the corner rushed forward, hurrying after the widow as she fairly skipped into the dressing room.

Her? Marguerite remained where she was, contemplating the bags she'd already packed and asked the butler to see collected from her room. She was so close to escaping. The need rose hot and thick inside her, climbing up her throat. Mrs. Danbury was a capricious creature, given to fits of laughing and weeping interchangeably. She drained the energy out of Marguerite. As mad as it sounded, Marguerite craved the predictability and calm of the dying.

Mrs. Danbury's voice drifted from the dressing room as she berated one of the maids, serving to confirm all of Marguerite's dread.

"I've just risen from my deathbed! I no longer need look a corpse, you daft girl. Put that horrid thing down and fetch me my blue silk tea gown."

Marguerite squeezed her eyes shut for a moment, hoping to block out the sound of her shrill, excitable voice.

A knock sounded at the suite's doors. The housekeeper stuck her head inside the room. Marguerite nodded toward the dressing room. The portly woman walked with a briskness that defied her girth for the dressing room door. With a knock, she announced, "Mrs. Danbury, Madame Foster has arrived."

"Excellent! Tell her that Miss Laurent and I shall be right down."

Madame Foster?

Moments later, Mrs. Danbury swept into the room in a flurry of blue silk. "Come, Marguerite, dear. We shall find out if I am truly on the mend and whether you can take your leave or not."

A knot in her throat, Marguerite followed. Uncharitable or not, she somehow suspected she would not care for this Madame Foster.

"Tell me, Madame Foster," Mrs. Danbury encouraged between bites of frosted biscuits. Marguerite watched as crumbs fell from her lips to her silk skirts. The widow didn't flicker an eye over the mess tumbling from her mouth, her attention trained on the garishly attired woman across from her. "What do you see?"

Madame Foster clucked her tongue and rotated the teacup in her heavily beringed fingers, even as she glanced furtively at the room's appointments, assessing with the rapacity of a predator.

Marguerite frowned from where she sat near the window, fairly certain the female was looking for anything she might pocket before leaving.

"Ahhh," the woman murmured, refocusing her attention on the cup.

"Yes? Yes?" Mrs. Danbury leaned forward eagerly.

Madame frowned slightly and turned the cup around, her movements suddenly quick. She glanced from the cup to Mrs. Danbury's animated face and released a heavy sigh. When she returned her attention to the dregs at the bottom of the teacup, her frown deepened into a scowl.

"What?" Mrs. Danbury asked shrilly. "Dear woman, tell me what you see!"

The woman set the cup down with a decided click on its saucer and motioned impatiently for Mrs. Danbury's hand. The widow quickly stretched her arm across the table, losing her lily-white fingers in the diviner's grasping ones.

Madame Foster bowed her turban-swathed head and closed her eyes as though in prayer. For moments, she said nothing. Only the ticking clock on the mantel could be heard in the hush.

Marguerite leaned forward in her chair, duly impressed with the intense expression on the woman's face. It was like she wasn't even in the room anymore but transported elsewhere. A truly affecting performance. To her credit, she was quite the convincing charlatan.

With a sharp breath, Madame Foster dropped Mrs. Danbury's hand. Shaking, she rose quickly to her feet, her many bracelets clanging together on her arms in her haste. "That is all for today," she said in clearly affected accents.

"What? No! No!" Mrs. Danbury lurched to her feet. "What did you see? You cannot leave. I'll pay you anything . . . you must tell me!"

With an unladylike mutter, Marguerite stood, unable to witness another moment of this farce, certain the female was only working at some ploy to extort more money from the pathetic and far too gullible widow.

Then something happened.

The diviner turned—looked away from the widow. Only Marguerite still saw her face. And she could not help wondering why she should feign such distress at that moment, free from the widow's view. Madame Foster's eyes, glassy and panicked, darted to the door, eager for escape. She skirted the table, avoided Mrs. Danbury's stretching hands. "I cannot—" she mumbled.

"Please, whatever you saw . . . whatever it was

. . . wouldn't you want to be told? To know?"

Halfway to the door, Madame Foster froze.

Feeling invisible, and not unhappy for that fact, Marguerite looked back and forth between the two women, wondering how she had ever come to be trapped in such a mad scene.

Slowly, Madame Foster turned, her gaze narrow and thoughtful. "That depends." She advanced slowly, moistening her lips. "Do you wish to know the hour of your death? Should anyone wish for such knowledge?"

Marguerite sucked in a breath, a shiver chasing down her spine. *Oh, no.* She wouldn't be so wicked, so irresponsible as to pretend . . .

Mrs. Danbury nodded doggedly. "I've lived half a century." She drew a deep, ragged breath. Marguerite read the fear in the lines of her face, heard it in the quaver of her voice, however much she presented an image of bravado. "However much time I've left, I would want to know."

Madame Foster nodded, pursing her lips. "Very well."

Marguerite strode forward, intent on putting an end to this madness and stop the swindler from placing an expiration on Mrs. Danbury's life. Except she didn't move swiftly enough.

"The truth, as I saw with my own eyes, is that you'll not live out the week."

Mrs. Danbury screamed, clutching a hand to her great bosom as she fell, plummeting like a sinking ship to the Persian rug.

With an inelegant snort, Marguerite wondered if the lady's death had not arrived upon that very moment. Prostrate on the rug, she greatly resembled a corpse.

Helping Mrs. Danbury to the settee, Marguerite glanced around to find the cause for all the trouble gone. Vanished like a wisp of smoke.

Determined to stop the culprit and bring her back, force her to confess that she was a liar and a charlatan, Marguerite patted her patient on the arm and raced from the room after her.

"Wait! Stop!"

Madame Foster shot a frightened look over her shoulder and pushed her considerable girth harder toward the front doors.

Younger and significantly lighter of foot, Marguerite caught up with her and snatched her by the end of her bright blue shawl. "Oh, no you don't!

You're not going anywhere until you march back up there and tell Mrs. Danbury she's not going to die *this* week!"

Madame Foster tugged on her colorful shawl, twisting it around her arm. "I won't do any such thing."

"You miserable wretch. This is not a game. Have you any idea what you've done to that woman?" Marguerite stabbed a finger toward the stairs.

"You think I enjoy this? You think I like letting people know their less than promising destinies? Usually, I lie. But not about something like this." She jerked her turbaned head toward the stairs. "Mark my words, that woman will be dead before the week is out, and she deserves to know she has so little time left. I'd wish to know."

"You mean to explain to me that *you* believe this rot?" Shaking her head, Marguerite hissed, "Never mind. I don't care. March up those stairs and take back everything you said before I call the Guard. Tell Mrs. Danbury it was a mistake." Marguerite waved a hand wildly. "Tell her you had another look into your crystal ball and you were wrong . . . you saw her eighty years old in a rocking chair—"

"Try to consider if it were you. Wouldn't you want to know?"

Marguerite shook her head, furious. "Spare me the ethical obligations of a *seer*," she scoffed. Snatching hold of the woman's arm, she tugged her toward the stairs, not about to give up. "You're going to tell that woman—"

Marguerite stopped, turning cold at the sudden look on Madame Foster's face. She'd seen the rapt, frightened expression before. Only moments before when she'd clutched Mrs. Danbury's hands.

A sick, wilting sensation twisted in her belly. Marguerite loosened her grip, eager to sever the contact, but then Madame Foster tightened her hold, keeping her hostage, her eyes eerie-bright, glassy and faraway.

"Let me go," she hissed, tugging at her hand and marveling at the older woman's strength.

Desperate, Marguerite stomped down on her foot, finally freeing herself. Rubbing her hand, she wondered if she shouldn't simply wash her hands of this madhouse and move on to her next assignment.

"You," Madame Foster whispered, her gaze focused again, eyes darting avidly over Marguerite's face in a way that reminded her of a wild animal. "I've seen your death."

Marguerite resisted the small chill the words elicited, reminding herself that this woman was a charlatan. Propping her hands on her hips, she asked, "Indeed? Mine, as well? This is an inauspicious day, is it not? Do I have but a week to live, too?"

"No." The woman readjusted her shawl around herself. "You have more time than that. Before the year is out, you'll meet your end. I have seen it with my own eyes. This Christmas shall be your last."

Marguerite could not stop her shiver. "I think you should leave."

Madame Foster nodded as though she couldn't agree more. "Aye, I've had enough of this house. I'm sorry for both of you. But you especially." Her gaze roamed her face, eyes brimming with pity. "So young. And such a terrible accident." She clucked her tongue. "Tragic."

Vexed beyond her limit, Marguerite pulled the front door open herself, with no care that she was effectively kicking one of Mrs. Danbury's guests from the house. Her further presence could bring no good. "Leave."

"Happily." Madame Foster departed. It took every effort not to slam the door behind her. Even from where she stood, the wails of her employer could be heard above stairs. She would not be easy to soothe. With a sigh, Marguerite started up the stairs, unable to credit the heaviness settling in her chest.

She didn't believe the swindler's claims for one moment. She didn't believe in spells or magic or people who predicted fate. Rubbish. If she could see it, touch it, taste it, then it was real.

At week's end, she would have her proof. Mrs. Danbury would be fine. Hale and hearty and sane. Sane, if not again, then perhaps for the first time in her life, with the evidence of her foolishness staring her in the face.

And Marguerite would be free to move on to her next assignment.

Chapter 2

A week later, Marguerite was free to move to her next assignment. Mrs. Danbury was dead.

Standing over the still warm body of her employer, she stared hard at the lifeless form until her eyes ached. She stared. And she stared. As if she could *will* the woman to rise and not be *dead*.

She'd witnessed countless deaths, stood alongside the families and friends as they mourned, shared stoically in their sorrow. And yet never had she felt like this. This was different.

This couldn't be happening.

Her chest constricted, air impossible to draw. Guilt, she realized, although she couldn't credit such an emotion. She had afforded her patient every care . . . even as she had not believed, up until the very end, that Mrs. Danbury was actually relapsing, actually *dying*. She had performed every measure to try and save her life. All for naught. Madame Foster had been right.

She blinked her dry, aching eyes. When Mrs. Danbury took a turn for the worse, declining swiftly over the course of three days, Marguerite had refused to believe that the *seer* could possibly have been correct. It was insupportable. For if she were correct . . .

Marguerite shook her head fiercely and swallowed against the terrible thickness in her throat. She directed her attention back to Mrs. Danbury's grieving daughter. An unfortunate creature with a too-large nose and a regrettable moustache. She had never wed. Before Marguerite's arrival, she had been her mother's constant companion. To say Marguerite's presence was a point of resentment would be an underestimation.

"Why? Why? She was so much better . . . on the mend, you said so!" Miss Danbury beat the bed beside her mother, very much like a child in a tantrum. "You said so, Marguerite, you said so!"

Marguerite flinched. She couldn't say a word, couldn't offer an explanation. Madame Foster's face materialized in her mind. *You'll not live out the week*. Her prophetic words had come to pass.

Shaking her head, Marguerite placed her hand on the young woman's shoulders, only to be shaken off.

She wet her lips to summon her customary words of sympathy. "I'm sorry. Your mother lived a good life. A full life . . . and a life lived is nothing to grieve."

She uttered the words every single time . . . had heard them once, when she'd first begun as a sick nurse. A friend of the bereaved family had offered the words of solace within her hearing and she thought them terribly wise. Now she thought them tragic. Tragic for someone like herself . . . because she hadn't lived a particularly *good* life. Thus far, she could not characterize her life as *full* either. Her life simply . . . *was*. A series of days passing, one after the other.

This realization had eluded her . . . perhaps because she had assumed she had so much time left. Time enough to live a *good* life. A *full* life. She folded her suddenly cold hands before her, looking away from the recently departed Mrs. Danbury enshrined in her bed and cursing Madame Foster for making her suddenly examine the state of her life.

All at once, the sight of death chilled her, affected her as never before, tangible as any hand that might reach out and seize hold of her.

"You're a liar!" Miss Danbury choked. "A liar! I hope you die, you dreadful creature!"

With a cold, humorless smile curving her lips, Marguerite turned and left the room, wondering in the darkest corner of her heart if Miss Danbury's wish might not soon come to fruition.

It was much later before Marguerite escaped to her room. The undertaker had come and left. The arrangements had been made. Miss Danbury had not been fit to cope, so the task fell to Marguerite. She knew the undertaker well and had been able to expedite matters with her usual efficiency, pretending there was nothing extraordinary about Widow Danbury's passing.

With a weary sigh, she fell back in the chair beside the window that overlooked the small courtyard situated behind the townhouse. Over the past few months, she'd enjoyed this room, particularly the view. Even in the grip of early winter, the trees looked lovely, the branches swimming in the breeze, their few remaining leaves clinging with laudable tenacity.

Her eyes drifted shut and she began to doze, the toll of the last days catching up with her. A knock sounded, and she rose with a start, smoothing her skirts before opening the door to the housekeeper.

"Mrs. Hannigan," she greeted. "Did you need something?"

"No, no, dear. Sorry to disturb you. I know it's been a long day, a right trial, and you've taken the brunt of Miss Danbury's pain, don't we all know it. But this letter arrived this morning." She pulled an envelope from her apron. "I thought you might like it now. Perhaps it's from one of those friends of yours." She shrugged one thick shoulder. "Thought you could tolerate a bit of cheer."

Marguerite's heart immediately lightened as she grasped the crisp envelope. A letter from either Fallon or Evie would certainly lift her spirits. Her friends were both happily wed . . . leading full lives. Despite their less than orthodox court-ships, they had found love and happiness in their marriages.

"Thank you, Mrs. Hannigan."

"Good night, dear. See you in the morning."

She nodded and this time her smile felt less forced, less tight on her face. "Good night."

Alone again, she sank to the bed, tearing open the letter with hands that shook in her excitement. Perhaps Fallon was back in London. She could stay with her for a few days before she took a new assignment and put this last week behind her, like a strange nightmare that would grow foggy and foggier until completely forgotten.

Her heart sank as her gaze settled on the page. She didn't recognize the handwriting. In fact, the scrawl was nearly illegible. Marguerite squinted to read:

Marguerite,

This letter likely comes as a shock to you. You may, in fact, believe I've quite neglected you over these many years. Let me assure you that is not the case. I funded you through Penwich, minding my responsibility to you as any dutiful father. It is not until this time that I have deemed a meeting

beneficial. I hazard to presume you may not agree,
but hope you may reconsider. Even if you have no
wish to acquaint yourself with me, think of your
sisters. They long to meet you . . .

The letter fluttered from Marguerite's limp fingers like a falling moth, the rest of the words detailing how she should contact her father insignificant, lost as her thoughts reeled.

Her father wanted to meet her? She snorted. Not likely. He had not deigned to see her all those years ago when her mother scraped by a humble existence in their small village.

Several times a year Marguerite's mother left her in the neighbor's care so that she might venture to London and the bed of her lover. She never recalled her mother sitting her down and explaining the purpose behind these trips, but she had somehow always understood. Her father was in London. That was never a secret. The carriage that arrived to collect her mother belonged to him. Her mother always returned with smiles, a new wardrobe, and a doll for Marguerite. The price of her dignity.

Following her mother's death, the same carriage

that had always collected her mother arrived to convey Marguerite to the Penwich School for Virtuous Girls.

Her father had never bothered to make her acquaintance in person before. She saw no reason to make his acquaintance now.

He was correct. She had no wish to meet him. But . . . *sisters*?

For so long she had counted herself alone. She moistened her lips and bent to collect the missive. Could it be true and not some fabrication? A ploy to bring her to her father's door? And why should he want to see her now? He'd had ample opportunity when her mother was alive. The opportunity had even been there when she was at Penwich's. Instead, she'd suffered there until her eighteenth year. Not even at Christmas had he sent for her. An orphan, for all intents and purposes.

Sisters. Her heart warmed at the possibility. Dropping back on the bed, she rolled to her side and curled her legs to her chest, feeling perhaps a little less alone, a little less chilled knowing that somewhere out there she had a family. Sisters who might wish to know her.

The echo of the diviner's words whispered

through her head like a sifting wind. *You shall not live out the year.*

She shivered. Rubbish, of course. Utter rot. Mrs. Danbury's passing was a mere coincidence. She had been ill, after all, clearly not recovered from her initial affliction.

Marguerite was not ill. She was not going to die. At least not at any time soon, and she wouldn't let some scheming swindler wreak havoc with her head. She would put Madame Foster firmly from her mind and get about her life. A life that looked suddenly brighter than it had moments before.

Chapter 3

Marguerite lifted her hand for a second round of knocking, ignoring the sting in her knuckles. *Blast!* She had to be home. Marguerite refused to believe she had made the trip to St. Giles for nothing.

Hawkers called loudly from the street behind her, selling their wares with hard, desperate voices. Carriages rattled past with noisy clatter. Despite the unseasonable cold, the streets were crowded. The only concession to weather appeared to be that passersby moved with haste, no doubt eager to reach the waiting fires and grates of their destinations. She, too, longed to return to Mrs. Dobbs's cozy boardinghouse. It was a familiar enough place. She frequently stayed there between assignments, if she was not visiting either Fallon or Evie.

At last the door swung open. A woman strolled

out, nearly knocking Marguerite aside where she stood on the stoop. Tucking her cloak more tightly around herself, the woman called back into the house, "See you next week, Madame."

Madame herself stepped within the threshold. "Aye, and mind what I told you, Francie. Stay away from that Tom fellow."

Francie fluttered her hand in the air as she descended the steps onto the cracked sidewalk.

Marguerite fixed her attention on the woman she had come to confront, despite all her attempts to put her from her head. Firming her lips, she gave a brisk nod. "Madame Foster. I've come to speak with you."

The woman settled a lingering gaze on Marguerite. "You," she said flatly. "I thought you would be here sooner."

Before Marguerite could respond, she shrugged and waved for her to follow. "This way. I expect you'll pay for my time. Just because you got the first reading for free—"

"I didn't solicit your service that day," Marguerite cut in sharply as she stepped into the dim shop that also served as the woman's residence.

"*You* touched *me*," she reminded Marguerite

as they passed through a set of swinging parlor doors. "Grabbed me most rudely, if I recall." Apparently she judged that tantamount to soliciting a reading.

Marguerite nodded her head doggedly. "Because you just informed my employer she would die—"

"That's correct." Madame Foster spun around with a militant gleam in her eye. "And was I or wasn't I correct on that matter?"

Marguerite pulled back her shoulders, loath to admit that Madame Foster had been correct, no matter that she had been. For if she had been correct once, it stood to reason she could be correct a second time.

The woman snorted, doubtlessly taking Marguerite's silence as affirmation. "Precisely what I thought. Well, whatever the case, you're here now. If you want more information, you'll have to pay like everyone else." With a huff, she seated herself behind a small table covered in a rich green velvet cloth.

Marguerite remained standing. "How did you know Mrs. Danbury would . . ." She swallowed, still unable to say *it*. She settled for, "How did you know she would become ill again?"

Eerily green eyes gazed up at her. "How did I know she would die? The same way I know you *will*. I saw it."

For several moments, Marguerite couldn't respond. She simply gazed at the woman she felt certain to be a fraud. Only why was she here then? Why had she come at all?

"Have a seat." Madame Foster motioned smoothly to the chair opposite her. "It's why you came. To listen. And I'm getting a pinch in my neck looking up at you."

Without a word, Marguerite sank down on the chair. Yes. She had come to listen. To find an explanation, something, anything. Perhaps Madame Foster possessed a better understanding of Mrs. Danbury's health condition.

Or perhaps it was merely coincidence. An educated guess. Anything except that this female with her cat eyes actually saw the future.

"What?" Marguerite motioned between them, desperate to ease the tension, to remind the other woman that she knew she was a fraud and would not be so easily duped simply because she sat across from her as a willing party. "No crystal ball?"

Madame Foster smirked. "Your hand should be sufficient to start with."

With great reluctance, Marguerite offered up her hand.

"Remove your glove, please."

"Of course." She slid each finger free, calling herself ten kinds of fool for even sitting in this woman's parlor. She forced herself to not fidget as her hand was held between the older woman's hands. She looked away, unable to watch her. Instead, she studied the contents of the cluttered room, noting that Madame Foster had a fondness for figurines of pug dogs. They covered every available surface.

After some moments, she sighed heavily, drawing Marguerite's attention back to her. "It's as I said. You'll not live out the year. I cannot see the precise time, but before this time next year, you'll be gone. Lost in a tragic accident. Sorry, love. This Christmas shall be your last."

These words, stated so matter-of-factly, chilled her to the core.

"Why?" she demanded. Only she wasn't sure what she was asking. *Why are you telling me such lies? Why do I almost believe you?*

The worst of it was perhaps that the woman did

look sorry, wearied all of a sudden. "I'm sorry. It never gets easier. I can't tell you how many times I've seen tragic fates in my mind . . . but you. You're so young, and you've lived so little yet—"

"Enough," Marguerite snapped, the words rooting with something raw and deep inside her. She'd heard enough. Rising to her feet, she fished a coin from her reticule. Dropping it to the table, she spun on her heels.

Had she hoped to feel better from this visit? Had she hoped for an apology? A retraction of the ridiculous prediction?

"Wait! If it's any solace, I saw some happiness in your future."

She shouldn't, but she hesitated, looking over her shoulder, hope blossoming in her chest, eager to hear something good, anything to give her hope . . .

"You'll be reunited with your family."

She jerked, just a small movement, which she quickly masked, stiffening, unwilling to give any sign to Madame Foster that she might have hit upon a possible truth. "I have no family."

Madame Foster shook her head. "I saw sisters. There were two." She grazed her temple with her fingers, concentrating. "Perhaps three. No, two."

No. It couldn't be. Marguerite felt as if the earth had been pulled out from under her. She grasped the back of a chair to stop from falling. She couldn't endure it, couldn't bear to ask for more, to hear another tidbit that would make her suspect the woman was not a fraud, but a genuine seer—one who had seen her death.

With her heart pounding in her ears, she turned to flee the room.

"There's something more . . ."

She stalled, glancing over her shoulder yet again and feeling the eeriest sensation at the quirk to Madame's lips. "I've seen a man. A fine specimen, to be sure. He'll be mad for you."

Her foolish heart tripped. Why should she want this to be true? If this was true, then so was all the rest—specifically her death. No, best that it all be inaccurate.

She pressed her fingertips to the center of her forehead and dragged her head side to side.

"Aye, you'll have a time of it with him." Madame waggled her brows. "Gor, the two of you! It's enough to make me blush, and I've seen everything. From the moment you both wed, you shall—"

Marguerite's head snapped up, her hand dropping away. "Wed? I'll marry him?" Her heart beat like a hammer against the wall of her chest.

"Busy year, eh?" Madame winked. "Yes, you'll have a grand time. Romance, adventure, *and* marriage."

"I cannot marry. It's impossible. I haven't any prospects. You're wrong," she said flatly, suddenly feeling a bit better, stronger again. As if she could once again breathe.

Madame Foster pulled back her shoulders, thrusting out her chest. "I am never wrong, but . . ."

"Yes?" Marguerite prompted. "But what?"

"I don't want to raise your hopes up, but no one's fate is etched in stone. A moment's decision can alter the course of fate."

She stared. "That's it?" *That would make her feel better*?

The woman shrugged. "It's something. All I can tell you."

This time Marguerite didn't hesitate. She fled the room. She didn't stop until she left the tiny shop and breathed air that smelled decidedly unclean. She stood there on the stoop, blinking in the feeble afternoon sunlight, grappling with the knowledge that Madame Foster knew about her sisters . . . knew even that Marguerite would meet with them, the very thing she had determined to do.

Feeling like a wounded animal, she felt the need to escape, hasten to her rented rooms across Town where she could reflect and reduce all that had just transpired into logical facts.

She needed to overcome her fears. Her next post would begin shortly, and she need not be dwelling on the distant and unlikely prospect of her own demise.

For the first time, sitting beside a dying woman and assisting her through *her* departure from this world turned Marguerite's stomach, leaving a foul taste in her mouth. She wanted nothing to do with death. She had no wish to be around it . . . she'd had her fill of it.

But what then?

She weighed this question as she worked her gloves back on her hands. What would she do? She'd tucked enough money away to live independently for some time, but that nest egg was intended for the future. So that she could acquire a home of her own some day. Just a small cottage.

Perhaps by the sea. If she spent that money now, her distant goal was all the more distant.

You'll not live out the year.

Madame Foster's unwanted voice rolled across her mind. Would it not be the height of irony to have saved her money so fastidiously only to die at a ripe young age? She felt the absurd urge to laugh, but bit back the impulse.

What would it hurt? Should not everyone live each day as though it was the last? In theory, it seemed a most excellent ambition. *Carpe diem* and all that rot. One could never look back with regret if she lived by that standard.

Indeed, what could it hurt?

A sudden determination swept over her. It was a rash scheme. Mad, but wonderful. The clinging fear she felt evaporated.

She would take a year off. A sabbatical of sorts.

This time next year, she would look back and see that Madame Foster had indeed been the grand swindler she believed, but Marguerite would have lived a splendid year at any rate. No harm.

She would have the year of all years.

As to Madame's absurd prediction that she would take a husband? Not likely. Marguerite knew she was moderately attractive, but she was little more than a servant, lacking all prospects. A husband? Unlikely. A lover . . .

Well. Now that was an interesting notion.

Since Fallon and Evie had married, she had begun to wonder, to speculate at the origins to the heated looks that passed between her friends and their husbands. Perhaps it was time to discover passion for herself. That should definitely be something experienced before one dies.

Standing on the stoop, she gave a decided nod and earned herself a strange look from a woman pushing a pram.

A lover. *Yes*. A brilliant notion.

And she already had one candidate in mind.

Chapter 4

Lost in thought, Marguerite lingered on the stoop of Madame Foster's shop and burrowed deeper into her cloak. She told herself it was merely the cold and not Madame Foster's prophetic words that shot ice through her veins . . . nor the rash decision she had just reached.

Shivering, she lifted her face to the air, determining that it had dropped several degrees since she first entered the shop. Unusually inclement weather this early in the season. It brought to mind her many cold winters in Yorkshire. The biting cold, the dwindling winter rations . . . the meager blankets that never quite warmed her.

A slow, freezing drizzle began to fall. Her hood failed to sufficiently cover her face and icy water dripped off the tip of her nose. She eyed the street, hoping to hail a hack quickly and escape the dismal weather. She longed for the cozy fire in her rooms back at the boardinghouse. Perhaps a decadent novel. She started down the steps.

Loud shouts attracted her notice. A small, harried-looking man raced past the front of the stoop where she stood, darting through bystanders like a scurrying street rat.

A moment later another man followed, his long strides easily overcoming the scrawny man's lead. He caught him by the scruff of the neck. The little man whirled around, swinging his arm wide in an attempt to defend himself, but the blow bounced off the bigger man's shoulder.

She gasped, freezing on her step as the younger, stronger man pulled back his arm and smashed it with brutal force into his victim's face.

A crowd gathered, vultures scenting their prey. Shouts drew more people to the fray, blocking her view several steps above the streets. Afraid the brute was killing the unfortunate man, she lifted her skirts and rushed down into the street.

"Stop! Stop it at once! What are you doing?" She charged through the crowd of gawking onlookers, elbowing past men jeering their support. Even a few ladies milled about. Although she could scarcely call them ladies. They shouted encouragement as crudely as any of the men, watching with glee as the large brute of a man beat the slighter one.

Even as she pushed her way through, she could hear the smack of fists. It was a horrible sound, like cracking wood. Each one jarred her to the core, shuddering along her bones.

Through the press of bodies, she glimpsed flashes of the assailant's white shirt. No vest. No jacket. The man was a primitive. Uncivilized. After several blows, the small man could no longer rise. The scoundrel wasn't done, however. He held him up by his crumpled cravat and delivered blow after blow to his lolling head.

With a grunt, she gave another push and broke through the circle of onlookers with a stumble, earning herself an unfettered view, much better than what she'd witnessed from Madame Foster's stoop. Or *worse*, depending on one's perspective.

She cringed. The beaten man's face was a mangled mess, his nose swollen and misshapen. Dark blood gushed from his nostrils. Her stomach heaved at the dreadful sight.

Reminding herself that she was no squeamish miss—she'd seen worse from her patients—she charged forward and caught the Goliath's arm as he hauled it back for another punch. The moment her fingers locked on the heavily muscled limb, she sensed she might be in trouble.

Through the thin lawn of his shirt, his arm felt hard and tight with raw strength. He was like no man she'd ever encountered . . . thankfully.

A warning bell clanged in her head that she duly ignored. It failed to matter anymore. As risky as her behavior was, she wasn't to die here . . . at least she didn't think so. According to Madame Foster she must meet her sisters first . . . and *marry*. Not that she planned on the latter happening. A simple-enough matter to control.

No. This wouldn't be the hour of her death. The realization emboldened her, made her hang on harder to the arm of rippling muscle.

The man tugged, practically lifting her off her feet. Still, she clung. Using her most ferocious tone, the one she used when dealing with an insensible patient, she barked, "You shall not harm this man, you brute! Do you hear me?"

The crowd guffawed, chortling and whistling.

A female's voice called out, "Looks like she could use the tap of your fist, too, Courtland!"

Courtland. His Christian name or surname, she knew not. She only knew that he was a popular fellow among this riffraff, and that couldn't bode well.

"Aye, maybe a tap of something else," a man crudely suggested.

"Well, Courtland there can certainly deliver 'er that, just ask Sally over there!"

"Aye, and if he won't, maybe I will!"

Marguerite's cheeks burned, perfectly mortified at the rough remarks.

The brute twisted so that she was no longer grasping his arm anymore. Instead *he* was holding onto *her*.

She squeaked. "How did you—"

Her words were lost as he hauled her close, their bodies flush, his face—handsome, in a rough-hewn, carved-from-stone sort of way—only inches from her own.

She swallowed, fighting the sudden thickness in her throat at the abrupt change in position, shaken to find the tables so easily turned . . . shaken that he would press himself so intimately against her.

Everything seemed to slow, the air crackling as the moment stretched out and she found herself in the grip of such a virile, dangerous man. *Courtland*. Ironic, she supposed, as there was nothing *courtly* about him. Certainly not in his chilling black eyes.

She glared down her nose at the hand on her arm, gulping at the sight of his bloody fist—the cut, raw knuckles flexing over her. Her stomach dipped and twisted.

Her gaze flicked back to his face. His eyes flashed dark obsidian down at her, the demon eyes a startling contrast to his golden hair. The sight undid her, robbed the last of her composure. It was this, everything, those last moments with Madame Foster when Marguerite accepted that the woman might not be a complete fraud after all. All of it sought to unravel her, take her apart bit by bit until she was naught but tiny motes of dust on the air.

She addressed the scoundrel with a hiss. "Unhand me, you wretch!" She swung her free arm around, her palm cracking solidly with his cheek. The blow carried more force than she suspected herself capable.

Her handprint stood stark white on his swarthy cheek. For a moment, the crowd stilled, all laughter and jeers dying. Then a whispering murmur broke out over the crowd.

She caught a snatch of words, a fractured phrase. *Dead woman.*

Irrational laughter bubbled up from her chest. She swallowed it back lest everyone deem her well and truly mad. She had no wish to be carted off to Bedlam. That's not where she imagined spending her final days.

"Wretch," he sneered, a questioning ring to his voice. His lips curled back to display a flash of shockingly white teeth. She blinked. Superb teeth for one of Society's dregs to possess. Even his speech did not mark him an uneducated lout given to thrashing helpless souls in the streets.

His fingers tightened around her wrist until she feared the bones would snap. She winced. From the corner of her eye, she watched as the hapless creature he'd beaten scampered away, disappearing into the crowd. At least there was that.

His gaze flicked to the retreating figure, then back to her. "You let him get away."

"You've already beaten him to an inch of his life . . . or was it your goal to kill him?" she bit out.

His angry gaze slid over her, insolent and furious. "What concern is it of a fine lady like you? Strayed a bit far from Bond Street, haven't you, sweetheart?"

"I've no wish to see an innocent man murdered before my eyes."

He thrust his face so close she thought their noses would bump. Startled, she pulled back as far as she could, craning her neck at an awkward angle.

"Innocent?" His mouth twisted cruelly and he laughed, the sound rough and deep, raising the tiny hairs on the nape of her neck. Even with that laughter, he looked furious, dangerous. Whipping his head about, he glared at their audience. "What are you all looking at? Show's over!"

Then she was moving, hauled after him by the wrist. A wrist she was certain would bear bruises later.

She dug in her heels, but it did no good. She moved, tripping after him. "Where are you taking me?"

He ignored her, his long strides taking them past Madame Foster's shop to the corner of the street. He waved a hand. His whistle pierced the air. Almost immediately, a hack swung to a stop beside them.

"Go home," he snapped as he yanked open the door and practically threw her inside. "Where you can delude yourself about the innocence of others."

Delude herself? Sprawled on the floor of the hack, her legs tangled awkwardly in her twisted skirts and petticoats, she blinked up at the stranger's fierce countenance and even fiercer words . . . and had the strangest feeling she was caught in the midst of a dream. Or rather a nightmare.

First Madame Foster, and now this dark angel glowering down at her and speaking to her with such rancor and condemnation. Would this horrid day never end?

"The next time you visit St. Giles, don't interfere in matters in which you know nothing. Not if you hope to return home as lily-white as when you arrived."

She snorted inelegantly. "The scene I just witnessed required little explanation."

Dark heat flashed in his gaze. He leaned inside the hack, angling his imposing body over hers like a finely stretched bow, taut with barely checked energy.

His fingers curled around the modest neckline of her bodice, pulling her up by his grip on the fabric. She gasped, certain he meant to rip her gown from her body and ravish her.

"That *innocent* man," he hissed, "very nearly beat a woman to death. A working woman, the likes you would cross the street to avoid." He scoured her with a contemptuous glare. "A woman with no family to protect her, no husband, and a small child to feed. An *innocent* child."

She absorbed his words, an awful heaviness settling into her chest. Her eyes stung and she blinked them fiercely.

Still, a part of her couldn't back down from him. Perhaps it was his manner, the rough way he handled her and spoke to her—his utter arrogance. "And beating him to death will improve matters? How will that help this woman and her innocent child?"

"Stubborn fool," he ground out, his grip tightening on the front of her dress. "You know nothing of how things work down here."

Heat scored her where the backs of his fingers slid down between the valley of her breasts. *The first time any man had touched her so intimately . . .*

Her heart hammered, beating like a drum in her too-tight chest. She didn't resist him, didn't blink, her eyes wide and aching in her face as he pulled her closer and closer . . . until no more than an inch separated their faces.

An arrested look came over him then.

She didn't move. Didn't breathe.

He stared at her, truly stared at her for the first time, it seemed. Everything else melted away. It felt like they were alone in the hack, even with half of him still standing in the street.

Street sounds faded, lost to the roaring in her head.

He lifted one hand between them, large and masculine. Not the hand of a gentleman. He brushed her lips with his fingers. "Such a beautiful mouth to spout such drivel," he mused.

She drew a ragged breath, her belly quivering with a twisting heat.

He eased her back down then. She propped her elbows on the carriage floor to stop herself from descending completely onto her back.

The back of his hand delved lower inside her bodice, knuckles grazing the swell of a breast. She gasped at the foreign sensation, at the sudden tightness of her chest. Her breasts grew heavier, the tips tightening, hardening. Embarrassing heat washed over her face, traveling all the way to the tips of her ears.

He watched her closely, moving his hand again, testing her, it seemed, with each graze of his knuckles against her goose-puckered skin.

"You like that." It was more a statement of fact than a question, but a denial rose swift and fiery to her lips just the same.

"I do *not*."

The look in his eyes told her he didn't believe her, which only increased her mortification. Mortification she would perhaps not feel so deeply if she did not suspect it to hold a grain of truth. She did like his touch, reveled in the way her belly twisted and clenched, enjoying the way her heart thundered inside her chest, reminding her that she was alive.

She needed this—had to find this magic with another man. A lover of her own. The idea had burrowed and rooted its way inside her already, but now it intensified its hold.

The notion would not go away, and she didn't want it to. It filled her with purpose. Led her to action she would otherwise have thought brazen and insane under ordinary circumstances. Only her circumstances were no longer ordinary.

"Yes," he rasped, dipping a single finger deep inside her bodice, beneath her shift, the tip daring to stroke a nipple. Her teeth clenched against the spike of sensation arcing through her. *Magic.*

A strangled sob escaped her.

His eyes flashed, darkly smug.

He continued, his voice a low rumble, physical, as tangible as that finger against her breast. "You like it," he declared. "What's your name?"

"Marguerite," she breathed before she could consider the wisdom of giving him her name.

His lips turned up slowly, flashing teeth too white for belief. That grin was all-knowing. It galled her, pulled her from whatever feelings and sensations had addled her head. She wanted this, true. Only not with him, a voice whispered, small and unconvincingly inside her head.

"Perhaps, Marguerite, you've no wish to return lily-white. Perhaps you came to the rook for a taste of what you can't get in your clean little world across the river." He cocked his head, studying her as if he had never seen anything quite of the like. "Is that it?" He brought a hand back to her face and stroked the soft flesh of her jaw.

Then she smelled it—blood. Coppery rich on his

knuckles. An inch from her mouth. Her stomach rolled, heaved.

It was all the reminder she needed. He was a savage. Seductive or not. Dark-angel mien and all. She was a fool to let such a scoundrel lull her with his mesmerizing gaze.

Without thinking, she turned her face and bit down on his finger.

He hissed and pulled his hand back, shaking it. She held her breath, waiting, certain he would strike her. Certain he would turn the savagery she had witnessed in him on her.

Instead, he merely glared at her, his glittering gaze furious. And something else. Something that made her belly fill with dancing butterflies.

She thrust out her chin. "Remove yourself from me!"

The driver shouted down. "Eh, we going any-where or you just going to shag the wench in there, guv'nor? Whatever yer business, I need coin for time in my hack!"

"If you know what's good for you, you won't come back to St. Giles. A pretty bit of muslin like you, with that saucy mouth . . ." He shook his head, frowning. "You'll only meet with trouble. Run into the sort of man you so gallantly saved from my fists this day."

"How considerate," she sneered, certain she would never come face-to-face with a greater threat to her person than he. "I thank you kindly for the advice."

He rose up, hovering, looming within the narrow carriage door, overfilling it, blocking out all light. His eyes gleamed from within his shadowed features. She loathed that she couldn't make herself move, that she lay on the floor of the carriage like a quivering mouse.

"Just do as I say. If you know what's good for you, stay out of St. Giles."

All her wrath bubbled to the surface at his terse command. How dare he speak to her like she was his to command? Words she'd never spoken before, dared not think—except perhaps when she was enduring one of Master Brocklehurst's unjustified beatings—rose on her lips. "*Go to hell.*"

For a moment he did not move. Did not speak. Then he threw back his head and laughed. "Perhaps the *lady* isn't such a lady, after all." She felt his gaze then, raking her, traveling over her with familiar insolence. "But then I don't find that such a surprise."

Sputtering, she clambered to the carriage seat. "You beast!"

His laughter scraped the air, dragged across her stinging nerves. "Never fear. I'm certain I shall find my way to those fiery pits someday. Just do me a favor, sweetheart, and don't wish me there before my time. And in case you didn't notice"—he waved a hand about them and her gaze drifted to an ugly lodging house with broken, gaping windows. Stained rags were stuffed into the cracks in a weak attempt to ward off the cold—"this is fairly close to hell."

He vanished from the hack then, his laughter receding, a drifting curl of sound, strangely provocative, winding itself around her where she shivered on the stiff squabs.

A sound, she would later learn, that would follow her to bed that night and haunt her dreams.

Chapter 5

Ash Courtland strode down the streets that stank of rot and acrid smoke from the nearby factory. The odor was as familiar to him as his own shape and form, and yet he smelled only the chit he left behind. The whiff of honey lingered in his nostrils.

Stepping over a gutter, he cursed low beneath his breath. He shouldn't have let her go, he realized with an uncustomary pang of regret. He shook his head at the irrational thought. She was not a puppy one discovered on the streets, to be kept and coddled.

Still, he could not shake the feeling that he left something behind as he strode along the uneven sidewalk. Rarely had he met a female to stand toe to toe to him. She brought out the primitive in him—perhaps the chief reason he let her go.

His primitive, savage nature was a thing of the past. He was a man of property now. Wealth. A respected businessman.

He and his partner owned two of London's most popular gaming hells. Not to mention a mine in Wales and a factory in the north, the latter two only acquired at his insistence. Jack would just as soon have kept their business to gaming. His partner did little these days aside of letting Ash run affairs and increase their wealth, something at which he was proving vastly superior. Jack's lack of involvement didn't trouble him. Without the older man taking him under his wing, Ash would never have gotten off the streets.

After all he had accomplished, Ash didn't need a female hanging about who looked at him as if he were still the lowest of street vermin—who, in fact made him behave that way.

He'd come far from the boy that skulked in the shadows committing all manner of vice and crime in order to survive. He possessed wealth and power that most men never knew. The only thing lacking was gentility, breeding. He vowed to have that, too. With a grimace, he acknowledged that snatching a female off the streets and mauling her in a hack like a caveman of old did not serve to that end. And yet those whiskey-hued eyes burned an imprint on his mind.

He sent a lingering glance over his shoulder, as if he would still find the hack sitting there. Feeling a stab of regret yet again, he cursed himself. So she was a pretty piece, with her black hair and flashing eyes. Pretty women were no rarity, he reminded himself. Beautiful women were common enough within the walls of his gaming hells. One interfering, hot-tempered virago didn't bear notice.

Go to hell.

He laughed. Again. Those ugly words had sounded absurd in her soft, cultured voice. He'd bet that she'd never uttered them before.

But the sound of that voice, whispering a much different variety of words, words that enticed with naughty, wicked suggestions, filled his imagination.

A sound, he would later learn, that would follow him to bed that night and haunt his dreams.

The grand façade of Hellfire appeared ahead, a porticoed palace amid the squalid dwellings. A steady stream of people passed through the grand double doors even at this time of day. Vowing to think of her no more and put his mind to more important matters of business, he entered the hell. The whirring of roulette wheels filled his ears as he stepped within the marble-floored interior. This, he mused, was all he needed. All he had left in the world.

"Miss Laurent! What a lovely surprise. Dear me, how long has it been?"

Lord Sommers swept inside the salon with a grace borne from years of aristocratic upbringing. His grandmother—may she rest in peace—had been a dowager marchioness and the most exalted patient Marguerite had ever served.

"Lord Sommers," she greeted.

He proved every inch of his breeding as he politely bowed before her. Not even in the deep brown of his gaze did he betray the awkwardness of their last meeting, that uncomfortable encounter when he dropped to bended knee and begged her to become his paramour. Indeed not. To stare into his eyes, one would never recognize what must be his undoubted surprise at finding the woman who so coolly rebuffed his advances and declined his proposition calling upon him in his drawing room.

Marguerite assessed him, trying to judge whether he could be the fine specimen Madame Foster described. His jacket required no padding. He was fit and fair of face, but possessed a somewhat weak chin and thinning hair.

The seer's affected accents rolled through her head. *A fine specimen, to be sure, mad over you. Yes, you'll have a grand time. Romance, adventure, and marriage. You will definitely wed.*

A frisson of alarm coursed through her, which she quickly dismissed. Certainly *that* fellow could not be Lord Roger Sommers. The nobleman would never offer marriage to the likes of her—even if he did once upon a time harbor a *tendre* for her. She was safe on that score. He could not be the one. She drew a deep, relieved breath, filling her lungs. Already she was averting the fate that would lead to her death . . . according to Madame Foster, at any rate.

As she surveyed him, an image of the brute from St. Giles rose in her mind. *Now he had been a fine specimen.* She gave herself a swift mental kick.

Roger scarcely—thankfully—did not look the sort capable of beating a man senseless in the streets, deservedly or not. Nor would he manhandle a woman and accuse her of enjoying it, *wanting* it. He wasn't that coarse, that brutish . . . that *raw*.

She pressed her fingers to her throat, noting the jumpy thread to her pulse there. Her body betrayed her, tightening at the core with the memory of being in the close confines of the hack with that scoundrel.

Shaking all thoughts of the stranger free of her thoughts, she answered Roger's original question with more bluntness than intended. "We've not seen each other since you visited my room in the dead of night a week after your grandmother's passing and requested that I become your mistress . . ." She paused to lick her lips, adding a courtesy: "My lord."

The young man's face burned brightly at her candid speech. He tugged at his cravat. "Ah, yes. I recall now . . ."

It had been over a year. She'd found the situation entirely embarrassing. Unprecedented for her. Such occurrences had been commonplace for Fallon. With her striking presence, men flocked to her like bees to the honey pot. But not Marguerite.

She did not inspire those types of urges in the opposite sex. At least she had believed so until Lord
Sommers.

His infatuation and subsequent proposition had
taken her unawares. She had not even shared the
details with Fallon and Evie, simply wishing to put
the incident from her mind.

"As it turns out, I've reconsidered your offer and
should like to accept, if you're still agreeable to an
arrangement." Chin held high, she marveled that
injecting passion into her life should sound like
such a negotiation. So officious and formal. Was
this how it was usually done?

"Er." The viscount blinked owlishly and looked
her up and down. "Can you be serious, Miss Laurent? I felt certain I had offended you with my
proposition."

She *had* been offended at the time. Naturally. But
that Marguerite seemed quite different from who
she was now. The new Marguerite lived each day
as if it might be her last.

She nodded briskly. "I am quite serious, my
lord."

"I . . . see." Not the ardent response she had been
anticipating.

"Have I changed so much then?" She spread her hands out before her, glancing down as if she might see something offensive. "Am I no longer appealing to you?"

"Oh, no. Nothing like that." He tugged at his cravat again and swept her a look of longing that made her feel once again certain of herself. "I've always had a penchant for dark-haired females. Sweet, biddable, and mild-mannered girls such as yourself . . . You quite fit my tastes." He frowned, and she shoved aside the sensation that he was describing his preferences of horseflesh.

She stared down at her hands, unliking the notion. His next words snapped her attention back to him.

"Forgive me for saying, but I can't seem to recall you being this forthright."

"Well, yes, on that score, I have changed." Not that she would have termed herself as mild-mannered before, but she would not dispute the point. If that's what he thought of her, then let him think it. "I've simply decided to make certain things happen in my life before—" She caught herself. The word *die* had almost slipped past.

"Before?" he prompted.

She wet her lips and adjusted herself on the settee. "Before I miss any opportunities."

He nodded, apparently satisfied with her vague reply. "I see. Well, I am quite taken with you. That has not changed." His gaze skimmed her. "Should we have a contract drawn up? I've a nice house in Daventry Square. Modest but quite above the cut."

She shook her head. "No. That won't do."

He blinked. "No?"

"I have requirements, my lord, and should you agree, I'll take you at your word. No contract necessary." She would rather not leave a written record of her moral descent. If she lived out the year—*when*—she would not continue on as a rich man's mistress. Marguerite would prefer the world know nothing of her adventure. The life of a paramour had been her mother's life-long vocation. Not hers. No, the handsome lord would do for her purposes for a while. For now.

"What is it you want, Miss Laurent?"

This time when he asked, his gaze was sober, focused and intent as any man entering a business deal. Again, she felt that stab of disappointment. Where was the passion she sought?

"I wish to spend the winter in Spain. Three

months, to be exact. I don't require a house, nothing permanent in nature. Three months. You. Me." She looked him starkly in the face. "I want adventure. I want passion. And after that . . ." her voice faded.

Courtland's face chose that moment to flash in her mind. Blast the man. Who was he to invade her thoughts? She supposed it was his virility, his very maleness. When she thought of passion, his unwelcome image rose in her head.

Lord Sommers's eyes warmed as he looked at her. "How can I refuse such a request?"

She released a shaky breath, not realizing until then how nervous she had been. "You agree with my requests then, my lord?"

He cocked his head, studying her. "I'm long overdue a holiday, and with Christmas upon us, well, I dread this time of year . . . all the blasted relations swarming the place. I would much rather escape to sunny Spain. With you, my dear. The notion strikes me as providential, in fact."

She winced at the description, deciding it either oddly apt or blasphemous.

Lord Sommers moved then, lowering himself down beside her, rearranging his bright blue jacket around him with a fastidiousness to rival any lady. She tried not to flinch when he lifted her hand from her lap and held it in his cold fingers. "How soon shall we do this?"

"I'm ready now. We can leave at once." Then she remembered she still needed to visit her sisters. She didn't care that she had vowed to do everything in opposition of Madame Foster's predictions. She could not *not* meet them. They were her sisters, the family she had always longed for. One brief meeting would not hurt.

He answered her before she could retract her statement. "I cannot leave until the following week, I'm afraid. I'll need some days to set my affairs in order and make arrangements for us." He grinned then, all at once boyish. "Sunny Spain! What a brilliant idea." His attention fixed on her, his gaze lowering to her lips. "And I cannot think of a better companion. We shall have a grand time of it. You'll have your passion. That and more, I daresay."

She smiled. *More* was what she was counting on. *More* was precisely what a dying woman craved, *needed*.

As he leaned down and pressed his mouth to

hers, she tried to convince herself that she felt alive, electrified at the touch of his lips—a bit like how she'd felt when that scoundrel from the rookery put his hands to her. A lie, unfortunately.

She felt nothing.

Still, she returned his kiss, determined to feel something. A fraction of the fire that sparked between her and Courtland.

Nothing.

When he ended the kiss and pulled away, she sighed. He apparently mistook the sound for rapture of his mediocre kissing.

"There will be more of that later, love," he promised.

She nodded and forced a smile. "I'm counting on it." Counting that next time it would be magic.

That night she dreamed. An uncommon occurrence.

Usually, she slept hard, a dead sleep, with no memory of dreams the following morning. They faded like wisps of smoke. It had been that way since Penwich. Weak and hungry, she'd always fallen into sleep like a rock dropped into deep water. Always waking in the exact position that she touched down, curled on her side, her night rail not even so much as tangled around one calf.

But this night was different. This time, she was alert to her dream. Her senses hummed as she lived it, *feeling*, tasting as a participant.

She was still in her room. At the boardinghouse. In her same bed, which might lead her to think she wasn't caught in the throes of a dream, but in all actuality awake. And yet she knew she dreamed. For no other reason would she have been sitting naked at the edge of her bed. Sitting, not lying down.

And she wasn't alone.

Strange, that. The only soul ever to occupy the room with her had been the proprietress, Mrs. Dobbs. Stranger yet, she held herself boldly, proud and comfortable in her skin, in her nudity. Poised at the edge of the bed, sitting still and ready, she pressed her hands against her thighs. And watched.

With her stare fixed straight ahead, she watched the large, shadowed shape by the window. The curtains fluttered behind him, moonlight streaming in pale ribbons, the streaks of light illuminating his dark trouser-clad legs.

Fear didn't exist at all. Even as she told herself to get up, to move, to rise. To demand that he leave her room. She couldn't voice the words. She couldn't budge. She couldn't even care enough to lift a hand and shield her nudity.

It was as though she gave herself permission to do anything, to do *everything*. In this dream that didn't feel like a dream, anything was possible.

He stepped forward with easy, decided steps. He wasn't even dressed properly. She saw that. No jacket. No vest. The lightness of his lawn-colored shirt matched the moon's glow. The fabric opened down the middle, leaving a deep vee of shadow. His trousers were dark, lost against the night, as obscured as his shadowed face.

He stopped before her. And yet she didn't move. Not even when his hands fell to her shoulders, drifting inward to her collarbone, stroking the delicate lines. Her breath escaped in a small gasp.

His broad palms fell to her shoulders again. With a single push, he forced her back down.

Cool air wafted over her breasts. Her nipples hardened, chilled and achy as she descended to the mattress.

He came over her so completely, like an enveloping blanket. His mouth closed over one nipple, drawing it deep as his hand gripped her other breast. She moaned, arched, dug her hand into silken hair. Even as her breasts tingled and throbbed, she looked down, stared at the dark golden head feasting on her breast. Her belly tightened, twisting with heaviness.

He lifted his mouth, blew warm air against the engorged tip, and raised his head to look at her, holding her gaze.

She released a strangled sob at the darkly familiar eyes. Taunting demon eyes. Devilish and seductive.

He shouldn't be here. It should be Roger, not him. Not him!

But it was just a dream. A mere dream. With that whisper coaxing its way through her head, she relaxed back on the bed again and accepted the magic of his mouth and hands, the delicious weight of his large body bearing her down.

Moaning, she let her head drop to the side, fisting the coverlet. And she saw the other pair of eyes then, watching from the dark still of the corner, a voyeur of her most intimate tryst. A chill chased through her at the flaming white eyes set in a face shadowed beneath a deep hood.

Gasping, she jerked upright, pushing at the warm male chest too muscled to belong to Roger. But not another. Not a certain brutish man of the streets.

"What? What is it?" her lover whispered, his hand skimming down her throat, focused on only her.

"Him." She pointed a shaking finger at the cloaked figure. So tall and thin, she doubted whether anything thicker than a rail stood beneath the voluminous folds of the cloak.

"Oh, him." Her lover's voice was all nonchalance. "He can wait. For now."

A niggling awareness curled with the rippling heat coursing through her body, distracting her from the full pleasure of her lover.

Her attention strayed back to that watchful figure, so stark, dark and faceless save the glowing eyes. He spoke to her. But not in any tangible way. Not with words. His voice reached inside her, into her mind.

I'm here for you . . . soon now . . . soon . . .

Understanding slammed into her with gale-force power.

She lurched upright, screaming, ready to flee, to run as far from that dark figure as her legs would carry her, even if it meant losing the lover whose mouth and hands worked magic upon her. It wasn't worth it. Not if it brought Death.

She blinked in the suddenly altered air, the scream still caught in her throat. She looked about her wildly, serrated breath tripping from her lips. She skimmed a hand down, feeling her night rail covering her body. *Just a dream.*

The curtains at her window fluttered as if a wind had just blown through. With the mullioned glass sealed tight?

Her flesh puckered to gooseflesh. She chafed her arms, running her hands over them, concentrating on steadying her hammering heart.

A swift rap sounded at her door. She jumped, swallowing down another cry.

"Miss Laurent!" Mrs. Dobbs's disembodied voice drifted through her bedchamber door. "Are you well?"

Marguerite cleared her throat, managing strangled speech. "I am fine, Mrs. Dobbs. Simply a nightmare. Forgive me. I did not mean to disturb your rest."

"Not at all, dear. Only wanted to assure myself you weren't being murdered in your bed."

She bit down on her fist at Mrs. Dobbs's flippant remark, feeling the words like a barb to her heart.

Not murdered. Not dead. Not yet, at any rate.

"I am well," she called again.

"Good night then, dear."

Marguerite fell back on the bed, sighing deeply as her head sank into the pillow. She listened to the heavy tread of the proprietress fade down the corridor. In the distance, a door opened and shut, the sound desolate as it echoed through the night.

Rolling to her side, she burrowed beneath the coverlet, seeking warmth, grasping the fleeting scraps of her resolve to do everything in her power to seize her life and mark it as her own, to avoid a fate like the one Madame Foster had described.

Chapter 6

Ash sat upright in bed and glared down at the large, blinking blue eyes of the tousled female beside him. "What did you just say?"

"Easy there, love." Mary smoothed a hand over his bare shoulder, her gaze hungrily following the stroke of her hand on his flesh, like she wanted her lips there instead, tasting everything she touched.

He leaned forward, draping his arms loosely upon his propped knees, and stared dazedly ahead as he absorbed her words, his blood simmering to a furious burn in his veins. "Are you certain it's true?"

"Aye." Mary fell back on the bed, mindless of her nudity. She and Ash had been lovers off and on for years. Long before Jack made him a partner. Hell, back when he was just one of Jack's managers.

Their long-standing friendship made her someone he could trust. A girl brought up alongside him on the streets, in the days when he picked pockets to survive, would always have his back.

"The great Jack Hadley has gone and gathered his entire flock. All girls. Daughters, can you believe it? It's almost amusing. For all his procreating, he never fathered a son. Suppose you're the closest he'll ever have to that."

With a growl, he shook his head. Not a son. A son was told things and kept apprised, and Jack had kept him in the dark over the matter of his daughters. Not an oversight, Ash was certain. Everything Jack did was with methodical deliberation.

Not that it shocked Ash to learn that Jack had fathered offspring. He only felt shock over the fact that he was suddenly interested in claiming his progeny—that they suddenly possessed value in his eyes.

Jack was no sentimentalist. He did nothing without benefit to himself. For no other reason had he made Ash his partner. He saw the advantage in it. Claiming his illegitimate offspring had to provide him with something. Ash knew Jack well enough to know that he cared for no one more than himself.

The sounds from his gaming hell floated from below stairs. The buzz of conversation, laughter, the occasional shout from a victor, all acted as a balm to his nerves. Even though he owned a grand townhouse in the City, he stayed at Hellfire, craving the sounds, the smells. His townhouse sat a lonely shell across the river, shrouded in silence. Only solitude and thoughts best left alone awaited him there.

His attention drifted back to Mary. She was talking, he realized. "They're all supposed to be under his roof together. Grier arrived over a week ago. A nice-enough girl, if not a bit outspoken. Another arrived just yesterday and another is supposed to show up this afternoon. Only that one's not staying as the other two are . . . that's why he's throwing together a little soiree tonight. He's hoping to convince the new one to stay for the grand event."

Three? The randy old goat had fathered three daughters?

"That a fact?" Ash dragged a hand though his too-long hair, watching Mary rise and begin to dress, his mind churning over the implications of what this development could mean for him. His partner suddenly had heirs. Three, to be exact.

"Reminds me that I need to get back," Mary muttered. "There's much to do. He wants everything spotless. He expects at least a dozen to attend . . ."

"A dozen . . . *who*?"

She shrugged. "Some fine gents, I hear. Real bluebloods."

The hairs on Ash's neck began to stand as he watched her shimmy into her gown. "What scheme has he concocted?"

"He ain't saying, but Grier can't keep her tongue behind her teeth."

"And what has this Grier said?"

Mary looked over her shoulder as if she expected the great Jack Hadley to materialize behind her. He was that way. Larger than life, an intimidating figure to many.

"Well . . . she thinks he's got it in his head to marry them off to some bluebloods. All three of them. Any swell will do, so long as his blunt has run dry and he's desperate enough to marry a bastard daughter of Jack Hadley."

"Bloody hell." He shook his head. "Why would any swell want to—"

Mary waved a hand about her fiercely. "For this, of course. All of it. The mine, the factory . . ."

Cold washed through Ash's veins. *Of course.* For everything *he* had worked so hard for.

It all came together then. He understood why Jack suddenly wished to claim the daughters he'd seen fit to forget. He wanted what they could bring him. Prestige. A door to the glittering world of the *ton*. The sneering aristocrats would have to welcome him into their drawing rooms if his daughters married men among their ranks. His hand curled into a fist at his side.

Mary must have seen something in his face. An uneasy look drifted across her features. She drew out his name on a heavy breath. "Ash."

"I've made this *this*," he said tightly, motioning to his elegant suite. "The hells were nothing before me. And the mine? The factory? It was my idea to invest—"

"I know, I know," Mary soothed.

"He means to hand over what is rightfully mine to some lily-handed prigs who suck up the nerve to marry his bastards?"

"Well, they are his heirs, Ash," Mary pointed out. "And their future husbands have a right—"

"Just because Jack shagged these chits' mothers doesn't give their future husbands the right to claim all I've worked for! All *I* have built!" His chest lifted on a deep breath.

"What can you do about it? You're partners. If Jack gives each of his princesses a share of all he owns, it's his right."

"*Princesses,*" Ash sneered and shook his head in disbelief. Jack Hadley had thieved, cheated, and murdered his way to the top. Everyone knew it. His daughters were no princesses.

"At least a dozen bluebloods will be in attendance tonight. Grier let it slide that one of them is even a real duke." She snorted. "Can you imagine that? A duke? Dining with ol' Jack Hadley. Maybe even becoming his kin?" She laughed.

And taking what is mine? The factory? The mine? The hells? All that Ash had in this world. "No," he bit out past his teeth. "I can't imagine."

And he couldn't. He didn't want to believe that the man who had taken him under his wing would discard him for a gaggle of females he'd never even met—daughters or not. After plucking Ash off the streets and giving him his start, how could he not consider Ash in any of this?

"Well, I'm off." Mary pressed a kiss to his cheek.

"Wait a moment," he murmured from chilled lips. "I'll drive you home."

"Oh." She arched her eyebrow, the look in her blue eyes decidedly wary. "You're not going to start any trouble, are you? I've no wish to get scolded for talking out of turn."

"Jack won't give you a thought," Ash assured her. "I'm coming," he said flatly. ·

He'd hear it from Jack's own lips that while he viewed Ash as a son, he didn't consider him good enough to be his heir . . . good enough to inherit all that he'd built for the two of them. Jack instead preferred for his share of wealth and property to go to a trio of blue-blooded dandies with nothing but birth and rank to their credit. Oh, and marriage to Jack's bastard princesses.

When Ash arrived at Jack's Mayfair house, it was to find double the usual servants buzzing about. Like an army of ants, they swept, dusted, and polished everything until it gleamed. Hothouse roses, fragrant and rich in color, covered every surface. Beyond extravagant for this time of year.

Amid the cloying bouquet, the butler led him

into Jack's office, a wood-paneled circular room of deep walnut that was as familiar to him as his own bed. He'd spent countless evenings in this room, a glass of Jack's finest brandy in his hand, discussing business, life, the politics about Town and how it all might affect their enterprises.

They were alike: both brought up from the gutters, both having tasted abuse at the cruel hands of the unforgiving and merciless London underworld. Both with an insatiable hunger to succeed, to win and prove that they were no longer gutter trash. Ash had always told himself that's why they worked so well together, why they'd become partners.

Apparently, he'd been wrong. They weren't alike.

Ash knew what he was, knew what drove him, and he felt not the slightest remorse or wish to change. Some men were built for domesticity and could content themselves with a simple life. A wife, home, children, church on Sundays. He wasn't one of them. He didn't aspire to be. Nor was he like Jack. Jack craved a place in Society, position, the final stamp of approval—and he would step on Ash to get it. That much was now clear to him.

Ash surveyed the familiar room with fresh eyes.

Even though Jack could scarcely read and do little more than pen his name, books lined the walls of his office, stretching to the domed ceiling.

He settled his gaze on Jack, sitting behind his desk, his secretary beside him, assisting him as they read over some documents.

Looking up, he greeted Ash as though nothing were out of the ordinary, as if gentlemen from Society's highest echelons were not about to descend upon this very house. "Ash. I didn't expect to see you today."

"Is it true?" he demanded, wasting little time.

Jack didn't even blink. He never did. Never gave an outward sign of what he was thinking. A trick Ash had learned from him. *Never show the world the true you. Cling to your guard.* "Is what true?"

"You have daughters. *Three* bloody daughters!"

Jack sighed and slid a glance to his assistant. "Give us a moment."

Ash watched him with narrowed eyes as the secretary left the room. Jack leaned back in his leather chair as the door clicked shut. "One of the maids, I presume? Every female on my staff falls into titters at the sight of you. Is there no woman you can't seduce?"

Ash snorted. Jack knew all about bedding women. His illegitimate offspring attested to that.

"Why are you here, Ash?" he demanded in a hard voice that told Ash he already knew.

"I want to hear the truth from you."

Jack studied him a long moment before speaking. "I'm a father. Is it so surprising that I should want to see my daughters? I'm not a young man anymore."

"I know you've gathered them all here to auction them off to some damned bluebloods." He felt his top lip curl back from his teeth in a sneer.

"Is it so wrong to want to see my girls well arranged—"

Ash broke out in laughter. He couldn't help himself. He knew Jack Hadley too well to believe he was a well-meaning father concerned with the welfare of his daughters.

"Come, Jack. Do you even know their names? This is about you. About getting yourself a duke for a son-in-law."

The older man's ruddy face burned vividly. "Of course, I know their names. I took pains to locate them, haven't I? They're all here . . ." A scowl swept his face. "Well, I believe so. The final one was to arrive today. She's been a bit elusive. Damned inconvenient. I have a big evening planned and I need her here."

The final one. She didn't even merit a name. She was without an identity. And yet Jack would hand over to her, to each of them, what Ash worked so hard to build. It was intolerable.

"So you don't deny you've claimed them as your heirs? That you intend to marry them off and give away all that I've labored to—"

"It's not all yours though, is it?" Jack cut in.

Ash ignored the question, pressing on. "The gaming hells were scarcely hanging on when you made me partner. The mine, the factory . . . I had to convince you to even agree to invest—"

"But I did agree," Jack inserted. "You couldn't have bought the mine or factory without me. And you've made me a very wealthy man. So wealthy I can buy myself any son-in-law I want."

Ash inhaled sharply. "What of me? Am I not to be considered a candidate?" The wild idea seized him, and he could not shake it loose. If marrying one of Jack's daughters helped him secure even a slight hold on the empire he'd built, then so be it. True, he'd still have two other daughters and their dandy husbands to contend with, but he'd cope—and all the better if he was married to a direct heir. One third of Jack's share would be his. Combined with the share he already possessed, he'd hold the greatest majority.

Jack arched a bushy brow. "You want to wed one of my daughters? *You?*"

The flesh near his eye ticked beneath Jack's appraisal. Of course he didn't want to marry one of the chits. He didn't want to marry anyone—much less some female he'd never clapped eyes on before. But in that moment he *did* want to know that this man who had saved him from starvation and abuse—this man who was the closest thing he would ever have to a father—*thought* he was good enough.

"Perhaps," he answered and held his breath as Jack regarded him with steady, unflinching eyes.

"Sorry, Ash. You know you're like a son to me, but I have big plans for these girls and you don't quite fit into them." His expression must have cracked, because Jack added, "I can't have you for a son-in-law. You're no different from me—another rat from the stews."

The words gouged him. "I see."

Nodding, he turned and strode from the room, each bite of his boots on the carpet driving the insult of Jack's words deeper home.

He did see. He saw everything clearly then. Jack had communicated his message perfectly. Ash wasn't good enough, and he didn't deserve to keep the empire he'd built up from two crumbling hells all to himself. He simply wasn't good enough to be Jack's sole heir.

Except no one told him he wasn't good enough. That he couldn't have something no matter what he did, no matter what he said or how hard he tried. He'd proven that over the years.

And he'd prove it again.

He may not want to marry, but he would.

He would have one of Jack's daughters, steal her right out from beneath his nose. Whatever bloody duke Jack had lined up for her would just have to miss out. Because Ash wasn't about to lose.

Not ever.

Chapter 7

She was vastly underdressed.

This regrettable thought flitted through Marguerite's mind as she entered Jack Hadley's drawing room to join her sisters. Her father, the butler informed her, was indisposed at the moment but would join them later. Just as well. She was not here for him, after all.

"Marguerite?" The older of the two girls rose to her feet, her elegant skirts swaying as she moved forward with an easy confidence. "I was afraid you would not come." She motioned to the other female sitting so silently, her slim hands folded neatly in her lap. "We'd begun to fear you did not wish to meet us."

"Of course I wanted to meet you. Both of you." *Especially before I leave.* Marguerite took a hesitant step, unsure where to sit.

"Come, seat yourself. I'm Grier and this is Cleopatra."

"Cleo," the one with hair nearly as dark as Marguerite's hastily corrected. A grim smile curved the lips. "My mother's a bit fanciful."

"You live with your mother?" It was on the tip of Marguerite's tongue to ask why she was here then, if she had a mother.

"Yes, and my stepfather." A grimace flickered across her pale face. "And my half brothers and half sisters."

"Fourteen, can you believe?" Grier volunteered, tucking an auburn strand back into her loosely arranged chignon. Her skin was unfashionably tan, but even that did not hide the spattering of brown freckles over her nose and cheeks.

Grier leaned forward. Reaching for the tea service, she poured a cup for Marguerite.

"Fourteen? How lovely," Marguerite murmured.

Cleo shrugged. "Not really. Why else would I answer the summons of a father who never sought to acknowledge me before?"

Marguerite nodded slowly, appreciating her candor and feeling the echo of that sentiment rush through her. "That's why you're here then?"

"That's why we're both here," Grier clarified. "We're both short on opportunities. Cleo is tired of being maid, cook, and nanny all rolled into one, and I'm . . . well. I just needed to get away from home." Grier's dark eyes took on a faraway glint. She tugged at her snug sleeve and scratched beneath at her wrist, convincing Marguerite she would be vastly more comfortable wearing something else. "I should have left a long time ago, but never had the opportunity before now. So, here we are then. And what of you? Are you here to stay?"

"It wasn't my intention. I came to meet you both." Marguerite cleared her throat, deciding now was as good a moment as any to explain that she would be leaving the country. "Before I go."

"Go?" Cleo asked. "Where are you going? You just arrived."

"I'm leaving. Tomorrow. For Spain."

"Spain? How exciting." Grier took a healthy swig of her tea and reached for a biscuit. "This is the farthest I've ever been from home. It's fair to assume then that you're not locked into sad circumstances that force you to accept the hospitality of the father who's neglected you all your life? Good for you."

Marguerite winced. She would scarcely consider her circumstances *good*.

"But what of tonight?" Cleo asked, her eyes bright with disappointment. "You do not intend to join us then?"

"Tonight?"

"Did you not receive my letter?" Cleo shook her head. The light streaming through the mullioned glass struck her dark hair, making it appear blue in places. "Jack gave me your address. I sent it two days ago. I thought that's why you were coming today."

Marguerite swallowed. She'd moved from the boardinghouse yesterday. Ever since her horrid nightmare, she'd been eager to leave the boardinghouse behind. Every time she glanced at the corner of the rented room, she expected to see the dark cloaked figure of Death again.

Aside from that, Roger insisted on putting her up at a hotel until they departed. His sisters resided with him in Town, so it was hardly appropriate to stay with him, but he was eager to begin his role of benefactor.

"What's tonight?" she repeated.

"Jack is throwing a little soiree for us." Cleo's

smile looked tight and brittle on her lips, as if the words hurt to speak.

"Oh, call it for what it is," Grier bit out, brushing the crumbs from her skirts as she finished her biscuit.

"I'm certain we can find you something to wear," Cleo offered, the hope rife in her voice.

"Did you not hear her?" Grier asked. "She's leaving for Spain. I don't think she wishes to snare a husband tonight. Not as we are meant to."

Husband. The word knifed through Marguerite, settling like a noose around her neck. It was as if Madame Foster was beside her now, whispering in her ear, *you will marry.*

"Snare a husband?" she managed to get out past dry lips.

"Jack has invited a few gentlemen to meet us this evening. It's to be a special gathering."

"Special." Grier snorted. "An auction more like it, so that these bluebloods may assess us as potential wives. It's why he's gathered us. He wants to wed us to some blue-blooded dandies, so he can call himself one of them." She sighed. "But the prospect of marrying well, security . . . never having to worry about the roof over my head . . ."

She gave a single hard nod. "I'd be a fool to pass up such an opportunity."

Marguerite stood on shaking legs, her head spinning. "I must go."

"You just got here."

"I'm sorry. This isn't what I thought . . . what I expected."

"Marguerite," Cleo settled her gaze on her. "You can't mean to leave so soon. We haven't even begun to acquaint ourselves."

"She's white as a ghost."

"I'm so sorry. I can't stay . . . I'll be back—"

"When? You're leaving for Spain," Grier reminded her.

She was correct, of course. Marguerite took a calming breath. She was leaving for Spain. She was not getting married. *Not getting married.* No need to dart from the room like a panicked hare at the mere mention of a husband. No need to react so irrationally. Still, the word hung there, too much, too close . . . too dangerous.

"I will call on you when I return." Hopefully, her father will have deserted all mad notions of marrying her off by then and satisfied himself with the more obliging Grier and Cleo. She nodded doggedly, backing out of the room. "I must go. Take care. Both of you."

She left them, intent on leaving before coming face-to-face with her father, before she had to hear his mad, selfish scheme from his own lips.

Free of the room, her heart calmed. Once she was free of Jack Hadley's house, she was certain her pulse would return to normal.

Sliding a shaking hand down her face, she started down the corridor. She hadn't taken very many steps before she sensed she was not alone. A floorboard creaked, and the hair at her nape tingled.

A memory flashed through her mind—the cloaked figure in her dream. A chill chased down her spine. Her heart hammered anew.

She turned around swiftly, intent on putting her fears to rest, certain she would find nothing more than an approaching servant.

A dark, blurred shape swept toward her like a great rolling tide. In less than a second, she was twisted around into arms that felt like steel bands, a brick wall of a chest at her back. Marguerite opened her mouth to scream, but managed only a brief shriek. Her cry was quickly cut off as a wad of fabric found its way in her open mouth. Speech was useless.

Something was thrown over her, sealing her in like a great cocoon. Caught, trapped, swathed in darkness, she kicked and clawed at heavy fabric, afraid she would be smothered.

"You're certain she's one of them?" A man's voice growled, velvet smooth despite the bite of his words.

She froze at the sound of it, a chill slithering through her and coiling around her heart.

A female voice, rushed and whispery as crackling parchment, quickly assured him. "Yes, yes, she's one of them. Now take her and go. Go before someone comes."

Then the thick voice returned, intruding in her dark, frightful world. She felt his face press close beside her head, imagined she felt his breath against her cheek.

"Hold silent and do not struggle. The sooner we're free of here, the sooner I'll lift this blanket from you. I've no wish to frighten you, nor is it in my practice to harm women. Understood?"

She nodded fiercely, anything to breathe again, to be rid of the suffocating fabric.

"Ash, be gone before someone comes. I'll not lose my post for you, no matter how far we go back." It was the whispering female again, a maid no doubt hired to assist the villain who dared to sneak into her father's household and make off with her. Marguerite could almost laugh—or weep—at the irony of it. Her first day as Jack Hadley's daughter—in a sense—and she suffered abduction. *Why?*

"Agreed then? You'll behave?" her assailant pressed.

Behave? Like a good little victim? Her temper simmering, she nodded yet again. Spots had begun to flash in and out before her eyes. She'd promise anything to be free of the smothering fabric.

Then his head moved from beside hers and she was swung up into his arms. The blanket shifted, loosened, freed more air near her nose, and breathing became easier. She had a sense that he must be very tall. It felt as though the ground loomed far below. She grasped what she could of him through the unwieldy volumes of the blanket shrouding her, praying she wouldn't fall.

They moved quickly. Before she knew it, cold, wet air curled around her dangling ankles and she knew they were outside. Panic rose in her chest, clawing through her. His footsteps fell louder, as though smacking on hard cobbles. She was free of her father's house. The very thing she had wished for moments ago, only not in such circumstances.

Beneath the many folds of her shroud, she worked her hands up and tugged the gag free. "I'm afraid there's been a dreadful mistake." Her voice was still muffled, but she felt certain he could understand her.

He ignored her and continued to move with hard, jarring strides.

She didn't allow his silence to defeat her. "I'm no one—nothing—to Jack Hadley. Whatever you hope to accomplish in seizing me, you will be sorely disappointed."

"You're one of his daughters," the deep voice rumbled low. A statement, not a question. She bit back the denial. His inside source, the maid, had him quite convinced of that truth, so there was no sense denying it.

"Scarcely so. I've never even met the man. I only called upon him today after receiving his summons to meet my half sisters. I was leaving, never to return—"

"Like I said, Jack Hadley *is* your father. That's all that matters to me."

She felt the tension in him as he uttered this, in the hard body holding her, so strong, so big, so . . . *male*. He enveloped her, carried her without the faintest hitch of breath.

He was a laborer. He must be. There wasn't an ounce of softness in the frame that held her so closely.

With a few more jarring steps, they stopped. She heard the squeak of a carriage door and then she was dumped unceremoniously upon soft squabs. As the door slammed shut, she fought free of her shroud. Tearing the fabric from her, she gulped air and woke to surroundings little changed from the dark world of moments ago.

The carriage was unlit. The curtains drawn. The barest light peeped out from the part. Even blind, she whipped her head around, blowing the hair that had fallen loose from her face.

Her fingers flexed on plush velvet squabs, digging until her knuckles ached. This was no hansom cab. The large shadow of a man sat across from her, still as marble, his eyes glowing faintly.

She stilled like prey caught in his watchful gaze. It was almost as though he could see her, even in this oppressive gloom.

Her nose flared. She smelled the faint whiff of mint. From him? And something else, something indefinable that made her quiver in a strange way.

Oddly enough fear eluded her. She should be terrified. She'd been abducted. Instead, she heard only Madame Foster's voice, her predictions ringing in her head. According to everything she had imparted, Marguerite would not die this day. It was too soon. Not enough time had passed, and she was unwed. She had not lived and loved as predicted. She would live through one more Christmas. This, she knew. For now, she was safe.

Fearless and calm, she squared her shoulders.

"No longer interested in screaming?" His voice rolled across the air like tendrils of smoke from a peat fire. She recalled that the treacherous maid had called him Ash. Fitting. Not only did his voice smolder like coals, he made her feel inexplicably warm inside.

"Should I scream?"

"Most women would."

"I'm not most women."

"I'm beginning to see that."

"You see nothing. What good would screaming do now? The only time it would have benefited me was back at Jack's house when I was gagged. It's pointless now and would likely only earn me a taste of your fist."

He chuckled softly, the low sound stroking something deep and unfamiliar inside her. "I would never strike you."

"No?" She angled her head. "You seemed quite threatening earlier."

She sensed his shoulder lift in the dark. "I needed you to fear me then. I wouldn't have that now."

Her hands balled into tight fists in her lap. "So you merely seed the fear of violence. And what do you think is worse? The fear or actuality of threat?" Before he had time to answer, she rushed to say, "I've lived with both and I can tell you it's a close race."

He was quiet for some time. She listened to the plod of hooves outside their carriage, sensing he was taking her measure. "You're not what I expected," he finally drawled.

She leaned forward on the seat and asked the question that she was almost too afraid to ask.

"And why should you expect anything of me?" They were nothing. Strangers. Predator and prey.

He inhaled, the soft sound deep and contemplative to her ears. "I assure you that I mean you no harm."

"And why should I take the word of my abductor?"

"Because I have never lifted a finger against a female . . . and I would die a miserable death before I ever assaulted my wife."

Wife. She jerked from the word, feeling it on a visceral level, a punch to her belly. Heat swelled over her face, making her skin itch. She fought to swallow the impossibly thick lump rising in her throat.

Madame Foster's voice was there again, a rushed whisper in her head, full of ominous warning. Turning her head slowly from side to side, she wet her numb lips and managed to whisper, "Wife?"

Was this it then? Her unavoidable fate? Would he force her to marry him? Was her life completely out of her hands?

"Yes. You and I shall marry. I've taken great pains to acquire one of Jack Hadley's daughters for that very purpose."

"Never," she hissed, fighting the warm wash of tremors his deep voice sent through her.

"I'm certain you'll come to see the advantages."

As suddenly as that, the fear that had eluded her, the fear that had seemed so pointless moments ago, found her and sealed her in, sinking its teeth deep.

Chapter 8

Ash observed the female within the deep shadows of the carriage, seeing only the hazy-dark smudge of her. He relaxed against the squabs, perfectly content to delay the moment when he clapped eyes on her. His future wife.

Triumph zinged through him at how easily he had stolen her from the partner who sought to steal everything from him, the empire he had created from two crumbling businesses.

Hopefully, she was at least passing fair. Not that he was marrying her for her face. Still, he hoped she bore little resemblance to her craggy-faced father.

Jack's daughter seemed to have stopped breathing from where she sat across from him. Curiosity rode hard in his chest, the urge rising to see what kind of woman he had shackled himself to. Before he'd captured her up in the blanket he'd glimpsed dark hair neatly arranged at the back of her head. There was that, at least, to look forward to in his future wife. He enjoyed dark hair, liked seeing it spread across his bed like spilled ink, trailing his fingers through the liquid dark . . .

Wife. The word left a bad taste in his mouth.

He'd never thought to marry. Had vowed against it, in fact. His earliest memories were of his parents' fighting, terrorizing and tormenting each other bit by bit until they finally succeeded in killing each other.

As for his sister, she was a casualty of their little war. Had they not been so obsessed in their rage for each other, they might have noticed their daughter slipping away from them, afflicted with rickets and dying in slow degrees. If they'd noticed, if they'd cared, they might have gotten her the proper nourishment she needed, might have saved her.

He shook off the unpleasant memories and faced the present. Getting leg-shackled was the last thing he desired, but he would not have a union like that of his parents. He wouldn't repeat their mistake. He would never possess such killing hatred for the female sitting so still and silent. It wasn't possible. To breed that kind of hate, one must first feel love. The sort of love his parents had shared at the beginning.

He squinted at her still shape. Jack's daughter— his future wife. His gut churned anew at the thought.

He need only remind himself that this marriage would help secure all he'd built—and would show Jack that he was not to be overlooked.

"What's your name?"

Silence answered him.

Now she would play silent? She'd been full of hot words earlier. "I'll have it from you eventually." He shrugged. "Something must go on the wedding register, after all."

"You cannot be serious." The croak of her voice scratched the air.

He flexed his fingers on his thigh. "Assuredly, I am."

"Why would you wish to marry me? You don't even know me."

"It is not *you*, specifically." He had every intention of being forthright with her. The simplest means to avoid confusion and disappointment.

"I've determined to wed one of Jack Hadley's daughters."

"Then choose another. Turn this carriage around. One of my half sisters may in fact be agreeable. Even now, they're preparing for a soiree of some sort where they will meet prospective suitors—"

"Which I am not considered to be," he growled, his hand squeezing into a fist. "Jack does not approve of me as a husband for any of his precious offspring."

"That's what this is about then? Some blasted grudge you harbor against my father?" She muttered something indecipherable beneath her breath in a language he suspected was not English. French, perhaps? Her words were too low for him to determine. "Has the world gone mad?"

"Has it ever been sane?" he asked. He had decided the world a far from logical place long ago, when he'd been lost to the streets at the tender age of eight. "When you mull it over, you and I marrying is scarcely absurd. Fitting perhaps. Face it, neither of us is a feted blueblood."

He caught the motion of her shaking head. "I'll not wed you."

Ash inhaled, gathering his patience close. It was

only fair to expect she would need a little coaxing, but as soon as she understood the advantages, he was confident she would cease her protests. He was a businessman. He knew how to negotiate a favorable arrangement. "Your agreement is desired, of course. I am certain you will—"

"Desired?" She laughed. The sound rang brokenly, fractured in the closed space. "You think I *might* desire such a fate? I have plans, and you, sir, shall not ruin them for me."

"What are your plans then?" He was certain he could counter any of her *plans* with far better prospects. He need only explain that she had landed herself a good catch, that his pockets ran deep enough to see her in jewels and satins for the rest of her life. "I'm not without means. You'll live a life of comfort. I have a magnificent home in the City awaiting a woman's touch."

She snorted.

He frowned at her shadow. "Consider my words. The situation I offer you would be the envy of many a woman. Home, security—a lifestyle that no doubt far exceeds your present circumstances." He had not missed the rough wool of her gown when he held her. Hardly the most sophisticated or elegant of wardrobe. "And I'm not exactly repulsive. I've been remarked handsome."

"Is there no end to your arrogance?"

His face burned—an entirely new and uncomfortable sensation. He detested this, this . . . entreaty. He'd never had to petition for a female's favors before. "I merely point out qualities that would appeal to a woman seeking a husband."

"You fail to understand me. I do not seek a husband. You're ruining everything! I leave tomorrow for Spain." Desperation tinged her voice. A sweet voice even in her anger. Her rushed vowels became more notable in her pique, evidence of a French background, perhaps. Perhaps her mother was an émigré. "The arrangements have all been made. Please let me go."

He frowned. This was not going as planned. She was not in the least obliging. Trust him to take the one daughter with no interest in finding a husband. "Tomorrow we'll be on our way to Scotland," he snapped, refusing to yet relinquish his agenda, convinced he could persuade her given the time to do so.

"Scotland," she hissed the word as if it were a

deprivation forced upon her, as though he'd threatened her with Newgate.

"Yes. It's the country to the north of us."

An outraged breath hissed past her lips at his mockery. "You cannot abduct me, drag me across the country and force me to wed you. These aren't the Middle Ages."

"In truth, I could . . . but I won't have to." Money, he'd learned, mixed with a fair bit of charm, won most anything. He was certain he could persuade her to marry him. He would never have bought the mine in Wales without his powers of persuasion. The sellers were very opposed to outsiders acquiring the mine. He'd overcome that challenge just as he'd overcome this one, too.

"My father—"

"Won't care once the deed is done," he finished. "He's a fairly old-fashioned man. He'll consider you well and truly mine once we're married. I know him. That will be the end of it."

"It won't be the end of it, because it's not going to happen!"

With that outraged cry, she flew for the carriage door.

He moved swiftly after her, hauling her back even as she strained for the door latch, a wild animal in his arms. He flung her down onto the seat. She turned on him in a sudden twist, throwing herself against him, spewing French curses.

His arms tightened around her slight frame, catching her as they fell to the floor of the carriage.

She tried to scramble up off him, but he locked his arms around her, trapping her sharp little fists between them, holding her tightly against him. She squirmed, wiggling, her skirts pooling over his thighs. He could not help himself. He took measure of the female in his arms.

She was small. Standing, she wouldn't reach his shoulder, and yet she was pleasantly formed, soft and well-rounded in all the right places. She still struggled—for the little good it did her—affording him the sensation of her soft body against his own, her breasts brushing him again and again. Until he had to bite back a groan.

"You'll only tire yourself," he murmured thickly.

"Let me go," she pleaded, her voice choked in a way that made him fear tears were close.

"Do you intend to vault from a moving carriage? Do you want to injure yourself? You're not going anywhere with a broken neck, I can assure you of that." He gave her a small shake, letting the words sink in. He had no wish to bind her hands and wrists. That wouldn't be comfortable, to say nothing of barbaric, but he'd do what he must to keep her from doing damage to herself.

She stilled then, her warm breath a pleasant fan on his face. "Very well," she whispered hoarsely. "I'm calm. I won't jump."

His chest tightened uncomfortably at the sound of her aggrieved voice. He'd given *her* very little thought when conceiving this scheme. She'd simply been one of Jack's bastard daughters. Now she was here, and he was faced with the reality of her.

Sighing, he gentled his voice and said, "Just hear my proposition—"

"I have a lover," she blurted. "I'm another man's mistress. Tomorrow I leave for Spain with m-m-my protector."

His chest lifted with a sharp breath at the un-expected words. Disappointment rooted deeply in his chest, settling there like a heavy rock. "You're a . . . kept woman?"

An emotion he could not identify followed

close on the heels of the realization that he knew nothing of this woman. Not her name. Not her face. Not even a hint of who she was. It had not occurred to him that she might possess entanglements. His hands loosened from her wrists and he pulled back. Her arms fell away from him, and she quickly scrambled back across the carriage.

The fleeting thought passed through his mind that he should return her and forget her sultry-soft voice. Then he heard Jack's voice, hard and matter-of-fact, whipping through his head, explaining that Ash was not good enough to be his heir. *Not good enough . . .*

Now, more than ever, he was convinced their marriage would be good for her. For the both of them. It would save her from her situation as some man's tart and grant her a life of legitimacy. He offered her freedom. He just had to make her see that.

"You *were* leaving for Spain," he began, his voice quiet but firm. "No longer. Now you are journeying to Scotland with me. On the way there, you'll realize that I'm offering you something this protector of yours never could." *He would convince her of that.*

"And what would that be?"

"Freedom. The means to be an independent woman. To go anywhere and do anything you want."

She held silent for a moment, and he knew he'd baited the hook. She was listening, perhaps for the first time. "You don't plan to *force* me to wed you . . ."

"I won't have to," he replied. "You'll see the wisdom in this. We'll use the journey to better acquaint ourselves." He heard her sigh, felt it ripple through him. A good sign. She was relenting. One more inducement and the deal was done. He was certain of it. "We need not even consummate the marriage. It will be assumed. After a few months, you can go anywhere you wish . . . fully funded."

"A few months," she echoed. He did not mistake the longing in her voice.

"Do yourself a favor and take the time to consider what I'm offering at the very least." His voice fell with a quiet hush, calm for all the tension riddling him as he awaited her response.

"Very well," she whispered at last. "I'll consider it."

His head dropped back on the seat. "You should

rest until we reach the inn," he suggested, feeling suddenly weary, none of the triumph he expected to feel present at her near agreement. None of this had gone quite as he thought . . . not that he had thought much about how they might interact—about *her* at all. He certainly hadn't considered that she might belong to another man. His hand curled unconsciously into a fist.

"When will we stop?"

"We had a late start. It's nearly dark. We'll stop just outside the city. Not too long."

Then everything would be better, he vowed, turning to gaze out the thin part in the curtains, watching the dark shapes fly past. It had to be. He couldn't accept defeat. Not on this. Even though he couldn't force some woman to wed him against her will, he would not give up until he persuaded her to agree.

He imagined the evening ahead. They would exchange pleasantries and come to an accord over a fine meal, a cozy fire crackling and warming the air. He would entertain her in a civil manner, charm her, compliment her fine eyes . . . woo her so that she fell readily into his lap and married him with little fuss.

There was no reason events shouldn't unfold amicably between them. Sighing, he relaxed back against his seat, letting the merry vision fill his head. And almost believing it.

As she gazed at the shadow of the man who abducted her, Marguerite could no longer deny the truth. No more lying or pretending to herself. It was there, staring back at her. Everything pointed to it. The signs were inescapable. As definite as the hard male body sitting across from her, reality stared her coldly in the face.

Madame Foster was no fraud.

Even as she confronted this bitter truth, Marguerite recalled something the woman had said in her cluttered parlor. Something that gave Marguerite hope and determination to push on, to thwart the scoundrel who sat across from her so confident in her surrender.

No one's fate is etched in stone. A moment's decision can alter the course of fate.

Marguerite would do that—she would alter her fate, do everything in her power to prevent the future Madame Foster had divined. She must. Whatever it took, she would *not* marry the arrogant brute with the mesmerizing voice. As long as that didn't happen, she would be safe. *That*, above all else, must not come to pass. Let him think she took his offer under consideration. If he deemed her compliant, it would make him easier to escape.

They sat in silence. She rocked with the carriage's rolling motion, biting the edge of her thumb, gnawing it the way she used to do when she was a child. First at the bedside of her ailing mother, and then later, cold and hungry, often ill as she slept in a tiny cot on the second floor of Penwich School for Virtuous Girls.

She felt that way again. Not ill, but cold, helpless, a fate not of her choosing pressing in around her, suffocating her in a tremendous dark fog.

Not again, she vowed. Never again.

She wasn't a helpless child anymore but a woman full-grown, and she wouldn't die without having fully lived.

She couldn't trust his promise for a temporary in-name-only marriage. Not for a moment. Too much depended on whether he spoke the truth—her very life. She wouldn't put anything past a man who dared to abduct her. Let him think she surrendered, agreed to his ridiculous proposition.

Then, when his guard was down, she'd leave him in the dust.

She'd have everything she ever planned for herself. Adventure, passion, the experiences she'd never allowed herself.

Life. Finally, life.

Chapter 9

Incredibly, Marguerite fell into a doze against the carriage wall. She napped fretfully, jostled awake from time to time when the carriage hit a rut. She would crack her eyes and assess the shadow across from her, a biting reminder that she was far from the safety of her bed at the Hotel Daventry. Far removed from a trip to Spain with Roger and the adventure of a lifetime she had promised herself.

The memory of her abductor's voice curled around her, smoky and deep. A bothersome and confusing reaction. Why should she feel anything but fear for the faceless stranger determined to make her his wife? He represented everything she must avoid.

Reminding herself they weren't too far from London, she rubbed the vestiges of sleep from her eyes. She could still manage to find her way back to her hotel in time for tomorrow's departure. Roger told her he would collect her at noon. She squinted at the dark outline across from her. He sat still as stone, but she did not deceive herself. She knew he was awake, had likely been watching her the entire time. A cat eyeing its prey. The hairs at her nape prickled. Rather irrationally, she wondered if he could *see* her. Did his gaze penetrate the dark like that of some predatory beast?

When the carriage finally slowed, she pulled upright, snapping alert, prepared for the first opportunity to escape no matter how the memory of his voice tumbled through her and settled like liquid heat in the pit of her belly. She told herself it was simply her decision to discard propriety, to embrace carnal pleasure that had awakened this hidden part of her. Nothing more. Not him specifically. Heavens, no. She had not even clapped eyes on his face.

"Where are we?" she asked the precise moment a groom pulled open the door.

A sudden draft whipped inside the carriage. She wore no cloak and her wool gown afforded scarce protection. Instantly her teeth clattered, and she hugged herself tightly, squeezing her arms.

Her abductor moved like a jungle cat then, proving that he was indeed quite awake. He descended the carriage with smooth movements, reaching back inside for her. He lowered her effortlessly to the ground, where she could appreciate the full height of him a scant moment before he turned and pulled her toward the waiting inn with its flickering windows that promised light and heat.

She sucked in a great, icy breath, preparing herself for what she knew she must do as her feet tripped, one after the other, through the slushy ground.

She held up her skirts, cold mud splattering up her calves, well past her half boots. With a deep breath, she fixed her sights on the inn's double doors. She could do this.

She envisioned the scene perfectly in her head. She would unleash an earful on the first person she saw on the other side. In minutes a magistrate would arrive, gripping her arm supportively while her captor was hauled off to the gaol.

She almost felt sorry for him. She almost felt guilty for breaking her promise to grant him time to convince her that marrying him was a good idea. *Almost*—had her happiness, her very life, not been at stake. Time was something she did not have.

As he guided her across the last half of the yard, she glanced up at his profile, steeped in the deep cover of night. The flickering lanterns hanging outside the inn afforded little relief.

A dog barked, rushing to greet them. Her blood pounded in cold-constricted veins as she practiced various dire proclamations in her head that would stir any soul to action.

She visualized three very large, very mean-looking men sitting inside the inn. The sort of men who loved their mothers and harbored deep-rooted protective instincts toward the fairer sex. They would surge to their feet on her behalf.

"Wait a moment." His hand on her arm pulled her to a stop.

She blinked at his shadowy form, trying to decipher his intent. A slight popping sound filled the air. She cocked her head, recognizing the sound but not quite placing it. At least not until he splashed her liberally with gin.

He'd uncorked a bottle.

She cried out as alcohol saturated the front of

her dress, sinking through her chemise into her very bones. The overpowering aroma wafted up, burning the inside of her nose.

"Forgive me," he said, popping the cork back in place, and not sounding in the least contrite. "A precautionary measure."

"What are you doing?" she demanded between chattering teeth. "You've ruined my dress."

"And, I imagine, your credibility. I don't intend to risk you prattling on that I've abducted you. I've spent a time or two behind bars as a lad. It's not an experience I relish repeating."

She sputtered, at a loss for words. Could he read minds? How had he conceived it was her intention to see him locked away?

He continued, "Should you heap pleas upon sympathetic ears, I shall confess, to my shame, that I have a very drunken wife." He mockingly clucked his tongue. "Have you ever heard of such a thing? Quite embarrassing. A sickness, really. I don't know what to do with her."

"You wouldn't dare!"

In the gloom, he waved a hand over her person. "Oh, it's quite done already, my love."

My love. The empty endearment puckered her

skin to gooseflesh. The cad was a stranger, an utter malcontent. His potent voice and empty endearments should not stir her in any way.

"No one would believe such drivel! I'm not a drunkard."

Taking hold of her arm again, he said lightly, "Why should this bother you so greatly? You promised you would hear me out and give us some time to become acquainted. Unless you *lied* and planned to escape me all along."

She snapped her lips shut, unwilling to admit that was precisely what she had hoped to do, and loathing that she should feel a flash of guilt.

Her captor strode toward the inn, his long fingers looped around her wrist. She stumbled after him, trying to recover her composure and not appear the drunkard he sought to portray her.

With the front of her gown soaked, she shivered as they entered the inn's toasty confines. Still, she suspected her trembling had more to do with her anger than the cold wet.

Stepping into the large well-lit room, she blinked like a mole emerging from the earth, searching, seeking a friendly face—someone who might aid her.

Her gaze locked on a cheery-faced man, nearly as round as he was tall, waddling toward her at what must be quite the clipped pace for him. He wiped meaty hands on his apron, exclaiming, "Welcome, welcome, my fine friends!"

Marguerite opened her mouth to declare the brute beside her the lowest scoundrel, an abductor of innocents. With those hot words burning on the tip of her tongue, she turned to face her accused, ready to condemn him before he bandied his lies about her.

Mouth open, words hovering so close, she froze. Utterly robbed of speech, she stared.

The hard lines of his face reflected her own surprise. Or was it horror?

The innkeeper had reached them by now, but still they continued to gawk at one another. Her abductor's dark eyes crawled over her as though he had never seen a female before.

It was he. *Him.* The man from the St. Giles. "Courtland," she whispered.

"Marguerite," he returned, mouthing her name so quietly she scarcely heard him.

Now the bothersome effect of his rumbling voice made sense. It had been the same then, when he'd pressed his body to hers, when he'd touched her so intimately and had spoken near her ear. On some level, she must have recognized him. She must have known.

"You," she hissed. She shook her head as though dizzy, struggling to reconcile the scoundrel from St. Giles with this man who claimed to possess great wealth. Wealth enough to tempt her into matrimony—at least to his thinking.

He blinked and whatever emotion she had awakened in him vanished. His dark gaze stared at her coolly, the light lost, dormant. Once again, he was in control.

"Of course, my dear," he soothed in the beleaguered voice of an afflicted husband. She followed his gaze to the watchful eyes of the innkeeper. "It's always me. By your side."

Understanding at once that he was attempting to establish the pretense that they were married, she pulled her arm free in a wild jerk. "Oh, no you don't," Marguerite hissed in low tones. She lunged for the innkeeper, eager to explain her predicament, but Courtland stepped on her hem, his boot firmly catching her in place.

She staggered, wobbled, struggling to right

herself, to pull her hem loose. And then suddenly, she was free. He removed his boot from her hem and she tripped against the innkeeper. A deliberate move, no doubt, to make her look all the more unstable.

"Umph!" the innkeeper exclaimed.

"I'm so sorry! My apologies," she babbled. "He made me do it . . ." her voice faded at the look on the innkeeper's face. He pressed one hand to his nose, the offending smell of her clearly devastating him. He placed his pudgy hands on her arms and quickly set her away from him. "There, there, now." He leveled both of them with a stern look. "I don't know what kind of establishment you think I'm operating here—"

"You'll have to forgive my wife," Courtland began, his tone placating and needling. Not at all *him*. That much she knew already. "We've returned from my great aunt's ninetieth birthday celebration. The dear old bird—can't believe she's still getting on. Walks to the village and back every day. She even walks to church on Sundays, weather permitting of course, and that's quite a distance. My wife here has difficulty controlling herself where spirits are concerned. It's been a lifelong battle. But what can I do? I married the girl. I protect her as much as I can from her demons, but I cannot stand guard of her every moment—"

Marguerite sputtered, her nails cutting painfully into her tender palms. What a display! He belonged on stage. "You bounder! Wretch!"

The innkeeper looked wide-eyed between them.

The scoundrel with his liquid dark eyes even managed to look angelic and contrite as he shook his head. Blast the man! "I promise if you just let us a room for the night, we shall not cause any disorder and we'll depart at first light." The silver-tongued devil pulled a healthy pouch of coins from his cloak and dangled it for the innkeeper. "I'll more than compensate you."

The portly innkeeper wet his lips and snatched up the sack. "So long as you don't disturb my other patrons."

" 'Course, the missus will no doubt succumb to sleep the moment she touches down on the bed. 'Tis the case in most these situations."

With a brisk, businesslike nod, the innkeeper led them up a narrow set of steps. Her captor clamped down on her arm, continuing to talk over her protests and mutterings about his great-aunt's birthday festivities and painting himself the veritable saint for so loyally abiding his sot of a wife.

At the door to their room, the innkeeper left them a lamp, offering the parting advice, "Appears she might need more of a firm hand from you."

Courtland actually deigned to look sheepish, smiling feebly. It was such a false expression, almost ridiculous on his face, a face carved from stone. "I do let my tender feelings for her at times stand in the way of sound judgment."

"It's a rigid hand she needs, either from you or in an asylum."

"I'll take that under advisement."

Oh, the miserable man! Marguerite looked around wildly. Any guilt for lying, for reneging on her promise to consider his offer of marriage fled. Her gaze scoured the room, landing on the pitcher sitting on the washstand. She tugged her arm free of her *alleged* husband.

Courtland released her, shutting the door with a click, isolating them.

This time, no masks. No darkness shrouding them. Just the two of them. She was alone in a bedroom with a very big, virile male intent on dragging her toward the fate she fought to avoid. And she had all but told him such a fate was acceptable to her. Of course, that was before she realized he was the scoundrel from St. Giles. Before he doused her in gin. She absolutely could not marry *him*.

Her gaze devoured the chipped pitcher, angrier than she had ever felt in her life. Her trembling hands closed around the heavy porcelain, her fingers curling over the curving handle.

Swinging around, she let the pitcher fly.

His eyes widened a fraction before ducking. The pitcher crashed against the wall.

With a grunt of disappointment, her gaze scanned the room for the next available object. Unfortunately, there wasn't time to seize anything before he grabbed her around the waist and lifted her off her feet. Air escaped her in a great gust as his shoulder ground into her belly. She beat him on the shoulders, the back, anywhere she could reach. He stalked across the room, hauling her like a sack of grain, not the least affected from her efforts.

He flung her down on the bed. "Enough," he growled, looming over her, a dark scowl on his face. Except the scowl did nothing to detract from his striking looks. Her heart tripped treacherously, tightening in her chest.

Staring at his too-beautiful visage, she sank into the soft mattress—and that made an entirely new kind of panic flare inside her.

His words fell clipped and hard from his well-carved lips. "I just promised the innkeeper to keep you in check, and I don't relish spending the night in the carriage when you get us thrown out."

"I don't care what you *relish*!"

His eyes narrowed to hooded slits, no less diminishing their brilliant darkness. His jaw clenched, a muscle feathering along the taut, shadowed flesh. "You've promised to consider my offer. I intend to see you keep that promise."

"I changed my mind. I have plans, a life—" She struggled beneath the hard line of his body, choking a bit on these words, at the ache beneath her breastbone. "A life to lead." A well-lived life. "You're ruining it all!"

His gaze crawled over her face, missing nothing. She recoiled, averse to him seeing anything at all within her. "Is this because of that bloody trip to Spain?" he demanded. "I've wealth for you to enjoy countless times over. Wed me and you can go anywhere in the world without being beholden to anyone."

She shook her head where she lay beneath him on the bed. "You don't understand." *I haven't the time.* Deciding to try a softer approach, she moistened her lips. Recalling his name, she murmured, "Ash, please. You must release me. You don't understand how important—"

"It's this lover then?" He shifted, settling deeper against her. His hard chest undulated in a way that made her breasts tighten. Her cheeks burned anew at their immodest position. Her gaze raked the broad line of his shoulders, the chest straining against his jacket. She blinked once, squeezing her eyes tightly, trying to block out his physicality. Opening her eyes, awareness of him hit her full force again and left her quivering. The memory of his strength, the raw power that she had witnessed in the streets of St. Giles invaded her thoughts, catching her breath in her throat.

"Do you love him then?" His voice lowered as he brought his face closer to her neck. She trembled at the warm rasp of his words on her throat. "Is that it? Are you afraid he will not wait for you? That after a few days he'll take another mistress? Take *her* to Spain when you go missing?"

She held her breath, unsure how to answer.

Should she claim to love Roger? Insist that he loved her in turn? What man, after all, wanted a wife who pined for another?

She watched him carefully, studied the shadows flickering over his face, dancing over the harsh lines. The nose that may have been broken at one time. The mouth sensual and beckoning. A stark contrast to the unyielding look of him.

Too bad he wanted marriage.

The thought came unbidden. If he didn't want to marry her, she could use him to exact all her desires. He was the perfect specimen. His hooded eyes promised all manner of illicit knowledge. A glance into them and she felt pulled, compelled, dragged into something dark and fathomless deep. A man like him could teach her a thing or two about passion. Even his name hinted at vice . . . *Ash.*

Like this, with his vital body pressed over hers, she felt more alive than she had in years. It was enough. Enticement enough to let madness seize her and take over, urging her to arch up against him, molding herself to all the warm male hardness.

He angled his face, watching her closely, studying her as she studied him. With a finger to her jaw, he tilted her face up and to the side. "I can see nothing of Jack in you." A smile twitched his lips, lips that dipped toward her, drawing ever closer. "Which is just as well. I don't really care to think about him at this particular moment."

His finger on her jaw slid to the corner of her mouth, brushing the bottom lip. She trembled, ached strangely, yearning from the center of her being.

Was this his plan then? Seduce her with the gentlest touch? Was this how he meant to persuade her to marry him?

Her body hummed, every nerve ending quivering fiercely, as if she might ignite.

He stroked the full length of her bottom lip in a gliding caress, his fingertip dipping inside her mouth just the barest hint. Enough for her to taste him.

"I think we'll get on just fine." His hoarse voice scratched the air. "This won't be such a bad arrangement for either one of us."

No words could have more effectively doused her ardor. In one breath he reminded her that he wanted marriage—a destiny tantamount to death for her.

She jerked her head away from his offending hand. "Get off me."

His eyes narrowed at her tone, but he didn't move. Remained a heavy wall atop her. "What? No sampling? It's not as if you've not freely given it before."

Her cheeks burned. "Freely given to a man of my choosing—that of which you'll never be."

"You might surprise yourself." His lip curled up over his teeth. "I've not been refused before."

"Well, you are now."

"I've not set about trying, my dear."

"Seems you just were."

"What? This?" He glanced between them, at the nonexistent space separating their bodies, and chuckled. The sound raised the tiny hairs on the nape of her neck. Everything about him did that, touched her, stroked her without actual contact. "This is scarcely seduction. You would know seduction. I can be very persuasive, I assure you."

She snorted and gave another shove at his chest. "What on earth makes you think I would want some blackguard from St. Giles to place his hands upon me?" The words burst from her lips.

However much she intended to be insulting, cruel even, her chest tightened uncomfortably at the look on his face. Like she had struck him. A flash of emotion glimmered in his dark eyes before vanishing, leaving flat blackness in its place. Once again, his face was cold, impassive marble.

He stood, peeled himself away from her as if he couldn't stand the contact. As he moved to the door, she scooted to the edge of the bed and rose to her feet, loathing how unsteady her legs felt.

"Where are you going?"

"Why should you care? I'm simply some primitive. A savage from the stews."

She held up her chin. "As it pertains to me, I care."

"We leave at dawn. That's the only thing you need concern yourself with." His voice rang sharply. "Get yourself some sleep. You look fit to collapse." He pulled open the door and stood there for a moment, looking to the side, avoiding her gaze, his profile etched in the sifting shadows. "You promised to consider my offer. I intend to see you keep that vow."

Already her mind raced, speculating on how long to wait before making her way downstairs to find help from someone besides the innkeeper, who had already formed his opinion of her.

Again, as though he knew the workings of her mind, he added, "And don't think of leaving this room. No doubt there's some servant whose services I can engage to guard the door . . . in order to prevent my poor, mindless wife from leaving and harming herself."

Oh! She lunged for the washstand and snatched the basin from its nest. With a cry of frustration, she lifted her arm to fling it in his direction, but he was already gone, the door clicking shut. The sound of his chuckle mingled with his fading tread.

The reprobate was clever, damn him.

Well, she would show him. She would show him just how clever she could be . . . just how clever a woman with nothing to lose could be.

Chapter 10

Ash stomped down the steps after cornering a maid in the corridor and offering her a generous amount of coin to guard the door.

Relieved of that concern, he descended to the main floor, where he spotted his driver and groom at a table, huddled over bowls of steaming stew. With a quick nod to them, he headed out into the night, indifferent to the biting cold. He'd talk with the men later and make certain they knew to be ready at first light.

He didn't think Jack would come after them. He'd have to know Ash even took his daughter for that to happen, and he doubted he did. According to Marguerite, she wasn't participating in her father's little marriage auction. She had, in fact, been leaving the house when he absconded with her. So that she might ready herself for her voyage.

The reminder whispered across his head, sliding down his throat in a bitter swallow, and he knew why. It had nothing to do with her trip to Spain, specifically, but it had everything to do with the fact that she had a lover.

His hands balled into fists, the knuckles painfully tight and aching at the thought of her locked in another man's embrace . . . at home in another man's bed. Absurd. He barely knew her, but possessiveness toward her curled low in his gut as he imagined her with this lover. Some man who probably paced the floors for her now. Ash lifted one shoulder against the cutting wind. Too bad. He felt no remorse for the faceless figure. If this man had wanted to keep her, if he had wanted to make certain no man snatched her away, he should have married her himself. Now she belonged to Ash, or soon would.

He walked directly into the wind's teeth, glad for the cold slash against his skin. It brought him back to earth. To reality, chilling the warm lust that ran through his veins. Inconvenient, that. Lust addled one's head, and he needed his thoughts clear and composed when it came to dealing with Marguerite.

She was a clever little witch. Hot-tempered, too. A dangerous combination. He could see the wheels turning behind those whiskey eyes and knew that she would escape if he gave her the chance. He couldn't let that happen.

He slid a glance to the inn, to the second floor, and then looked away, as if he indulged in weakness by looking back.

The girl in that second-floor room was nothing like he had expected. He had assumed from what Mary told him that Jack's daughters were *all* in the market for a husband. But this one—the spitfire with fiery eyes and night-black hair—was hardly the agreeable female he'd imagined. Just his luck that he'd grabbed the one daughter who didn't wish to be married off.

He should take her back as she suggested and trade her in for one of her more willing sisters. A malleable female who knew a good arrangement when presented with it.

He stopped abruptly and swung around to glare at the inn, specifically the dimly glowing window on the second floor where he knew her to be.

The only problem with that plan was that she had gotten beneath his skin. And not tonight. It was that day in St. Giles. From the beginning, from that first encounter, she'd lingered in his head, with her hot accusations and eyes that burned. And now he had her.

He need only convince her that marrying him was to her benefit and not just his. Once her temper cooled, she'd start to see the logic, the wisdom behind their union.

If he believed in things like fate, he would say their paths had been destined to intersect again. He wouldn't throw her back like some puny fish. He had her. And he wasn't letting go.

The carriage rumbled beneath Marguerite with an unsettling rhythm she was coming to know much too well. With a small sigh, she parted the curtains and stared miserably out at the snow-covered landscape.

They'd been together for three days now. Her ship for Spain would have long since departed without her. Roger probably thought she had changed her mind and lacked the courage to face him and tell him so herself.

Courtland had been true to his word. He presented her with a sound argument for a name-in-only marriage at every opportunity. Independence, freedom to do what she wished, go where she wished. Tempting indeed. Only Madame Foster's words gave her pause, stopped her from agreeing to what was sounding more and more an ideal arrangement.

Of course, she wondered if eschewing intimacy meant she would avert her fated death. Sighing, she rubbed her temples. It was enough to make her head throb.

Escape was her only recourse.

Courtland never left her unguarded. Whenever he stepped from her side he made certain someone was there. Either the driver, the footman, or someone else he paid to hover over her.

"Just seeing that you keep your word," he had archly reminded her when she protested.

Blast her for promising to consider his offer! "I retract my promise. Take me home."

Those dark eyes of his had drilled into her so darkly then, flat and motionless as a midnight sea. She'd strained for a glimpse of something beneath the liquid dark, a flicker of his thoughts. "Is that honor to you? Making promises and then discarding them when convenient?"

Rather than scream, she had looked away then, reminding herself that she was not a woman given to tantrums. They had not spoken since.

She supposed an ordinary woman might have accepted her fate. It wasn't as though she was being forced to wed a hideous figure of a man, after all. He was handsome. He possessed funds enough to outfit her in a lifestyle she never dared dream for herself.

And yet, ever since her collision with Madame Foster, her life had taken a decidedly extraordinary turn.

Ash seemed to relax as London fell farther and farther behind. His shoulders lost some of their rigidity. Not that she thought anyone would follow them. Certainly, the father she had yet to meet would care little for the daughter who failed to fall in line with his schemes.

Courtland's growing ease would be to her advantage. She was resourceful. She had not survived years at Penwich without using her wits. She'd outsmart Ash yet. She could still break free and find her way back to London, back to Roger. Once she explained everything, he would doubtless reschedule their adventure. There was still time.

"A village lies ahead. We'll rest and dine there while we change out the horses."

She nodded, a cloud of breath fogging at her lips. Winter managed to penetrate the well-appointed carriage. She couldn't imagine the level of cold she'd be enduring if she weren't traveling in such comfort. Heated bricks warmed her feet and a thick blanket covered her lap. Every morning he draped the blanket on her lap, tucking it around her as if she were a child. She always sat still, astounded at the care he took, struggling to refrain from softening toward him. She couldn't forget this was the same ruthless man who had abducted her.

She flexed her gloved fingers inside the soft ermine muff atop her lap and stared at him, searching for something unlikeable in his handsome face. A hard-eyed cruelty, a tight-lipped savagery ready to unleash itself on her. Not that she wanted to be harmed . . . she simply wanted him to be less . . . *appealing*.

He'd found her appropriate attire for the cold climate and days of hard travel. That he had taken such consideration of her added to her unease.

No one had ever taken care of her before. Her

earliest memories were of spending all her energies on her mother, seeing that she did not languish in the neglect of Jack Hadley. It was a full-time occupation, keeping Mama from wilting and withering away entirely between her visits to Jack.

Marguerite was good at taking care of others. It's what she did, after all. All she knew how to do.

But *this*? A man caring for her . . .

She shook her head, refusing to let that affect her. Tender feelings for Courtland would only weaken her from her purpose. From what she must do. As enticing as his offer was, she could not risk marriage to him. In-name-only or not.

She hardened her heart, warning herself not to be duped into liking him because he provided her with clothes and a blanket. He likely had no wish for her to die from exposure. She moved her gaze from the window, studying his profile.

Aside of his kind gestures, his sound arguments, he'd held himself distant as they traveled north. She was certain it was what she had said that first night at the inn.

What on earth makes you think I would want some blackguard from St. Giles to place his hands upon me?

Ever since she'd flung that insult in a desperate

attempt to remove his person from her, he'd held himself aloof. Distant. She'd struck a nerve. Who he was, what he was, where he came from . . . apparently, those were sensitive points for him.

Or it could just be that he offered her a marriage founded in cool practicality, and he felt no emotion regarding the matter. Regarding her.

The carriage came to a stop. Frigid wind buffeted her as she stepped down. With every mile north they plunged deeper into the teeth of winter.

She shivered and burrowed into her cloak and hood. Walking alongside Courtland, she paused to watch a family walking past with arms full of greenery. For boughs, she assumed, recalling that it was Christmastime. The mother exclaimed as the youngest tripped and fell into his armload of pine and holly. She and the older two children hurried over to the little one, dusting the needles off him and putting a stop to the tears.

"Come," Courtland tugged on her arm. "There's a fire inside."

She pulled her gaze from the mother and children and permitted him to guide her inside the inn, holding silent as they were shown to their room. *Her* room rather. Since that first night when she'd insulted him, he didn't so much as step inside her room. She supposed she should feel relieved.

The few times she'd tried to leave her room, she'd opened the door only to find someone standing guard. The groom, the driver, a barmaid. Never him though. And she couldn't help wondering where he spent his nights.

Did he bed down with a willing female? One of the many maids who followed him hungrily with their eyes? She shouldn't care, but the notion pricked at her.

His deep voice rumbled over the air. "I'll have a tray sent up." The same words he'd uttered the last several nights. "Do you need anything?" He asked that each time, too.

She moved to the center of the room, rotating in a small circle to face him.

He didn't bother moving deeper into the room. Standing with one hand on the door latch, he waited for her response, appearing anxious to escape her company.

Rubbing her arms, she lifted her chin and stared at him coolly. "My freedom would be nice."

His lips twitched and for a moment she thought his implacable exterior might crack, that he might actually smile. Then his lips stilled, his mouth a hard line again.

She hugged herself, shivering.

"Are you cold?" he asked, his gaze flickering to the smoldering fire in the hearth. "I'll have someone fetch more wood."

"Where are you going?" she asked abruptly.

He stared at her with his black gaze. "Why? Will you miss me?" There was no teasing in the question, no humor. His intense stare only made her flinch.

"Of course not," she replied, her voice quick, overly loud. "Why should I care?"

"It's not unheard of for a woman to care about the whereabouts of her soon-to-be husband."

"Indeed, a wife *would* care. But according to you, I shall be a wife in name only."

He cocked his head, dark eyes glinting. "You accept my proposal then?"

"I did not say that," she retorted, cheeks warming. It did sound as though she were relenting. Her gaze drifted over the long length of him, standing so strong in the threshold. Perhaps she was.

She could not deny that he drew her, affected that part of her she had thought immune to men.

The secret part that longed to know the mysteries that passed between a man and a woman. Except, according to Madame Foster, experiencing those mysteries with her husband would lead only to her demise.

Fortunate for her he did not appear the least inclined to make their union anything more than the business arrangement he proposed. She swallowed against the bitter taste in her mouth.

"You need to decide. We'll reach Scotland tomorrow."

Tomorrow.

She shrugged, pretending not to care, pretending that his announcement had not spiked her pulse against her throat. "I'll decide tomorrow then."

He cocked his golden-dark head. The move struck her as somehow dangerous, menacing, like a predator evaluating its prey before the final pounce. How was she to trust him? If she were wrong . . . the price was too high. How was she to believe he would return her to London if she refused him? Or try not to seduce her if they wed?

As little as she knew her father, he'd taught her much about men. They were not to be relied upon for anything.

She inhaled a wet breath, a sob caught thickly in her throat. Nothing about this was simple. Her head pounded. She pressed her fingertips to her temples, where the dull ache throbbed.

She only wished she knew whether marrying him would set her on a course to certain death.

If she wasn't so convinced he would stick her in an asylum, she would explain everything to him. Except she wasn't so certain she wasn't mad to believe it all herself.

"Tomorrow then." With a nod, he pulled the door shut after him, leaving her with the image of his handsome face. Her thoughts a wild jumble, she paced the small space. Tossing her muff down, she pulled a glove free and began gnawing at the edge of her thumb.

She couldn't marry him. Nor could she refuse him and trust him to accept her refusal. There was doubtless any number of unscrupulous reverends that wouldn't bat an eye over a reticent bride.

She didn't bother trying for the door. Her gaze flicked along its length reproachfully. It would be pointless. Someone likely already guarded the outside.

But she would escape. Tonight was her last

chance. She moved to the window, wiping her bare hand over the frosted panes with a squeak, clearing it enough to peer outside.

The back of the inn loomed beneath her, bare mostly, except for a shed and a pen with four fat hogs.

A servant girl emerged, dumping a bucket full of scraps into a bowl near the shed. Two dogs snarled at each other for the fine fare. The girl's voice lifted on the evening air with hard words of reprimand for the scrapping mongrels.

Marguerite eyed the sloping porch swooping out beneath her window. Even if she fell off the edge, it wouldn't be such a steep drop. She couldn't injure herself. Much.

She nodded determinedly. She'd do it. Time had run out.

A knock alerted her that her dinner had arrived. Turning, she bade entrance, a calmness suffusing her that hadn't been there before, a peace with the decision she'd reached.

She'd be sure to eat every bite. She'd need her strength for what lay ahead.

Chapter 11

Ash sat at a table alone the following morning, staring through the window at the flurrying fall of white, wondering if the snowfall would delay their journey.

"Can I get you anything else, sir?"

He turned at the sound of the hopeful voice. It was the same saucy barmaid from the night before. She'd been most solicitous, offering more than a warm meal as she repeatedly leaned close, revealing a view down her cleavage.

"I'm fine, thank you." Dropping several coins on the table for her, he stood, stretching his tight muscles. No doubt he would have slept more peaceably with a certain raven-haired imp in his bed. Shaking his head, he cautioned himself. Their marriage would not involve any of that.

Deciding it time to collect Marguerite and be on

his way, he asked, "Have you already delivered a breakfast tray upstairs then?"

"Oh, yes, but the lady wasn't there."

Ice shot through his veins at this bit of news delivered so blithely. "What do you mean, she wasn't there?"

She shrugged, looking annoyed. "The room was empty—"

"Bloody hell." He stormed up the stairs, his boots pounding on the steps. It must be a mistake. Marguerite couldn't have gotten past the guard.

He didn't bother knocking. Storming past the groom, he flung open the door. Immediately, the chill of the room hit him, whipped straight through his clothes, biting into his flesh and sinking into his bones. The curtains at the window fluttered in the wind, taunting bits of lace damp with snow. He strode ahead. Gripping the sill in numb hands, he glared down at the yard, staring at the sloping roof with reproach.

Damn her.

He shook his head. God help her when he caught up with her. He'd been patient with her, extended her every courtesy and believed her sincere when she claimed to consider his offer. The female lacked all sanity. She would rather jump from a window than face him with her refusal. Did she think he would drag her by her hair to the altar?

With a curse, he pushed off the sill and stalked from the room, barking for the wide-eyed groom to follow. Hopefully, someone saw something. A female like Marguerite would stand out. She held herself with a quiet grace. Her raven-winged hair and whiskey eyes gave her an otherworldly quality, feylike. As though she sprang from earth and woods. She could not go unnoticed. Useful for him to trail her, but not good for her. Not good for her at all.

Buried within his anger lurked fear. Metallic and bitter on his tongue, he worried that she would come to harm without an escort. He knew first-hand how rough and merciless the world could be. A woman alone was especially vulnerable. No more so than in this part of the country, thick with thieves and highwaymen and all manner of desperate individuals.

Swallowing down his apprehension, he told himself she couldn't have gotten far. He would find her soon, and make her regret she ever toyed with him.

* * *

Marguerite woke with a start, disoriented, surrounded in a blanket of darkness, pricked and scratched on every side. She swatted at the offending bramble scraping her face and wondered wildly if she had woken within a thornbush.

Then she heard the driver call out and the horses' responding whinnies. The wagon pulled to a stop, wheels creaking. She stilled, ceasing her squirming as she recalled that she had stowed away in the back of the wagon.

She'd slipped from the inn window after dinner and spent the night hiding from sight, awaiting her chance, eyeing all the travelers passing through the village. That chance arrived in the early hours of dawn when she spotted a farmer rolling through the village with his wagon of hay. He hadn't spotted her. Not even when she slipped into the back of his wagon, folding herself carefully beneath the hay.

She blew at a particularly thick piece of hay stabbing her lip, hoping to dislodge it. Had she thought hay soft? The stuff felt like needles pricking her flesh.

She burrowed a peephole through the hay with

her fingers to peer out at her surroundings. Marguerite couldn't achieve a good look from her vantage, but she spotted several thatched roofs. Her gaze slid upward, eyeing curling chimney smoke against a gray-washed sky.

The driver called out and she jumped, pressing back into her prickly bed, fearful that she'd been discovered. A moment passed, and she realized he only called a greeting. Listening, she heard another voice and then her driver accepting an invitation for a pint. The wagon stilled and shifted weight, and she guessed that the farmer was no longer at his perch.

Holding her breath, she forced herself to wait several more moments and endure her scratchy nest. Convinced the driver was well and truly gone and ensconced with his ale, she climbed down from the wagon, hay flying from her person like feathers from a molting bird. Marguerite landed unsteadily on her feet and brushed at her impossibly wrinkled skirts. The skin-eating hay might have kept her warm, but it had worked horrors on her attire.

Deciding her dress beyond help, she turned her attention to her hair. Plucking hay from her tumbled locks, she eyed her surroundings, recognizing the village as one they had stopped at yesterday to change horses. Well, at least the farmer had traveled south with her. There was that to appreciate.

A modest church loomed across the road, its spire the tallest point in the small hamlet. The humble vicarage nestled beside it. Certainly one kindly soul existed within its walls. She took a fortifying breath and strode ahead, looking left and right in the road before crossing—

And that's when she saw him. A hazy silhouette against the misty morning.

He stood in the gently falling snow like a character stepped from the pages of a fairy tale. He looked virile and dangerous, snow piling atop his broad shoulders. Sketched in the gray-brushed twilight, he appeared large and muscular even with the road stretching between them.

The familiar carriage sat behind him, the door yawning open. Evidently he had just stepped down. The team of horses huffed foggy breaths and pawed the earth, their dark necks shining from exertion.

He'd pressed them hard . . . all to catch up with her. A sick feeling churned in her stomach.

She longed to toss back her head and shout at the injustice of it all. First a death sentence, then an abduction, and now this. Her escape thwarted with disgusting ease. She hadn't even managed to put a day between them.

She quaked where she stood—from anger, from panic, feeling like a rabbit caught in the sights of a predator. She swallowed her suddenly dry throat.

He hadn't spotted her yet, but he would. Any moment.

Heart hammering, she looked around desperately for somewhere to run. A cottage sat to her right. To her left a field stretched, edged with a rickety fence. Beyond this fence, woods crowded thick and heavy. Woods where she might lose herself.

She dove for the field, intent on hurdling the distant fence and losing herself in the trees.

Courtland roared her name, the sound as angry and hot as the furious rush of blood to her face. *He'd seen her.*

Legs pumping beneath her skirts, she risked a glance over her shoulder and shrieked. He was closer than expected. One glimpse of his thunderous visage coming after her, closing in with such speed, and her heart jumped to her throat.

She ran harder. Icy wind stung her cheeks and made her eyes tear. The landscape blurred white and gray as she pushed. Pushed until her lungs ached from inhaling the cold-burned air.

She cleared the fence with a graceless stumble, her skirts and cloak a tangle at her feet, nearly bringing her down to the snow-covered earth. Kicking her legs free, she regained her footing. The heavy pounding of his tread was upon her. This time she did not look behind her, too afraid of what she might see.

She dove for the tree line, refusing to entertain the notion that she was well and truly caught. That she had endured a cold, bumpy ride in a wagonload of miserable hay for naught. If she had learned anything in the last fortnight, it was that supernatural forces were at work in this world. Perhaps if she wished it, *willed* it, she could sprout wings and fly.

The heartening thought did not save her.

A great weight struck her in the back. She hit the ground with bone-jarring force. Sputtering, snow filled her mouth, eating up her nostrils.

A hard hand gripped her shoulder and rolled her over, but he didn't lift off her. His great weight bore her down into the cold.

"Owwww!" She beat him in the chest and shoulder with both fists and arched, attempting to throw him off. A vain endeavor. He was a veritable boulder atop her. "Are you trying to kill me?"

"Oh," he sneered, his savage expression no less handsome as he pushed his face close, "and you care so much for your life? A woman who jumps from a second-floor window and braves the north road alone is scarcely someone I would describe as mindful of self-preservation."

"A necessary risk to preserve myself from the villain who abducted me and thinks to force me to marry him, thank you very much. Now! Get! Off! Me!"

"Force?" he barked. "I gave you a choice—I've been endlessly patient while you make up your mind, woman!"

Helpless rage swept over her. Helplessness because she couldn't explain her desperate need to escape him. Not unless she wanted him to believe her mad.

"What is it you're running from?" he growled,

his gleaming dark eyes crawling over her face with an intensity that made her throat constrict.

You, she wanted to shout. And yet it wasn't him. She could no longer deny it. She didn't want to run from him. He was temptation incarnate.

"I hate you!" The words burst from some place deep within her. And that moment she did hate him. She loathed him for tempting her with what she couldn't have.

If possible, the roiling emotion bled from his eyes. His gaze turned to dead ice. His strong jaw locked, a muscle feathering along the taut flesh. "There now. See," he murmured with deceptive calm. "We're already behaving as a married couple. Shouldn't be too difficult to make the transition."

"Never!" she shouted, thrusting her face close to his. Foolish, she knew. She should at least feign submission. The man was crushing her in a snowy field.

"Come now," he mocked bitterly. "We've already come this far." He angled his head closer. The cold tip of his nose brushed her cheek. A hissed breath escaped from her lips. "Why such the fuss?" His rasping breath felt warm as peat smoke on her face.

She couldn't help herself, she inched her face closer into him, into that delicious heat.

His voice continued at a purr. "My pockets run deep enough. I'm no fortune hunter, as all the others sniffing about your father are. And best of all—I won't try to dominate you as any other husband would."

As far as solace went, it wasn't much. It wasn't anything at all. She had other motives for escaping Ash Courtland that he couldn't even begin to guess. Life and death motives. This very moment she was supposed to be on a ship bound for Spain. He ruined that. The reminder fueled her fury.

"No thanks."

He looked angry again, his dark eyes burning. "Obstinate female. It's not as though you're some green girl. You've done this before. At least I'll make an honest woman of you and not demand you serve me on your back—"

"Oh!" Heat flamed her face. She resumed her struggles in earnest then, wedging her arms between their bodies, marveling at the breadth of him, solid and firm and so unyielding.

"Marguerite, *enough*," he snapped. "You'll only hurt yourself." He grabbed her wrists and stretched them out on either side of her head. The position thrust her breasts up into his chest. Her cheeks burned at the provocative sensation. The tips of her breasts hardened. Mortification swept through her. Hopefully, he could not feel the aching tips through her gown. Her breath fell in spurts, little gasps of air that betrayed her, revealing exactly how he affected her.

"You needn't fight this, you know." His voice dipped to a husky pitch, confirming her worst fears. He was aware of how he compelled her. "Perhaps we should discard the idea of a name-in-only marriage and strive for the real thing—"

"Never," she cried, her voice a desperate whip on the frigid air. In truth, his suggestion sparked something deep inside her, fanning the flame he'd started upon their first encounter. She tugged at her wrists, more desperate than ever to be free of him.

He angled his head. Waning sunlight filtered through the heavy clouds, gilding his hair. "You're not some chaste creature—"

She laughed hoarsely, the sound dry and broken. "So because I'm damaged goods I shouldn't concern myself with whose bed I share?"

"You're far from damaged goods to me," he said, his voice oddly thick, breathless to her ears.

He lowered his head, his dark eyes, fathomlessly deep, melting her where she lay on the cold earth.

She scarcely heard her whispered, "What are you doing?"

"Something you've been wondering about from the moment we met." His lips brushed hers as he spoke, butterfly soft but no less shocking. She jerked back reflexively, air shuddering past her lips.

"I have not," she managed to get out, her voice so shaky she didn't even believe in her own denial.

"Something," he continued as if she had not spoken, *"I've* wanted to do since I saw you that first day in the rook."

She sucked in a breath . . . his breath, and tasted a hint of coffee. And something else subtle—mint?

His lips lowered again. This time she didn't pull away as his mouth claimed her. She didn't move, simply held herself still.

His mouth was firm but gentle in a way that she hadn't expected. His lips moved slowly, leisurely, coaxing her own to move in response. The sensitive skin of her lips warmed, tingled. Her entire body heated despite the snowy earth under her, soaking through her clothes and wetting her to the bone.

She didn't care. She didn't feel the cold or wet. She was lost to it. Lost to anything but him. She felt only the delicious hardness of him against her every curve and swell.

His hold on her wrists loosened, his fingers softening to a silken caress, gliding down the length of her arms . . . grazing the sides of her breasts.

She sighed, her arms looping around his neck. The heavy weight of him sank deeper into her. He groaned, deepening the kiss, both hands sliding up to cup her face. His thumbs pressed into her cheeks as he angled his head, his wicked tongue tracing the crease of her lips, opening her to him. She moaned at the first taste of his velvet tongue on hers. Wild as the wind and snow-scraped gorse around them. She moaned, bringing him deeper, hungry for more.

One of his hands slipped around her neck, tilting her face closer. His other hand dragged a burning trail down her bare throat. His thumb grazed the delicately hammering pulse there.

She placed her palm on the plane of his face,

relishing the scrape of his bristly jaw against her palm. She savored it all. The press of him over her, the hot fusion of their mouths, the way his hands moved over her, always touching, brushing, caressing her like she was something special . . . fine crystal to be cherished. An illusion all, but she savored it nonetheless. The first time she ever found herself in a man's arms. Perhaps the last.

He angled his head, slanting his mouth and deepening the kiss yet again. As if it could never be deep enough. Heat curled through her, sinking into her belly and coiling there, twisting. She wiggled against him, pulled his head closer, her fingers stroking the rich strands of his hair, like silk to her touch.

He groaned and the sound rippled through her, reverberated deep within, as though it had come from herself.

"Marguerite." He breathed her name into her mouth. She drank the sound, loving it. On his lips, her name sounded raw, hungry and desperate with need.

The same need she felt pumping through her. *God, I am my mother's daughter.* All these years, she had thought herself so unlike her, so immune to the desires of the flesh. It must be the specter of death hovering over her. It made her bold, reckless.

His lips broke from hers, gently nibbling the side of her mouth. His hand at the back of her neck anchored her, a feast for his mouth. "So sweet," he whispered, dragging feathery kisses along her jaw, scalding a path down her throat.

His other hand palmed a single achingly heavy breast, chafing it until it throbbed within her suddenly constrictive gown. She purred, arching her body closer to his.

"Mr. Courtland!" The sudden shout ripped through her haze of lust. She blinked. The call came again. "Mr. Courtland!"

Pounding feet shook the ground beneath her.

Ash's head lifted from her with a jerk. She glanced around, brushing a hand to her bruised lips and eyeing the trembling arms braced on either side of her.

"What?" he bit out from above her, a wild tic feathering his cheek.

She followed his stare to the driver and groom running through the field toward them. The portly driver clutched his side as if suffering from a stitch. The groom, concern writ upon his face, was a good yard ahead of him. As he neared, the concern lifted and his expression turned sheepish as he marked their scandalous position on the ground.

"Oh, forgive me, sir! Thought you had fallen and injured yourself . . ." his voice faded. He grabbed hold of the panting driver. Together, they turned back toward the lane, tromping clumsily across the field.

The spell had been broken.

Her lips still tingling, she squeezed out from beneath Courtland. Fortunately, he made no move to stop her.

Teeth chattering, she fell an arm's length from him, watching him warily, prepared to bolt if he made a move to touch her.

He sat back, studying her. When he reached to swipe an inky wet strand that drooped in her face, she jerked away and swatted at his hand.

His lips pressed into a hard line, his dark gaze dead again, looking straight through her, giving nothing of himself away.

"You're shaking," he announced coolly.

She didn't bother telling him that it wasn't the cold as much as him that made her shiver, or rather the memory of him—his kiss, his body pressed to her own, the stark, feverish way he whispered her name. There would never be a moment when the memory of that did not make her shiver.

Rising to his feet, he reached for her arm. "Come along. I've brought your things. Let's get you into some dry clothes, and then we'll be on our way."

He tugged her along, not waiting for her response. He was all brusqueness, yet again the businessman who first offered her an *arrangement* of marriage. He in no way resembled the man who had kissed her so passionately moments before. The man she just might be willing to risk everything for.

Chapter 12

Ash led Marguerite into the room he'd procured for the evening. Naturally, they hadn't reached Gretna Green as planned. Not after backtracking to find her. He dropped *both* their bags—hers and *his*—beside the fire and gazed at her with an arch of his eyebrow, waiting for her protest.

She stared from her bag to his. They had spoken very little in the carriage, but he fully expected her to break that silence now.

True to form, her lips parted with hot words. "What is your bag doing—" Her whiskey eyes shot to his face, brimming with understanding. "You're sleeping in here?"

He cocked his head. "I believe that might be the only way to make certain you don't do yourself harm." He sent the window a wry glance. "You may very well break your neck at this drop."

She stepped toward him, then stopped herself abruptly, as though she realized she had come too close. She shook her head, her eyes straying to the bed. "I promise I won't run again—"

"I know. You won't." He took a seat and shrugged out of his jacket. Panic filled her eyes at the sight of him getting comfortable, settling in for the night. "Tomorrow, if you wish to return, I will take you back myself."

She moistened her lips, and his gut tightened, his gaze following the pink tip of that tongue. He remembered that tongue, remembered tasting it against his own.

His blood heated, looking at her, standing so small and yet proud. Men twice her size took more caution around him than she did. It was reckless, to say nothing of baffling. Why should she resist him so greatly? Did her situation as a mistress appeal so much more to her than the respectability he offered?

A knock sounded at the door. He called out, bidding entrance. A serving girl arrived, balancing a tray laden with food. Steam wafted from the crockery, making his stomach rumble. He'd scarcely eaten from the hamper he'd stowed on the floor of the carriage, too tied into knots over the female who thwarted him at every turn.

Instead he'd watched as Marguerite nibbled on a wedge of cheese, his muscles still tense and tangled over her escape. A woman alone, without a protector . . . anything could have happened to her. He'd seen many a female abused and maltreated. Friends, girls that he had fancied even. Their faces flashed through his head . . . each one looking a little like Marguerite in his mind. His hand curled into a fist. As long as she was in his care, he would not leave her side again.

He held out a chair at the small table where the serving girl arranged their plates. He motioned for Marguerite to sit. She lowered herself onto the chair, her gaze lowered from his.

The servant girl left them, and they ate in silence: him watching her; her watching the snow fall outside.

"You don't see that very often," he murmured, nodding his head at the snow, marveling that he should make light conversation with her—that he felt compelled to woo her as if she were a lady he sought to court and not daughter to the king of London's underbelly. As if he hadn't come one breath from ravaging her on a snow-swathed field today.

He stared at her lips as she slowly chewed, his flesh tightening as he contemplated leaning across the table and kissing her again, swinging her into his arms and depositing her on the bed, ending what had begun today. Hell, what had begun the first time they exchanged insults in St. Giles.

She had completely addled his head. In the short time he'd known her, she'd gotten beneath his skin.

Likely it was this cat-and-mouse game. The *hunt* was entirely new to him. He wasn't accustomed to women refusing him.

Ever since he had taken to the streets, scraping to survive, he'd had his share of lovers. For a time, it was how he survived. Many a lonely widow with coin to spare would beckon him within her darkened carriage for a foray beneath her skirts. He'd walked the ugly, seamy side of life. Had perhaps forgotten anything else existed. This, he realized, is what Jack had spoken of. What made him fall short and undeserving of any female with a modicum of gentility. Fortunate for him, Marguerite was no tender maiden. Perhaps they were well suited for each other.

"I've seen my share of snow," she volunteered. "It's never very lovely though, when you're cold and hungry."

He cocked his head, staring hard at her, trying to see beneath the delicate lines and hollows of her face. "When did the daughter of Jack Hadley ever go hungry?"

"My surname is Laurent. I was not raised Jack Hadley's daughter. My father never recognized me, never gave me his name."

He nodded slowly. "How is it then that Marguerite *Laurent* should know the pains of hunger and cold?"

"After my mother died, Jack sent someone to fetch me." She shrugged, paused as if she needed to catch her breath before continuing. "A servant collected me and deposited me at the Penwich School for Virtuous Girls. Maybe Jack was too busy to care. I don't. I don't know him." And from the tone of her voice, he gathered she had no wish to.

She continued, speaking so quietly he had to lean in closer. "Let us just say that Penwich was not the type of school a father would send a daughter he loved . . . not after her first letter home, not after the first time he visited and observed how thin and listless his little girl had become. Yorkshire winters can be hard enough with warm clothing and food in your belly. Without that, well . . ."

"And Jack never visited," he surmised.

"No, he did not."

He nodded grimly, imagining Marguerite as a little girl with little food and little clothing to abide a Yorkshire winter. Damn Jack.

His hand curled into a fist beneath the table. He almost wished he didn't know this. Wished he didn't know that he and Marguerite had anything in common, that she had known suffering and depravity as he had.

He lifted his glass of claret, extending it to her for a toast.

She looked from the glass to his face. With an arch of her dark eyebrow, she lifted her own glass. Everything in the motion struck him as reluctant. She was still fighting this, fighting him. She wouldn't even let herself contemplate a moment of accord between them.

"To a better future," he murmured.

Her face paled, all color bleeding from her olive complexion. She set her glass down without drinking.

One would have thought he had toasted to her death.

"You can't toast to the future?" he bit out. "Are you that stubborn? That determined to hate me? I did not say it had to be with me."

She shook her head. "You don't understand."

"Explain it then."

"My future isn't . . ." her voice faded. She tore her gaze from him.

He snatched up her glass and thrust it toward her. "Bloody hell. *Toast*," he hissed. "If I'm not part of your future, you should merrily drink then, correct?"

She dragged her gaze to his face. Her eyes were luminous, shining like sunlight through stained glass.

"And who is your future with?" he continued with a sneer, a dangerous fury burning through him. "Your fine gentleman back in Town?"

"No," she whispered, her eyes reminding him of a wounded animal. "My future is with no one."

"You make no sense," he growled.

She nodded. "I know." She turned her gaze back to the window then, staring raptly at the falling snow.

And he stared at her just as raptly, wondering if she might not be a little mad—and marveling why that did nothing to cool his ardor for her. Why the thought of returning her to Town and saying good-bye made his chest ache uncomfortably.

After dinner, Marguerite changed behind the screen in the corner, berating herself for skirting so close to the truth with Ash. Those kisses must have addled her head. A part of her wanted him to know, to understand. Except he would never believe her. She could scarcely believe it herself.

Sighing, she slipped the cool fabric over her head, disgruntled at having to wear one of the night rails Ash provided. Especially in his presence. The silk whispered over her skin, hardly appropriate armor for winter in the north of England. Clearly he had not shopped with practicality in mind. It had been one thing to sleep in the scanty attire alone, but another thing entirely to face him wearing the garment.

She released a shuddery breath and lingered behind the screen, gathering her composure.

She had thought she might wed someday. A possibility, yes. Marriage to a staid, hardworking, respectable man. Someone safe in his very predictability.

Exciting men only ever led to trouble. Her mother taught her that. Fallon and Evie were the exceptions. Marguerite was not a fool. Nor was she arrogant enough to count herself as an exception.

She had no use for a scoundrel—a disreputable gaming hell owner who lived on the most distant edge of Society alongside her guttersnipe of a father.

She ran a hand over the sheer fabric hugging her hip. Indeed, a scenario like this had never entered her mind. A union with a brute who more resembled fantasy than reality. His demon eyes, sun-kissed hair and a body fashioned from a sculptor's hands were the stuff of novels. Not the substance of Marguerite Laurent's life.

Gulping down a breath, she darted from the safety of the screen, reminding herself that *she* made her life. She alone chose her fate.

She raced the few steps and dove beneath the coverlet, yanking it up to her chin. Too late, of course. She felt the imprint of his gaze burning every inch of her. He had missed nothing. She cursed the champagne-hued peignoir she wore.

With lace panels up the sides, she knew it blended with her flesh and made her appear naked.

Heat crawled over her face. Her heart beat a furious rhythm in her chest. She recalled that snowy field—his lips, his hands, the heavy, wonderful press of him on top of her. There would be nothing to interrupt them this time should they repeat their tryst. No servants calling out. No reason to stop. Unless she gave him that reason. Could she? Could she be that strong when her body acted of its own volition of late?

A dark whisper shivered across her mind: *How badly do you wish to live?*

Even beneath the coverlet she trembled, longing for the familiarity of the white cotton nightgowns abandoned in her hotel room, waiting alongside the rest of her belongings to board a ship for Spain.

The familiar was gone. Nothing would be as it was before.

Peeking out from the blanket's edge, she watched him in the glow of firelight as he stripped his clothing. He moved with a bold grace, unmindful of himself, of his strength, his appeal. He possessed an animal beauty, reminding her of a jungle panther she'd watched one afternoon at a zoological exhibition in Town. The raw power was the same, ready to spring at will.

As he approached the bed with his feral strides, the air froze in her lungs and she wondered if she could really do this. Was it worth it? A life filled with passion, opposed to a safe, dull life. That was one manner of death, was it not?

She burrowed deeper into the soft mattress. Even with the crackling fire, the room was frigid. The wind howled at the window panes, seeking entrance.

She hardened her jaw. She wouldn't be cowardly. She wouldn't cower like the Marguerite of old.

He wouldn't ravish her. Such savagery was not in him. After days together, he could have performed any number of dastardly deeds and depravities on her person, but he had not. No, if she willed intimacy, she would have to alert him of the fact.

He doused the lamp. The bed dipped as he slid beneath the coverlet. Cringing, she hugged the edge, turning on her side to stare out the window, the image of his bronzed flesh permanently branded in her mind. The contours of his shoulders and biceps. The cut of muscles ridging his belly.

A deep throbbing began at her core. She brought her knees to her chest, biting her lip against the sensation.

His voice reached across the small space between them, plucking at her frayed nerves, making the tiny hairs along her nape prickle. "We'll turn back for Town on the morrow."

Unless she spoke. Unless she dared say what tempted her thoughts.

Silence stretched, hung suspended between them. She watched the snow fall in perfect fat flakes, and realized this would likely be her last Christmas. In days, it would arrive, this special time of year that had never been particularly special for her. Apparently, it never would be.

Her chest grew tight, thinking of that. Thinking of all the Christmases she'd spent alone, telling herself that next year would be better. That her next Christmas might be the one in which she didn't feel so wretchedly alone.

Even when she visited Fallon or Evie, she'd always been a visitor, a spectator. That feeling only grew since they'd married. No matter how welcoming or warmly they treated her, she was a guest. Not family.

All her life she'd felt apart from the world and everyone in it. Alone. Isolated. Even when her mother lived, she'd been absent from Marguerite, staring into the distance, dreaming of Jack. At Christmas especially. Her mother would spend many an evening weeping for the lover who had forgotten to send a gift.

Clinging to the side of the bed, Marguerite imagined she felt Ash's breath at her neck and shuddered. If she remained, if she accepted Ash's proposal, she wouldn't be alone this Christmas. She would be with him. Strange as it was, that might make for her best Christmas yet. She certainly couldn't claim loneliness.

His hand closed around the curve of her hip, and she jumped. Warm fingers slid inward, following the dip to her belly. "I imagined you wearing this. Golden all over . . ."

Her breath fell harder.

There was no misunderstanding his intention. She understood perfectly. She felt the same. Felt alive, craving intimacy. Needed it. Needed him.

She drew a shuddery breath, caught in the struggle of wanting him . . . even if it led her further down the path she was trying to avoid at all costs.

He tugged, attempting to roll her onto her back. She resisted, curling her fingers tightly around the edge of the bed, not yet ready.

He relaxed his grip on her hip until his strong fingers slid free. She lay there half relieved and half regretting that he had released her. She uncurled her fingers from the edge of the bed, let her hand dangle.

After some moments, he sighed. The sound shuddered through her. "What are you so afraid of, Marguerite?"

She inhaled a panicky breath, alarmed that he should be able to read her so well. "Who said I'm afraid of anything? I'm not."

"Maybe I'd believe that," he replied, his voice a feather's stroke down her spine. "If I hadn't kissed you. If I hadn't pulled you to me, felt the way your body responded—"

"Stop," she snapped, squeezing her eyes as if she could block out his words, stop the rush of warmth they ignited in her, the longing that tugged her toward him. "You mustn't speak like that."

"Why not? This all ends tomorrow. If I'm to take you back, I'll at least speak the truth."

She closed her eyes, squeezing them tight. Tempted. So tempted.

"I *want* to marry you," he growled. "This doesn't have to be some sordid affair. It can be—"

She punched the mattress. "Don't make this into something it isn't. You don't want to marry me. Not really. You wish to speak the truth, then do so." Emotion burned a fiery trail up her chest. "You merely wish to satisfy your ego and marry Jack Hadley's daughter."

"That's how this began, true, but—"

"Don't fool me into thinking you've had a change of heart and actually feel some affection for me." She laughed brokenly, the miserable sound curdling through her. Indeed not. That, unfortunately, was her. He wanted her for reasons that had nothing to do with *her* specifically, and he wouldn't persuade her to believe otherwise.

"When would this *affection* between us have started?" she sneered. "When I admitted to being another man's mistress? When I struck you in the face? Or was it when I ran away and sent you on a merry chase across the countryside? All acts that have endeared me to you, I am certain." She paused for breath, chest heaving from the bitter rush of words. "I'm not some gullible, green girl."

Heavy silence fell. His body thrummed beside her, the air crackling, rife with tension.

A hot tear slid down her cheek that she darted furiously away, swiping it to the pillow. For all her heated words, she wanted to be wrong. She wanted to think he felt something genuine for her. That would make the risk of marrying him tolerable.

Passion and a grand adventure might make her last days meaningful, but genuine affection and love would make her life worthwhile. A shame that love should be so elusive.

He sighed again. This time it was a tired sound, and she felt a little at fault for that—to know that she wearied him. "Good night, Marguerite." She felt the bed shift and knew he had rolled so that his back was to her. Instantly, she felt colder, as if he'd taken the warmth with him. Left her alone. She felt a chasm yawn between them.

Morosely, she lay still for a long time and watched the snow fall in lovely plump flakes, sleep the last thing on her mind.

"I accept."

For a moment, he said nothing and she thought

he had not heard her. Perhaps he already slept.

"What did you say?"

A sigh rattled loose at the sound of his voice. She moistened her lips. "I accept."

The bed shifted with his weight. "Accept what?" he asked, his voice full of hard demand.

She swallowed. "Your offer of marriage." *And the passion to come.* She would have that. Assuming he wanted to pick up where they had left off this morning. But she couldn't bring herself to confess that to him yet. One declaration a night was enough. For now. There would be time for passion later. After their vows.

Grasping her shoulder, he rolled her onto her back. His dark eyes glittered obsidian down at her. "Just like that? You accept? After all your refusals? After risking your neck and running away?"

She strove for a mild tone. "You offered a sound arrangement. I'd be a fool not to accept, a fact you pointed out on more than one occasion." She'd be a fool to run from the prospect of more kisses like the one he had treated her to.

"Indeed," he murmured doubtfully.

"Indeed," she echoed.

His fingers flexed on her arm, each one a burning imprint. "What are you at, Marguerite? You don't want to marry me."

"There are a great many things I want. Marriage to you shall help me achieve them." Most of them, anyway. At his continued silence, she challenged. "Have *you* changed *your* mind?"

He pulled back slightly. "Of course not."

"Excellent." Pulling free of his grasp, she rolled onto her side, presenting him with her back and telling herself she had not just signed away her life. "Good night, Ash."

After several moments, in which she felt his dark-eyed stare boring into her back, he replied in a voice that reflected his total mystification with her, "You're the most contrary female I've ever met."

A humorless smile curved her lips. Ironic that the reliable, ever-practical Marguerite should be viewed as anything but a meek and passive creature. She did not entirely regret the designation. To her ears contrary meant . . . *alive*.

"What cat-and-mouse game are you playing with me?"

"I play no games." None, at least, that she did not intend to win.

Chapter 13

They made their way along the snow-laden north highway and crossed the border into Scotland with slow progress. Marguerite stared out of the carriage window at the rising snow, fearing they would become mired deeply at any moment. A curse or blessing, she could not decide.

When they at last arrived at the village, her resolve tottered precariously. She supposed misgivings weren't unusual for a bride . . . but she wasn't the usual bride. Marrying, embracing passion—according to Madame Foster—heralded her demise. Shaking off the sense that a noose was looping itself about her neck, she permitted Ash to guide her into the inn. Madame Foster also said her fate could be averted. It was not an impossibility.

Shortly after securing her into their room, Ash absented himself. A maid soon arrived with a package. Lifting the lid to the box, Marguerite gasped to find a dress within the delicate wrapping. He'd bought her a dress for their wedding day?

With shaking hands, she lifted the gown from the box. The dress overflowed in her palms, a rich plum with gold trim. She'd never owned anything so fine in her life. She fingered the delicate material, spreading it out upon the bed. It seemed to stare back at her, dazzlingly lavish, beckoning her to slip it on.

The most beautiful gown she had ever possessed—and the prospect of wearing it terrified her.

She swallowed tightly and took a step back, her head spinning. Perhaps they would bury her in it, too. She shuddered at the morbid thought. This wasn't over yet. *She* wasn't over.

She closed her eyes in a tight, pained blink. Suddenly, the memory of his mouth on hers, the titillating slide of his hands over her body, wasn't enough. She could *not* do this. Not even to live out the passion she felt in his arms.

Panic feeding her heart, she glanced around the room, desperation knotting her stomach. She must act fast. He was likely fetching the reverend this very moment.

A knock sounded at the door, and she whipped around, praying it was not Ash.

She bade entrance, loathing the quiver in her voice. When a serving girl and two young men entered the room hauling steaming buckets of water, the tension in her shoulders lessened. Not Ash. Not yet, at any rate.

One of the lads, much younger than herself, gave her a saucy wink as he paused, sloshing water on the floor for all of his inattention to his task. She stared down her nose, marveling at his impertinence.

"They'll be back," the maid explained when the boys left the room with their buckets. As if Marguerite was concerned she would not have enough water for her bath.

As the maid busied herself about the room, tending the fire, Marguerite tried to devise a way out of the untenable situation. She stared longingly at the cracked door.

"Can I help you, miss?" the maid queried in the sharp voice of a schoolmistress, and Marguerite wondered if the girl had been assigned the task of guarding her. Did Ash suspect she would bolt? He had called her contrary after all.

The young men returned then. The arrogant one smiled at her and winked again. This time she didn't look down her nose—she didn't look away at all.

She gazed directly at him, even summoning a smile she hoped he would read as enticing. Perhaps even flirtatious. At this point, she couldn't be too choosy. She'd take help where she could find it. Even from gangly youths.

His eyes widened a bit at her inviting smile. Encouraged, his gaze grew bolder, skimming her from head to toe with a new thoroughness. She abided his stare, deepening her welcoming smile as an idea took shape.

"Robbie, hop to it!" the girl snapped.

Robbie blinked and moved to the copper tub, pouring in the steaming water. Marguerite glanced at the serving girl, happy to see she was looking away, busy stacking linens.

Sidling near the boy, Marguerite whispered for his ears alone, "Interested in some company?" She winced as the words left her lips, wondering if he could possibly believe in the sincerity of such terrible tripe. There could be no worse dialogue at Vauxhall.

Terrible but apparently believable. His eyes widened and a smile hugged his lips. "Aye, love," he whispered back. "I'd like that very much."

She flicked an anxious glance to the maid. "Can you do something about her?"

"Och, my sister, Fiona?" He snorted. "I can handle 'er."

Marguerite lightly brushed his arm with her fingers. "I should like that. Until then, I eagerly await." She glided from his side the moment his sister looked up. The maid's expression turned cloudy as she stared at her brother. "Robbie, what are you still doing here? Get on with you. You've duties to attend."

With a parting wink for Marguerite, Robbie departed the room. Triumph swelled inside her chest. But that was not the only sensation. Anxiety fluttered her belly. Was she mad to place herself in the hands of a boy? A stranger, no less?

"Can I get you anything else, Miss? Help you undress?"

"No, thank you." Her hands moved to the buttons at the front of her gown.

With a brusque nod, Fiona took her leave.

Marguerite hurriedly undressed, her pulse a panicked jump at her throat. Would Robbie really manage to lure his sister away? She flew to action, sinking into the copper tub. It had been days since she'd had the luxury of a bath. She wasn't about to pass up the opportunity.

She worked quickly, sloshing water over the sides of the tub without care. When she hopped free, she stood for a moment, biting her lip and staring at the gown waiting for her on the bed. Not exactly appropriate attire for an escape.

Putting her faith in Robbie's quickly formed *tendre* for her, she donned a riding habit instead and packed a few things she would need for the journey back to London.

She was in the process of lacing up her half boots when a gentle knock sounded at the door. She hastened forward, opening it a crack to peer out.

Robbie stood there. "I got rid of Fiona, but she'll be back any moment. Come quickly."

Marguerite snatched up her small valise at the foot of the bed. Stepping out into the hall, she told herself trusting this boy was the right thing to do. Her only choice, considering her fate if she remained at this inn.

"Quickly, then," she said. "Lead the way."

Young Robbie took her hand and led her down the servants' stairs. On the bottom step, he paused and stuck his head into a room. From the heavenly aroma of bread, stewing meat, and wassail, she presumed it was the kitchen. Apparently, Robbie judged it safe, for he yanked her down the last step and into the warm room.

She swallowed back a gasp at the sight of the cook—her back to them—peeling potatoes into a large bowl. As the thick-shouldered woman started to turn, Robbie dragged Marguerite from the room. They plunged out the door into the crisp cold.

They ran across the yard into the stables, their quick tread crunching over the packed snow. The pungent scent of horseflesh and cut hay filled her nose as they took shelter in an empty stall.

"Here we are, love." Robbie boldly took both her hands into his and chafed them together. Leaning down, he blew on them for warmth. "We'll have you right warmed up." His hands slid up her arms, pulling her closer. The lascivious light in his eyes was unmistakable.

She stifled her indignant snort. Did he think the odor of horse manure appealing to a female's senses?

"Robbie," she quickly said, pressing a hand to his chest inches before his lips descended onto hers. "I knew at once you were a gallant, chivalrous man."

He halted. "Chivalrous?"

"Of course. At a glance, I saw that in you. You're so kind to come to my aid this way."

"Your aid? You're in trouble, miss?" He frowned.

She glanced over her shoulder. She couldn't help it. She didn't have long. Ash would learn she was missing soon, and she didn't want to be anywhere around when he did. The last thing she wanted was to come face-to-face with him. Her willpower all but vanished in his presence. One look in his mesmerizing dark eyes, and she wanted only to crawl into his arms, fate be damned.

With a sniff, she swiped at the corner of her eye in what she hoped was an affecting manner. "He's a brute."

"Who?" he demanded. A militant gleam entered in his eyes.

"The man who brought me here," she explained, guilt stinging her heart for talking about Ash in such a way. "Forgive me if I misled you, but I needed to escape that room before he returned. Will you help me?" She squeezed his hand.

He looked uncertain, glancing over his shoulder. "Fiona would have my hide if—"

"Please." She clutched his hand in both of hers, gazing beseechingly upon him. "There must be some way you can help me."

He looked at his hand clutched in hers. "I suppose they wouldn't miss me for an hour. I can get you to an old hunting cottage south of town. My da sometimes lets it out, but it's vacant right now." He nodded as if the idea were growing on him. "I can settle you in there and then come back for you later . . . take you to the nearest rail station—"

"That sounds splendid," she breathed, thinking she might truly have done it, truly escaped Ash and the temptation he represented. "Thank you." Again, she glanced over her shoulder, almost certain to find his imposing figure looming there. It couldn't be so simple. "We must leave now though. He will return any moment."

A frown pulled at her lips. A sudden tightness filled her chest as she realized she would never see Ash once she was free of this place. Foolishly, she had let herself grow attached. Why else would she have almost convinced herself to marry him?

Roger seemed only a poor replacement now. How could she return to him and enjoy his kisses, his touch? She laced her fingers tightly together.

Robbie pulled her into another stall. She watched as he saddled a mount. Tightening the cinch, he tossed a smile over his shoulder. "We'll be gone before he ever knows you're missing."

Securing her valise at the back, he assisted her onto the horse, then climbed up after her. With a click of his tongue, they plunged back into the cold. She spotted the cook at the kitchen's back door, emptying a bucket of dirty water. As they burst through the yard, she looked up with a scowl.

Robbie ignored her, turning them hard into the wind. With a dig of his heels, the horse surged forth into the dusk in a bolt of speed. She grasped the horse's mane to keep from falling as they dashed down the lane. Away from the inn. Away from her fate.

The lodge was a comfortable abode and could not have been too long neglected for all its lack of dusts and cobwebs. Either that or Robbie's father took great pains to keep the residence in fine order. A fireplace gave heat to the house's two rooms. She could have stood within the hearth, it was so vast. A comfort, given the fierce winter winds outside. Still, she hoped she would not be here for long.

Robbie started a fire for her. Dusting off his hands, he rose as it grew to a crackling nest of flames. "Be certain to tend it. Don't want you to freeze tonight." He approached her, chafing his hands. "Perhaps if I can get away you won't have to spend the night alone." Stopping before her, he laid a hand awkwardly on her shoulder and squeezed.

"Robbie," she began, hoping to dissuade him from any notions of intimacy. "Please understand that nothing untoward may pass between us."

A shutter fell over his eyes and he ducked his head, burying his hands in his pocket and looking every bit a callow youth. "Aye, I understand. You needed a pigeon—"

"Please, it's not like that. You've been so kind to me, truly. I appreciate your willingness to help me from the goodness of your—"

"And I'll likely get caught for it. Da will take his strap to me," he grumbled.

She tried to speak again and offer some reassurance, but he waved her off. "I'll be back as soon as I can," he said, his voice tight with resignation.

"Thank you, Robbie," she called over the slam of the door. She moved to the window in order to watch him ride away. The snow was falling thickly now, coming down in a slanted veil. Horse and rider dove back into the white-dappled trees, vanishing from sight.

Outside, the whistling wind released a howl. Marguerite tried not to shiver at the prospect of spending the night alone in a strange cottage. She was quite accustomed to spending her nights alone in one room or another. How should this time matter?

Rubbing her arms, she moved to the fire and added several more logs for good measure. Standing, she eyed the bed. It looked comfortable with its thick, colorful afghan and several plump pillows.

Removing the extra quilt folded at the foot of

the bed, she wrapped it around herself and sank down onto the plush armchair before the fire. Staring into the rising flames, she twisted around until she found a comfortable position, settling in to wait . . . and trying not to think about Ash and his reaction when he learned she had eluded him twice now.

He wouldn't find her this time. It would be as though she had disappeared, not a trace of her life left. Nothing but the echo of her broken promise to marry him. Nothing of her left at all.

Nothing of her left at all.

She shivered and regretted that precise thought. That's what this was all about after all. Making certain *she* remained, that *she* continued to exist. Even if it was to secure a passionless existence for herself.

With a grimace, she bent down and unlaced her boots, kicking her feet free to bring her knees to her chest. Wrapping the blanket around her, she hugged herself close and sank even deeper into the overstuffed chair, silently congratulating herself.

If she hadn't acted when she had, she'd be married by now. Ash Courtland's wife. A man cut from the same cloth as her father. Someone who grew up in the stews and earned a living exploiting the weaknesses of others. Even if Ash did bring her body to life with a single touch, a single dark-eyed look, she should feel nothing but triumph, relief . . .

And yet for some reason, she felt only a deep, numbing cold.

Chapter 14

Marguerite woke with a sense of bewilderment, chilled and huddled uncomfortably, a quilt clutched to her chin. Disoriented, she shook her head, blinking the sleep from her eyes. She moved carefully, testing her stiff and aching muscles, regretting falling asleep in a chair.

For a moment, glancing around, she wondered how her rooms at Mrs. Dobbs's had changed so greatly. Then she remembered.

The howling wind outside brought it all back. With a moan, she dragged a hand over her face, wincing at the rawness of her chapped cheeks. Dropping her head back in the chair, she sighed heartily, her gaze settling on the window.

Dusk had come and gone. It must have stopped snowing. An inky black pressed on the panes of glass and made her feel adrift, as if she floated lost in a night sea. She glanced around the hunting lodge, staring at the walls with their strange, clawing shadows. The fire burned low, casting a dim red glow that seemed demonic. What had looked quaint before now struck her as ominous.

Squeezing the quilt even tighter about her, she rose to add more wood to the fire. That done, she poked it several times until sparks danced.

A horse's whinny broke over the keening wind. She stilled, straining her ears for any other sound. The jingle of a harness soon followed. She set the poker back in place and turned, her heart light.

Robbie had managed to get away, after all. She didn't care for the impropriety of it, she was simply glad he would save her from a night alone in this eerily still place that sent her imagination darkly awhirl.

She moved eagerly for the door, jerking to a stop as it burst open.

She cringed within the embrace of her quilt, a single hand lifting to her mouth—as though a scream might burst forth. Of course, it didn't. Only a breathy croak escaped as she stared at the man looming in the threshold.

Ash stood there, more furious than she'd ever

seen him. The small scar beneath his eye stood out starkly, a jagged white crescent on his swarthy skin.

"Surprised?" he growled, nostrils flaring. His dark gold hair gleamed wet with snow, tousled wildly about his head.

She edged back several steps, shaking her head, gaping like a fish.

Beneath her astonishment and fear, another emotion lurked, humming just beneath her skin at the sight of the man she never thought to see again.

Ash moved into the room like an invading storm. Behind him, Robbie hovered, his eyes bright and fearful.

"Robbie . . ." she began.

"He can't help you." Ash flicked the boy an angry glance. "Not if he knows what's good for him."

"Apologies," Robbie called, shaking his head. "Cook saw me leave with you. I tried—"

"You may go now, boy." Ash did not even look at him as he said this, instead fixing his frigid gaze on her.

Robbie hovered uncertainly, looking back and forth between Ash's imposing figure and Marguerite.

She searched the boy's gaze, desperate to reach him, evoke the sense of protection she had stirred in him earlier. This was her last chance. She knew it with a deep conviction as she gazed at the intractable set of Ash's jaw. She would not escape again. He would not let it happen. Nor could she rouse the will to resist him yet again.

Ash continued, clearly sensing Robbie still behind him, "Or you can stay and I can knock your teeth in." Robbie's face blanched. "You're in over your head. She's safe with me, whether she realizes it or not. She'll not come to harm."

Harm? Marguerite didn't know whether to laugh or weep. She shook her head fiercely at Robbie, trying to convey that she was anything but safe in the company of Ash Courtland. Without knowing it, the man was the bringer of death.

Robbie gave a single nod. His gaze connected with hers again, regretful, apologetic, but nonetheless defeated. Without another word, he turned and disappeared, swallowed up by the dark night. Ash shut the door, facing her grimly.

She edged back another step, putting herself behind the oversized chair where she had stolen a nap. Cold acceptance slipped over her, firming her jaw. Marrying him might be inevitable, but not the rest. Not dying. She hadn't given up on life simply because he'd won this night.

He advanced and stopped, the chair a much needed buffer between them. He began shedding his jacket, his vest, dropping them one by one into the chair.

Her pulse spiked with the fall of each discarded item. "What are you doing?"

"What I should have done last night."

She moistened her lips, inclined not to ask for an explanation. Swallowing her fear, she braved the question anyway. "And what is that?"

Whipping his cravat free, his lip curled back from his teeth wickedly, revealing a flash of white. "You don't know? Come, you're a clever girl, even if you can't seem to make up your mind about whether or not you wish to marry me."

"It's complicated," she hedged.

"You continue to get the best of me," he said as if she hadn't spoken. "A matter most annoying . . . especially when you risk your neck in the process."

"I was never in any danger," she quickly denied.

"No?" He thumbed behind. "And what if that

boy had gotten it into his head to collect a little recompense for assisting you?"

"Robbie wouldn't—"

"You permitted him to take you to this isolated lodge where he could have committed all manner of depravity on your person." His faced burned an angry red now, his dark eyes frightening. "Things you have no sense of, but I do. I've seen women after such miseries . . ." His gaze raked her. "You're small, Marguerite. You would have had no hope of fighting him off."

She squared her shoulders in an attempt to look taller. "I don't see the point in discussing what *could* have happened when nothing untoward did."

"I see the point in discussing why you continually expose yourself to danger." Ash grabbed her wrist and hauled her around the chair, angled his face so close she could study the glinting black of his eyes, see that there was almost no difference between the dark of his pupils and irises. "Have you no thought to your person? No care for your life?"

His words hit her hard, struck deeply to a raw wound. "Yes," she hissed, thrusting out her chin.

"I do! Which is why I seek to avoid marrying you."

He pulled back, still keeping a hold on her wrist. "You think me a danger?"

"Marriage to you will most decidedly place me at peril." She nodded fiercely. "Yes." It was as much as she dared to explain.

His eyes glowed an impossible black. "I agreed to release you. I hold no knife to your throat."

She laughed then, a wild, broken sound.

His dark gaze scoured her face. "Are you daft? Is that it? Wanting me one moment, running away the next—"

"I don't *want* you!" A lie, of course. She ached with want for him. "I'm sure you possess many admirers in St. Giles . . . a score of them are doubtlessly in your employ. Do not count me among those females."

Angry color burned beneath the swarthy skin of his cheeks. "You are deluding yourself, denying what's between us—"

She shook her head, a single dark strand of hair catching in her mouth. "There is nothing," she hissed, swiping the hair from her lips.

"Nothing?" He dropped his hand from her wrist with a snort. "We are quite past the name-in-only marriage I proposed at the start of this journey. Shall I prove you a liar yet again and give us both what we want?"

Panic quickened her breath. She stumbled away, maneuvering herself back around the chair, her fingers clutching tightly on its curved back, eyes widening as he pulled his shirt up over his head and let it puddle to the chair with the rest of his garments, leaving him standing before her bare-chested. Her mouth dried and watered invariably.

He glanced around the cozy lodge, nodding. "Such privacy you've obtained for us." He motioned to a hamper by the door. "I've even brought us a repast." She had not noticed he carried it into the lodge, too fixated was she on his person. "It will tide us over until we return to the village in the morning."

"We'll stay the night here?" she asked with incredulity. "Together?" *Alone.*

"It's fearsome cold, and late. I do not relish the idea of braving the outdoors again this eve. Not when I might stay warm here with you."

She swallowed at the decidedly lascivious look in his eyes and swung her head from side to side with denial. "You cannot mean—"

"If I did what everyone ever told me, I would have long ago died on the streets." His hand shot over the chair then and seized hold of her arm. "I'll not start now. Even for the woman I am to marry."

She yelped as he dragged her to him. Sliding an arm beneath her knees, he lifted her high off her feet and carried her into the bedchamber.

Against her will, her hand came to rest on his chest, palm down on the smooth expanse. Silken marble beneath her fingers. Her body automatically softened in his arms, settling into the easy rocking motion of being carried.

"I've quite finished letting you lead me on a merry chase, Marguerite. You and I are going to happen."

His words sank in, terrifying and thrilling. She trembled in his arms and closed her eyes in a long, pained blink, hating the flash of excitement that made her belly drop and twist.

The whisper-soft sound of his voice made her eyes drift open again. "What are you so afraid of?"

He'd asked her this before. She stared at him bleakly, unable to answer with the truth. *Everything*. Afraid of dying without having really lived. Afraid she will not leave any mark on this world.

That there will be nothing to say that Marguerite Laurent was ever here, that she had lived. Gazing up at him, she wondered how he would react to such words.

When it became clear she would not answer, he lowered her down on the bed and proceeded to remove the last of his clothes, shamelessly and unabashedly revealing the muscled perfection of his body. Firelight danced over his taut flesh, licking every inch of his smooth skin, every scar, every hollow and curving muscle. Her palms tingled, imagining the texture, the feel of him.

He stood before her gloriously naked. More beautiful than any statue she'd seen in a museum . . . and certainly more generously proportioned. Heat flooded her face as that particular part of his anatomy expanded before her eyes.

Her breath fell sharply, eyes burning for lack of blinking. She couldn't look away. Not if her life depended on it. A painful sob built in her throat at that ironic thought.

Then a tempting voice rose within her, whispering darkly across her mind. *You're not married. This isn't following the course Madame Foster had predicted.*

Accept him, take what he's offering—what you want.
What you've wanted all along.

Moving forward, he stroked her upturned face, sliding the rough pads of his fingers down the curve of her cheek. His entire hand spanned half her face. Everything about him was large. Imposing. He could crush her with the smallest effort, and yet she didn't fear that from him.

Her eyes strayed to his manhood again, jutting forward so close now that she could reach out and touch it. And yet it didn't frighten her. She wanted to touch it, *him*, with a fierceness that might have shamed her a fortnight past, but not now. Now she yearned. Now she craved his strength, his power working over her.

Perhaps this was it. *He* was it. Her taste of life. The *living* that she sought if her time on earth was limited. How many women could say they made love to a man like him? That he craved her in turn? No matter what happened to her, she'd have that.

Perhaps that would be enough.

She'd make it enough. Make it count, make it last forever.

Holding his gaze, she slid back on her elbows,

her arms quivering with tension, scarcely able to support her weight.

He stilled, angling his head and watching her for a long moment, as though he expected her to resume her arguments—or jump up and flee from the bed into the snow-buried wilderness.

When it appeared he would make no further move, she lifted her hands to the front of her gown, signaling her decision. Her fingers fumbled before getting a grip on the brocade-covered buttons. She followed the trail of them to her waist, parting her bodice wide, baring her delicate chemise to his view.

She stilled, expecting he would make a move now.

"Finish," he rasped, his voice a husky rumble.

With a shaky nod, she resumed working at her skirts and petticoats, unfastening them and kicking them down her trembling legs. Her pantaloons followed. Her breath fell fast and hard. It took all of her will not to dive beneath the coverlet and hide from his eyes.

Knees locked together, she bent her legs in front of her, shielding as much of herself as she could. The intensity of his gaze, the looming presence of him so near, so deliciously, shockingly naked, utterly destroyed her. Her legs trembled so badly, she could barely hold them up.

His voice rumbled through the shadows. "Continue."

With a shuddering breath, she pulled the ribbon at the front of her chemise, wondering if he really intended for her to strip herself naked. Was that the normal course of intimacy? Would he not call a halt and invite her beneath the coverlet where they could then proceed with some vestige of modesty?

She'd always thought couples did this sort of thing in the dark. That they went about lovemaking in a reticent fashion, sensitive to the other's sensibilities.

From his unflinching stare, she gathered Ash did not put a great deal of weight in attending to her sensibilities. Perhaps that was how it was done. When it came to this sort of business, she was vastly uninformed, after all. She knew there was pleasure to be had. Excitement. Why else would all manner of people pursue physical pleasure with such single-minded focus? Her mother had been a perfect slave to it. Even Fallon and Evie had succumbed. Marguerite would at least finally know.

She would discover carnal pleasure for herself.

"If you mean to torment me with your leisurely actions, you have succeeded," he growled, his voice a stroke on the still air. "I think it only fair to inform you that if you do not finish undressing in the next five seconds, I shall handle the matter of ridding you of your clothes myself."

Chapter 15

Marguerite's hands flew, stripping off the last of her garments with feverish speed. Only once naked, she wondered why she did not let him finish the chore. She might have enjoyed that.

He chuckled and the low sound rippled over her bared flesh enticingly—and then his laughter died. He fell silent, his gaze crawling over every inch of her, missing nothing. No curve, no hollow, no flaw went unnoticed. His dark eyes seemed to liquefy within his intense stare.

She folded her hands across her breasts in an attempt to shield herself from his hot-eyed perusal. She pressed her legs together, turning and angling them so that he could glimpse little of her womanhood.

"Don't hide from me," he commanded in a quiet

murmur, his dark eyes snapping with a need she couldn't refuse.

With a deep breath, she lowered her arms. If she was going to do this, she was going to do it. No half measures.

He stared at her for an endless moment. She forgot to breathe altogether in that time, waiting anxiously as his gaze devoured her. All of her.

"Beautiful," he murmured.

Heat flared over her face, spreading throughout her. She scooted back on the bed, maneuvering herself carefully so that her legs stayed firmly together. She wasn't so bold as to endure his gaze *there*. She stopped at the head of the bed, realizing she had nowhere else to go.

Ash smiled wickedly, knowingly, lowering to his knees on the bed.

"You look like a scared virgin," he teased.

She smiled back at him, her lips wobbly on her face. Now wasn't the time to tell him that was a fairly accurate assessment. Not if she wished to explain the true nature of her relationship with Roger. And that would lead to other uncomfortable admissions.

He crawled toward her on the bed like some

kind of stalking jungle cat, muscles undulating beneath smooth, taut skin that gleamed golden in the firelight. Her heart thumped madly against her breast.

She gave the barest jump when his hand circled her ankle. The hot press of his fingers singed her, branding her skin.

He smiled again . . . that wicked grin coiling and twisting her insides tighter, melting her bones to butter.

"Relax," he drawled.

Then, in one fluid motion, he pulled her by the ankle, sliding her down until she was square in the middle of the bed, her hair a great fan around her. She gasped.

He came over her, a great weight carefully balanced on quivering forearms. She was certain it wasn't from a struggle to support his weight but more from his restraint. His large hands rested near her face. He turned them slightly inward so that his fingers tenderly brushed her cheeks, pushing dark tendrils back from her face and tucking them behind her ears.

No part of her was free of him. His chest covered her, abrading her sensitive nipples into hard peaks. His legs slid between hers, the crisp leg hair an erotic scrape against her tender thighs.

The intimacy of this—of *him*—on her, over her, between her splayed thighs left her breathless. His manhood prodded at her core, the hardness of him rubbing intimately against the most private part of her, creating a delicious friction that made her inner muscles clench with an aching need.

That must be it. The start of it all. A delightful torment that would only intensify until he relieved the ache and buried himself inside her.

He lowered his head, seized her lips in a deep kiss. There was no easing into it. Nothing gentle.

His tongue delved into her mouth, mating with her tongue, his lips moving expertly, loving and sucking and nipping at her lips with a thoroughness that had her arching against him, parting her thighs and thrusting her aching heat up toward him in a motion derived solely from instinct.

He held her head in both hands, his grip strengthening as their kiss grew feverish, bold and desperate.

He slid one hand from her head, his broad palm dragging down her face, her jaw, her neck, descending to her bared breast.

She cried out into his mouth as he seized the aching mound, kneading it until her passion coiled higher, tighter. She felt the head of him poised and ready and wiggled her hips until his manhood pushed at her weeping opening.

She gasped at the sensation of him there, just the tip of him. Unsatisfied, desperate for all of him to fill her, she pushed up against him, hungry for something elusive but near. She knew it was near.

Moaning in need, she dug her fingers into the straining bulge of his biceps. Still, he would not give himself to her.

Releasing a bicep, she dragged his hand to her neglected breast.

He obliged, caressing and fondling the mound until she was a gasping, writhing wreck beneath him. When he dipped his head and sucked the tip deep into his warm mouth, she shrieked.

Hot tears leaked from the corners of her eyes as his tongue circled the burgeoning tip. His teeth scraped the hard point, spiking her need into something dark and violent and a little frightening. She screamed at the intense pleasure, felt something rupture and burst inside her. Gray edged her vision and moisture rushed between her legs. She dropped back on the bed, her body a boneless heap. Her chest heaved, gasping and winded as though she'd run a great distance.

And still, a desperate need clawed her. The center of her ached more sharply, throbbed more insistently, almost near pain.

She felt a shift in him. He pulled back slightly. His face loomed farther away, the firelight illuminating half his face while casting the other half into deep shadow.

Then she felt him, no longer the teasing tip, but all of him pushing inside her bit by slow bit. The deep pressure increased between her legs, filling her, stretching her.

She raked her nails down his back, clawing him closer, arching for the strange joy of it.

And then it swiftly ended.

With a snap, something ripped deep inside her. The pressure gave way, twisting into a burning pain. She pulled away, instinctively trying to break free, escape.

"Marguerite," he ground out, grabbing onto her shoulders, holding her immobile under him. He stilled above her, utterly motionless inside her.

Except buried deep, his member throbbed, pulsed alien and large. His eyes gleamed with an angry fire, and she knew. She understood what had happened. *Stupid, stupid.* Why had she not considered the matter of her maidenhead?

"Stop," she whispered, not certain what she was asking.

"You lied to me," he said, the accusation sharp.

She shook her head, wincing at the ebbing pain inside her. "You assumed," she defended weakly.

"What was there to assume? You claimed to be another man's mistress."

She blinked burning eyes and arched her spine, hoping to launch him off her. The action only succeeded in moving him inside her. She hissed at the discomfort.

"I suggest you stop moving. You're the one causing yourself pain. You're small, Marguerite. Give your body time to adjust." He brushed the hair from her neck, his voice gentling. "I might have proceeded differently had I known. I can't stop now. You'll never want to try again."

"Indeed, I won't," she ground out, digging her nails into his shoulders. He made a sound of discomfort, but didn't object.

She shook her head, lying perfectly still, determined to avoid the ripping agony again. It had all been a lie. The passion, the desire. Nothing but a cruel fairy tale. This was misery. Nothing exciting about the reality of it all. Those earlier sensations had been a trick. A lure so that women would go along with the whole lovemaking deed and the human race would not die out.

She relaxed her fingers over his sweat-dampened skin, thinking he might oblige her more if she wasn't clawing his back to shreds. "Let me up."

He lowered his head, his dark-bright gaze intent and level with hers. "Can you stand it if I just hold still?" Taking her mouth in a nibbling kiss, he promised, "I won't move."

She held herself motionless, feeling, checking her body. The pain had dulled to a low ache. Uncomfortable but not unbearable. "Just don't move," she warned, then almost laughed. She was in no position to be issuing demands.

His breath escaped in a chuckle against her mouth. "I won't move unless you ask me to."

"I won't," she vowed fervently.

Ash laced his fingers with her hands and stretched them above her head, settling himself into her . . . but not moving—not insinuating *that* part of him any deeper. Just as he promised.

She felt herself relax, trusting him. For whatever reason. Scoundrel she knew him to be, he would not harm her. A man did not chase another man down for mistreating a woman and then turn around and do the same.

His lips at her mouth deepened, the kiss turning harder, more demanding. He sucked her bottom lip, took it into his mouth with a gentle bite, then followed by licking the bruised flesh. His lips traveled along her jaw. At her neck he found her pulse and sucked.

A breathy sigh escaped her. Her heart felt as though it might burst from her chest. She turned her head, granting him better access. This was nice. *This* he could do all night.

The throbbing once again grew at her core. She stiffened at the first sensation, remembering only the pain to follow. But no pain ensued.

She gave the barest shift of her hips, testing. No pain. Just a spike of sensation. Her belly clenched and she groaned, the sound stark with longing.

True to his word, he didn't move. Even when his breathing grew irregular, his body a hard, rigid board of tension above her. He dragged his mouth to her ear, and she shuddered as he blew hot air over the sensitive lobe.

Of their own volition her knees bent, rose up on either side of his hips. The movement brought him deeper, sank him farther inside her.

"Oh!" She skimmed her hand down his back, fingertips tracing the dip of his spine. Sensation rippled through her. Her body felt good, marvelous.

Still, he held himself as unmoving as marble inside her.

Emboldened, a slight smile curving her lips, she drifted her hands farther down, cupped his taut buttocks in her hands, lightly scoring her nails over the smooth flesh.

He groaned, dropping his head in the nook of her neck. "Marguerite." Her name filled her ears, a guttural plea. The sound empowered her. She moved herself against him, experimenting, marveling at the sensation of their flesh dragging against each other.

Sucking in a breath, she pulled back, away from him, sinking into the mattress. She held herself for a moment before surging forward. Up. Delightful friction arced through her, racing along every nerve ending in her body. She cried out, shocked, delighted at the deep thrust. This was it then. What she'd been waiting for. She pushed up her hips, demanding more, all he had to give.

"Now," she begged, understanding what was necessary to relieve the dark burn at her core. She understood enough. Enough to know only he could fulfill her.

"Marguerite," he whispered into her ear, and he sounded different. A stranger. As wrecked and shaken as she was. He trembled against her, and her need for him only burned hotter.

"Now, Ash, now," she gasped in his ear, saying what she hoped were the words to set him free and unleash the savage from its cage.

Ash needed no further encouragement. He let himself go. The hot need that had pumped through him from the moment their bodies first joined rushed free.

Grasping her hips in both hands, he unleashed himself, drawing in and out of her silken warmth and plunging back inside, seating himself to the hilt with an exultant shout.

He felt as if he weren't himself. As if he were possessed by some strange entity, a spirit, a semblance of himself that had never known pain or loss. The deprivations and torment of his past fled as if they didn't exist, as if shadows never dwelled inside him, haunting him and dictating his every move.

For the first time in his life, he felt free and unencumbered.

This—his coming together with this woman—was no random occurrence. It didn't matter to him anymore that she was Jack's daughter.

He fought to ease his strokes, gentle the hard slam of his cock into her tight body, but easy movements eluded him, tender lovemaking impossible. A force he'd never known before compelled him. No matter how much, how desperately he wanted to make this good for her, he was too far gone with need.

Marguerite arched, offering her body for him in complete surrender, lifting her slim legs higher.

He grasped her thigh, circling it around his hips. A quick learner, she wrapped her other leg around him, coming off the bed and shouting her pleasure with each thrust of him inside her.

She gasped his name, over and over, a wild,

bewildered sound that echoed in the still lodge. He reveled in it, in her. He struggled to cling to his anger, his sense of betrayal over her lies, but it was pointless. He felt only triumph, a deep sinking pleasure that he was the first man to do this with her. *And the last*, he vowed, pumping harder, need and possession spiraling his passion out of control.

Naked beneath him, she looked magnificent, shadows licking the curves and hollows of her delicate body, her hair fanning out in a black nimbus around her head. Who knew he would find such a responsive creature in the female who had treated him to such contempt and berated him before half of St. Giles?

He reached between their bodies, found her slick heat, that tiny nub of sensitivity and put his fingers to it, pressing, rubbing until he felt her shudder.

She shouted, nearly bucking him off from the force of her climax. He pulled her up, hauled her into his arms and clutched her tightly as he released himself, found utter fulfillment at last.

"How precisely does a mistress remain a virgin?" Marguerite's hand stilled from tracing slow patterns on Ash's bare chest, wincing even as she had known the question was coming. "I guess I wasn't exactly his mistress. Yet."

"Yet." The word dropped heavily on the air. "What of this grand trip to Spain?"

"Oh, I was going to Spain with Roger . . . I imagine the matter of my virginity would have been dispensed with sometime on the voyage across."

His chest seemed to harden beneath her cheek. "Do you love him?" he asked, his voice void of emotion.

She shook her head, not wanting to confess the truth, unwilling to admit that she knew Roger less than Ash. She had picked Roger for reasons that had nothing to do with love.

"Could you not find anything else to do? Something other than . . . than becoming some man's paramour? Were there no other options left to you?"

How she had come to be a mistress would require explanations . . . catapulting her into a complicated mire that would probably land her in an asylum.

"You could have gone to Jack," he suggested.

"No," she snapped, going cold at the mention of

her father. "I don't want help from him. Besides, his answer would have been to marry me off to some blueblood." A smile twisted her lips. "It's doubtful I would be here with you then."

His hand glided down her back in a possessive caress.

She slid her body over him, thrilling at the press of her bare breasts against the hard wall of his chest. "None of it matters anymore," she murmured, her lips close to his.

"Roger doesn't matter?" Ash pressed, apparently intent on that clarification. His eyes glittered in the shadows, bright with a hunger that echoed in the marrow of her bones.

She hesitated only a moment. "No. He doesn't," she answered. And he didn't, she realized with a start. Even if she returned to London and found Roger waiting, she could never be with him. Could never resume her grand plans and hop on a ship bound for Spain. She could never be his lover. Not after this.

Not after Ash.

Apparently, Madame Foster was right. Some fates cannot be avoided.

Lowering her head, she kissed him with warm

thoroughness. He stilled, as though he wasn't certain what provoked the tender attention.

Finally he moved, cupping the back of her head. Threading his fingers through her hair, he intensified the kiss, keeping it deep and slow until all thoughts fled from her head.

Chapter 16

Marguerite woke with a long stretch, sore in places she never knew existed. She rolled her head on the pillow with a happy sigh, settling her gaze on the thick gray air hugging the window panes.

Suddenly, she stilled, recalling the reason why she was so sore. The events of the previous night flooded over her. *Ash.* She inhaled and his musky scent filled her nose, surrounding her.

It had been wondrous. Aside from the initial pain, losing herself in passion had been everything she ever dreamed it could be. This was the reason Fallon's and Evie's faces glowed pink when their husbands entered the room. Now she understood. She had been a fool to judge them as tiresome in their feelings.

One could die peaceably having lived the night

she shared with Ash. It almost made the notion of facing death something she could abide. *Almost.* One hard fact pressed down upon her. *She still wasn't married.* Madame Foster insisted she would be married when the accident claimed her.

A chance remained. A chance to live. She couldn't toss aside that hope now. She had her night with Ash, her taste of passion. She needn't marry him now.

Her mind raced as she gazed up at the shadows dancing on the rafters. Ash slept beside her. A horse waited outside. She could just slip away— provided she was quiet and did not wake him.

Heart hammering in her chest at the audacity of such a move—to sneak away beneath his very nose—she turned her head to observe him in his sleep, as if she could find the answer in his handsome, well-carved face. As if one glimpse of him and she would know what to do. Would she regret walking away?

Her gaze fell on the bed. Empty space yawned beside her.

With a gasp, she lurched upright, clutching the coverlet to her breasts. He was gone. Her gaze swept the dim room.

"Ash?" she called, her voice small and thready. She swallowed, the thought of escape fading with the last of the clinging night.

No answer. Rising to her feet, she slipped on her chemise. Ignoring her chilled feet, she padded about the lodge, moving into the other room, chafing her bare arms. "Ash?"

At no sight of him, she moved to the large mullioned window. Thick snow blanketed the ground. She couldn't see into the shadowed interior of the small stable, but she imagined his mount was gone.

Still, never for a moment did she think he abandoned her. Even without the intimacies of the night before, even without the tenderness in which he'd loved her body, he wouldn't walk away from her. If nothing else, he'd invested too much time in her, and there was the score he wished to settle with her father.

She scanned the landscape. Where had he gone then?

Trapped, defenseless as any animal in a cage awaiting the return of its captor, she turned from the window. Past caring that she'd slept little the night before and should rest to gather her strength, she strode into the bedroom and dressed herself. With a deep breath, she settled down before the fire to wait.

Ash shook the snow from his great cape and led the reverend and the requisite witnesses—his driver and groom—toward the hunting lodge, pausing outside the door to kick snow from his boots.

He'd left at the first hint of dawn while Marguerite still slept, determined, now more than ever, to see them wed. As far as he was concerned, the only thing missing from last night was that he could not yet call her wife. A matter he intended to rectify within the next few moments.

With a single knock, in case Marguerite was still in the delectable state of nakedness he had left her in, he entered the warm confines of the lodge.

She sat before the hearth in the overstuffed chair, leveling her wide eyes on him and his small party. She rose quickly to her feet, brushing at her mussed skirts. She'd attempted to arrange her hair, but he guessed she had been unable to locate all the pins. Only half of the thick mass was pulled up, the rest trailed over her shoulder in a meandering stream of liquid black. He remembered all that hair twisting like silk between his skin and hers, and his body tensed in eagerness, ready to repeat last night. Relive every delicious moment.

"Marguerite," he greeted, unable to stop the thickness from entering his voice. The sight of her did that to him. Had he ever thought her anything less than soul-stirringly beautiful? Had he only thought her a means to secure his business? To get back at her father? He snorted. If he wasn't careful, he would start reciting poetry to her beauty.

She said nothing. Her darting eyes reminded him of a panicked animal, skipping past him to the three lurking men. She thrust out her chin defiantly, once again girded in her invisible armor . . . almost as though last night hadn't happened, hadn't softened her toward him. Contrary yet again. He sighed. At least she would never bore him. There was no predicting with her. Unlike any other female of his acquaintance.

Ash motioned to the lanky man with mutton-chop sideburns, stepping aside so that he could move forward. "This is the Reverend James, Marguerite."

"Miss," the gentleman greeted, removing his

hat and stepping fully inside, patting his gloved hands to his face for warmth. "Dismal weather, but with your happy festivity upon us, I am certain brighter weather is on the horizon. The Almighty shall see it so."

Ash swallowed a snort.

"Reverend," she murmured, her voice skeptical as she crossed her arms over her chest. Her boot peeped out from her hem, tapping out her ire. Fire sparked in her eyes, reminding him of the Marguerite he first met in St. Giles, ready to blast him with her venomous tongue.

The reverend tipped his head. "Indeed I am."

"Then I am sorry for your trouble. There is no need of your services here."

Ash cast a glance heavenward and strove for patience and understanding. After she had given herself so ardently to him—multiple times—he believed she had accepted their union. Apparently, he was under a misapprehension.

Her gaze drifted to him, as though sensing his annoyance. Her whiskey-eyed stare was flat, devoid of emotion. Nothing of the passionate creature from last night lurked there.

The reverend clucked good-naturedly. "Well,

now, I've never forced a truly unwilling maid to take vows. That would be unethical." Mr. James flicked his wrist. "However, sometimes a lass simply doesn't know her mind until I help her along."

Marguerite's gaze snapped back to the reverend. "Indeed? And you credit yourself with the insight to know a woman's mind?"

He nodded cheerfully. "Precisely."

Ash winced, wishing the imbecile would hold his tongue. The fool wasn't helping matters. Ash wasn't going to force Marguerite to wed him.

She cocked her head, a dangerous glint in her eyes. She no longer looked at the reverend but at him. "Do you deem me incapable of knowing my mind, Ash?"

He couldn't resist. "A more contrary female I never knew."

Heat colored her cheeks, but she didn't deny his claim.

"You want to marry me, Marguerite," he murmured, staring intently into her eyes, certain of this but still seeking confirmation. After a short moment she nodded, the motion jerky, reluctant.

"Shall we proceed?" Ash asked before she

changed her mind again. He moved beside Marguerite's stiff form. "Where shall we stand? Is this adequate?" he asked, taking Marguerite's elbow and steering her before the hearth with him.

"Ah, yes." The reverend chuckled. "I've performed this ceremony in settings far worse than this simple abode."

"I'm certain," Marguerite muttered, a hard statue beside him.

Reaching down, Ash took her hand. Her fingers felt cold in his grasp, limp and lifeless. His gaze drifted to her face, only to find her already looking at him. Her fiery gaze locked with his eyes. Beneath the fire an emotion lurked he could not quite identify.

He couldn't fathom it. After yesterday, he knew she felt something for him. He could admit to the same. He felt something for her. Something real. Something besides the cold wrath that had compelled him to abduct her at the start of their journey.

As shocking as it was, he'd come to believe they could have a real marriage, something based on desire if not actual affection. It was more than he had ever hoped for. It was reason enough for him to face the reverend and repeat the vows prompted without qualms.

But *not* enough for him to stand beside Marguerite with her lips pressed shut in silent reproach, clearly refusing to repeat her vows.

The reverend stared at her, waiting for her to repeat the words he had intoned. Nothing. Finally, he shrugged a bone-thin shoulder and skimmed over her part as though she had declared her vows.

With a snarl of disgust, Ash started from her side. He would not marry an unwilling woman. He couldn't do it.

He didn't know what angered him more. Marguerite for her stubborn refusal, or himself for giving a damn. After last night he knew she wanted him. He was proposing an honorable arrangement. He should simply make the choice for her—he should just marry the blasted female who didn't seem to know her own mind and be done with it.

And yet he couldn't. He'd spent too much of his life lacking choices. Upon the death of his parents, his first choice hadn't been any choice at all. The streets or a foundling home. Even if he thought Marguerite daft to reject what he was offering, he wouldn't deprive her of one shred of freedom.

He stopped suddenly at the feel of her fingers on his arm, stalling him, urging him back.

Her eyes locked with his, still full of that bewildering emotion. Watching him intensely, as though memorizing every line and hollow of his face, she repeated her vows with a slow solemnity that made his breath catch.

For a moment no one moved, no one spoke. Her small hand on his arm could have been a burning vise for all that it immobilized him.

She'd done it. She'd said the words that bound her to him with no prompting.

A strange tightness seized his chest, locking his breath in his lungs. He took her chilled hands in his, squeezing the delicate fingers. With a tug, she tumbled into his arms and he kissed her hungrily, uncaring for their audience. He released her hands to grip her face, savoring her lips, determined that she not regret it. She returned his kiss, matching his fire.

And that, he told himself, was enough. For now.

Mr. James's tones rang out. "I now pronounce you man and wife."

They broke apart at this announcement. Marguerite slipped from his arms, blinking in a dazed manner as if waking from a dream.

Moments passed, blurred. He scarcely recalled signing the register alongside Marguerite . . . could only stare at her, his *wife*, trying to detect regret anywhere in her face, struggling to understand why she had changed her mind, and if she would do so again.

"How long are we staying here?" she inquired, sinking down onto the chair after the others had left and they were alone once again.

He shrugged as he added more wood to the fire. "A few days. I thought some time together would not be remiss. Have no fear. We won't starve." He gestured to the second, larger hamper by the door. "If need be I can cook, but I cannot promise to the degree of palatability." He tossed her a self-deprecating grin. "We are husband and wife now. It would behoove us to get acquainted."

One corner of her mouth twisted into a half smile. "Don't couples usually do that beforehand?"

"I can't claim to know. I only care for how we do things, Marguerite." He circled to stand before her, and she resisted fidgeting. After last night there was hardly any call for shyness. After *marrying* him there was little call.

His boots slid to a stop before her chair. "Why did you say those vows?" he asked.

She shrugged, unsure what to say. Unsure if she even knew the reason why herself. Perhaps she wanted some control. If she was to believe Madame Foster, certain events were already decided, out of her control and destined through actions she had yet to commit but most assuredly would.

So why fight it? Why fight this—*him*? Especially as her body and heart no longer wished to? Her body ached for him. She'd never felt such an attraction, never been affected by a man like this before. Perhaps they were destined.

Feasting her gaze on him, she couldn't abide the notion of never being with him again. However many days were left to her, she wanted to spend them with him. She could embrace their marriage and still work to avoid the path that led to her demise. She believed that. She had to. It wasn't hopeless.

She simply needed more information, more details from Madame Foster, so that she knew what future events to avoid in order to avert the accident leading to her death.

"I don't know," she hedged, not yet willing to tell him that she married him because she *wished* to. Because her toes curled in her slippers at the mere sound of his voice.

She still didn't know how he felt about her. His motivation for marrying her was based on business. She wasn't about to bare her heart to him just to suffer his pitying stare.

His gaze scoured her face, almost as though he could see within her, to all she hid. She looked away, alarmed at just what he might find.

His voice rolled across the air between them, rippling her flesh. "It was the last thing I expected . . ."

Agreeing to marry him? She laughed, the sound parchment-thin. "Well, I didn't quite expect it of myself, either."

Madame Foster was right. There were choices along the way, opportunities, chances for her to change her fate. Except as far as she could tell, she continued to make choices leading to the fate Madame Foster predicted.

He placed his hands on the arms of her chair, leaning his face close, caging her in. The breadth of him overwhelmed her, his sheer masculinity flooding her senses. "I don't want you to regret this."

I don't want to regret this either. Emotion surged inside her. She nodded her head fiercely. "I won't."

"Good." With a nod, he pushed up from the chair and strode toward the door, his Hessians biting into the wood planks.

She rose to her feet, calling after him. "Where are you going?" A quick glance to the window revealed that it had started snowing again. "It's practically a storm out there."

"And why we need more wood."

At the door he stopped, pausing there for a moment before turning back around and sweeping her into his arms for a kiss that left her panting and aching for more.

Coming up for air, his eyes glittered obsidian down at her. "I could grow used to this," he drawled.

"What?" she whispered, her tongue darting out to wet her bruised lips.

"*You.*"

Then he was gone. She stared around the silent room, her throat thick, her eyes stinging.

She would have that, too. Have him growing used to her. For many years to come.

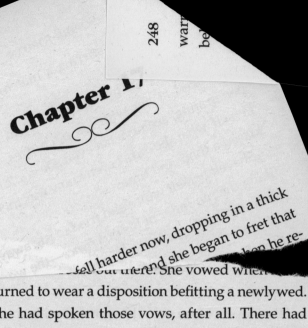

Chapter 1

...fell harder now, dropping in a thick
...and she began to fret that
...hen he re-
...out there. She vowed when...
turned to wear a disposition befitting a newlywed.
She had spoken those vows, after all. There had
been no coercion.

She vaulted to her feet when the door banged
open. A gust of wind swirled in the room with
Ash. He shook the snow from his broad shoulders
and stomped his boots on the rug.

She fixed a smile to her lips and helped his great
cape from his shoulders. Hanging the dark coat on
a peg by the door, she turned back around with
cheerful words on her lips. The words never came.

He hauled her into his arms, lifting her off her
feet in a breath-robbing kiss. His cold lips quickly

...ned on hers, stirring a matching fire in her
...ly.

He broke away for a moment. Holding her face,
he looked at her with his pitch eyes, deep and
penetrating, seeing what even she couldn't see of
herself, what she didn't even know was there. "I've
kissed a thousand times—"

She felt herself wince and tried to tug her face,
liking the reminder of his *experie...* on her face,
who doubtlessly pleased hi... ...made
skill than she. His ...forward with a fierceness that made

...her forward with a fierceness that made
her gasp.

"But never before you," he growled with an intensity that made her belly quiver. "Never before
you. Everything with you is new. Fresher and
sweeter. I won't give that up. I don't care that I said
I wanted a name-in-only marriage. Now I want
this. I want you. I want it all."

It was too much. She didn't let him finish. She
couldn't. She pushed her face the last few inches
separating him and kissed him, pressed her lips to
his in clumsy eagerness. Hunger soon melted away
any awkwardness. He groaned into her mouth.
After several moments, she came up for air,

murmuring against his lips, "Whatever shall we do? This is a honeymoon of sorts, is it not?"

"Indeed it is," his voice rumbled against her lips. "And Christmastime, too."

Her smile threatened to slip. She had almost forgotten. Christmastime had only ever been a series of days, one following another, much like any other time. Only cold.

"Yes," she murmured.

He kissed the corner of her mouth, looping his arms comfortably around her waist. It felt natural, right. Like he'd held her just this way countless times before. "I'm afraid it will be a quiet affair with just the two of us. How do you usually celebrate it? Parties? Caroling?"

"In recent years, I have visited friends." In her youth, she had done nothing. Sometimes she had even been left alone if her mother was fortunate enough to be called to Town to join Jack. "What of you?"

"Actually, your father usually has me to dinner. Quite a grand affair with several people."

She inhaled a stinging breath through her nose, thinking of how she had never spent a Christmas with her father. Because he never wanted her there.

"Was there a goose?" she asked, her throat unaccountably tight.

At Penwich, during the cold winter nights, she had always envisioned being called home for the holiday and sitting down to a fat, succulent goose on Christmas Eve.

"I suppose so, yes. Although we are always so befuddled from his housekeeper's deliciously potent wassail that I hardly recall the food." The humor in his voice was contagious and she began to smile. Until she recalled she was discussing her father. And the Christmases he never invited her to share. Her smile faded.

As if sensing her change in mood, he brushed her cheek with his thumb, staring at her deeply, his gaze uncomfortably probing. Fearful that he'd glimpsed some of her thoughts, she forced a smile.

"I'm quite certain we'll find a way to enjoy this holiday with each other," he said with a slow nod. She did not mistake the glint in his dark eyes. Nor did she miss the tightening in her own belly.

They had days alone together. What else was there to do but occupy themselves with each other? Her cheeks heated at what all that might involve. After last night, her mind raced and her body burned at the possibilities.

He pulled both their cloaks off the pegs. Spinning her around, he helped her into hers. "Come."

"Where are we going?" she asked, feeling dizzy and not a little giddy.

"To gather holly, of course. And boughs."

"Holly?" She looked over her shoulder at him. "Surely, you jest?"

Eyes dancing, he gave her a mockingly stern look as he bundled her into his coat. "We've much to do." With a wave of his hand, he gestured around them. "Do you not see the barren spots requiring festive embellishment? We've much to do in preparation."

She glanced about the room, speechless. He intended for them to decorate for the season? Here?

Snatching her scarf, he wrapped it around both her head and neck. He then helped her with her gloves, paying particular attention to each of her fingers. She studied his bent head, admiring the sun-kissed strands and wondering if anyone had ever shown her such care.

Finished, he looked up at her, a ready smile on

his face that melted her heart. Their eyes held, clung, and she realized with a sinking sensation that she was quite done for.

She'd fallen in love with the very man who abducted her and married her. The one man above all she should not lose her heart to.

"What is it?" he asked softly, his gaze crawling her face, leaving a burn trail in its wake.

She shook her head. "Nothing," she murmured. "Let's hurry. Before all the pine is gone."

With a chuckle, he held open the door and led them out into the sweeping cold.

Freezing air hissed past him as Ash fell from the tree and hit the ground. He laid there for a moment, stunned, the wind knocked from him, arms still full of itchy pine. He credited most of his astonishment to the fact that he had been so clumsy to lose his balance and fall in the first place—not that he had seriously harmed himself. The snow cushioned his fall.

"Ash!" Marguerite cried. He marveled at the panicked sound of the cry, inordinately pleased that his wife of one day should care so much for his safety.

"Ash!" Her boots pounded the snow-covered earth, crossing the distance from where she had been gathering holly. "Are you hurt?"

Perhaps it was wicked of him, but he did not hasten to reassure her, instead he held still, eyes shut, waiting for her tender ministrations, eager for the first touch of her hands.

She dropped beside him, bringing an icy breeze with her. Her urgent little hands flattened against his chest, exerting the slightest pressure as she patted him, checking for life. He stifled a laugh when her hands arrived at a ticklish spot low on his ribs. He bit back the sound.

A glove warmed over his cheek, chafing fiercely. "Ash, darling, can you hear me? Speak to me!"

Darling.

Her sweet breath fanned his face, a puff of warmth on his chilled lips, so close and misty-sweet he couldn't resist.

In one swift move, he grabbed hold of her and rolled her beneath him. She yelped, clinging to his shoulders.

She blinked wide eyes up at him. "You—you—"

"Marvelous man," he supplied. "World's best lover?"

She swatted him in the shoulder, scowling. "Fraud! I thought you were hurt. I was already envisioning how I was going to drag the great hulk of you back to the lodge."

Chuckling, he lowered his head and kissed her chilled, sputtering mouth. He deepened the kiss until he'd chased the cold from both their lips. Until his body warmed from the inside.

He slipped a hand beneath her body, bringing her up toward him and off the cold ground. Moaning, she circled her arms around his neck, clinging to him as if she would never let go.

He cursed their cumbersome clothes, thick and unwieldy between them. Mindless of the snow, he tugged her cloak open and pulled at her scarf, baring her throat for his lips. He kissed her neck, grazing the delicate arch with his teeth. She shivered. From him or exposure to cold, he didn't know. He only knew he had to have her.

Vaulting to his feet, he dragged her up with him. Clutching her hand, he strode swiftly back toward the lodge.

"The holly, the boughs," she cried breathlessly.

"I'll come back for them," he growled, increasing his pace.

Several times, she tripped and he pulled her upright. After a moment, he finally gave up on dragging her through the snow with so little regard. Without pause, he swept her up into his arms and carried her the last of the way.

His breath fell fast and hard, blood pumping as he entered the lodge, kicking the door shut behind them.

Her mouth already worked its magic on him, kissing up his neck, feathering along his jaw. Their hands worked in a frenzy, tugging and tearing clothes off of each other.

Her eagerness heightened his, and he freed himself with savage movements. Naked first, his hands darted to her hair, tugging the pins free and running his fingers through the strands, loosening the dark mass. He pulled her to him, kissing her, open mouth to open mouth.

She squirmed against him with a laughing moan, her hands managing to shed the last of her garments until she was flush against him. Bare flesh to bare flesh.

In their frenzy, they did not reach the bed. Limbs entangled, they fell on the fur rug before the fire in a pile.

Ash laughed against her neck. Rolling, kissing, crawling over each other, their hands never stopped—clinging, gripping, seizing, stroking.

Ash slid between her parted thighs. She wiggled herself up until she was perfectly positioned for him, her heat cradling his hardness in welcome. He slid inside her with one slick thrust.

She cried out, arching beneath him, her neck falling back, exposing the fine curve of her throat to his mouth. She shuddered at the first press of his lips there, at the gentle nip of his teeth on the cords of her neck as he moved in and out of her, setting a slow, sinuous pace.

She clawed his back, nails scoring his flesh. She thrust her hips up to meet him, pushing him to increase his pace, to take her swifter. His strokes quickened, drove deeper, wringing him of his control.

He buried his face in her neck, breathing in the sweet milk and honey of her skin, certain he had never smelled a woman like her before. "Marguerite," he panted, wondering how every inch of him could feel so hot with winter sweeping outside.

Her hands slid down his back, seized his buttocks and squeezed. He bucked against her, growling out his release as he slammed inside her a final time.

She shivered, convulsed in his arms as her own release swept her. He fell atop her, still buried inside her delicious warmth, the aftershock of his climax ripping through him in shudders.

After a moment, he rolled off her, an arm still wrapped around her waist. On her side, eyes shut, her breath labored as if she'd sprinted a great distance.

He stared at her face, flushed from their love-making, the tip of her nose still pink from the cold outdoors.

He stretched his arm to the nearby chair and grabbed the quilt folded there, pulling it over them, making certain she was fully covered.

"Hmm," she murmured contentedly, nestling against him as she settled deeper into the fur rug. "I could grow accustomed to this."

Making love in the middle of the day? Napping like a fat cat without a care or responsibility? Despite the wealth and power he'd acquired over the last few years, he'd never permitted himself the indulgence. He'd always prided himself on his labors, working more than he rested or played.

He was no blue-blooded aristocrat who inherited a silver spoon in his mouth. And yet he knew what she meant.

As her breathing evened to slow pulls, he studied her face, so relaxed and young in repose.

"Me, too," he murmured, an odd tightness squeezing in his chest. "Me, too."

Chapter 18

When Marguerite woke, dusk was settling in a soft blanket over the day, tingeing the air sifting through the window to soft pinks, purples, and grays. She yawned, surprised at how long she'd napped. A quick glance around revealed the bed empty. Ash was gone.

Although she knew he couldn't have gone far, an odd pang penetrated her chest. Rising, she quickly dressed, heat creeping over her face to realize she had slept these several hours naked. She'd never slept completely nude before. At Penwich, forty odd girls slept in one large dormitory. Even with little privacy to be had, she'd clung to her modesty and managed to reveal very little of herself when undressing. Somehow, with Ash, she lacked all such modesty.

Now she was a veritable siren, forsaking her

clothes as though accustomed to sharing a bed, her body, with a man.

Dressed, she entered the lodge's main room and found Ash bent over the table, pulling a loaf of bread from the hamper.

She sniffed the air. "Something smells heavenly."

"I've made a stew."

Her eyes widened, landing on a large pot beside him on the table. "You cook?"

His lips twitched. "I do a great many things."

It was then she noticed the holly and boughs sitting in a great pile by the door. "You fetched our holly," she murmured.

He shrugged one shoulder. "Thought you might like to arrange them this evening."

She seated herself across from him at the table. "Of course, I *should* do something. While I slept the day away, you've been quite productive."

"I've dragged you across the country. You're due your rest." His eyes took on that seductive glint she was coming to expect. "Especially as you have a long night ahead of you."

"Oh," she murmured, watching with her heart in her throat as he lifted the lid from the pot and stirred its steaming contents. A man waiting on her was quite an unfamiliar sensation.

Her stomach growled, a reminder that she hadn't eaten since that morning. As he spooned the savory-looking stew into bowls, she cut the loaf of bread into thick slices, feeling the need to occupy her hands, to ease her discomfort at having her new husband wait on her.

They ate in silence.

"This is very good," she finally remarked.

"Not the finest Christmas Eve dinner you've ever had, I'm certain."

She started. "It's Christmas Eve?" She'd lost track of days in the last week, so intent was she on escaping him . . . escaping her fate. Her gaze swung sharply to the window, as if she would see some evidence of the day in the softly falling snow.

"Yes."

Unbidden, the thought came to her. *Her last Christmas.* She shook her head fiercely in denial and blinked suddenly burning eyes. Not the last. This would *not* be the last. She would cease such dismal thinking. Especially with a man she was coming to . . .

She gave herself a mental shake. *What*? What was it she was coming to feel for Ash? Love? The word whispered across her mind. She squeezed her eyes in a tight blink. Yes, that was the sum of it. She'd already realized as much. How else could she take such a risk with him?

"I'm sorry," he said roughly, almost angrily, clearly misreading her reaction as she sat across from him in stunned silence. His spoon clanked against the inside of the bowl. "I'm sure there were countless ways you would have preferred to spend the holiday. I did not think of the timing when I took you from your father's—"

"Don't be sorry," she rushed to say, almost astounding herself with her next words, but needing to say them. "I'm not. I'm glad you came when you did. If you had come a day later, a moment later, you would have missed me entirely."

And that was the truth. He would have missed her. One of her sisters would be sitting here on Christmas Eve with him.

She wouldn't have been abducted. She wouldn't have married him . . . wouldn't have this. So much, she realized, was left to chance. Or fate.

And she wasn't sorry for it. Wasn't sorry for any of this—for him.

No matter what the year brought her, she would hold no regret. Everyone faced death sooner or later. If she faced it sooner, at least she would have truly tasted life. And love.

His features relaxed at her words, the harshly cut lines softening in the flickering firelight. "Very well then. I'm not sorry either. Not that I ever really was." With a grimace, he motioned to their bowls of stew, their simple surroundings. "I simply wanted something better than this for you on our first Christmas."

Lifting the spoon to her lips, she held his gaze and took a sip. "This is the best Christmas I've ever had."

Later that night, Marguerite woke to an empty bed and wondered if skulking from beds was a habit when it came to Ash. Did the man never sleep?

Slipping her shift over her head, she padded out into the larger room, chafing her chilled arms and marveling at how comfortable the little lodge had become to her. The idea of staying, lingering here forever, didn't strike her as altogether . . . *bad*. Perhaps danger wouldn't find her here . . . or whatever accident was meant to befall her. Perhaps here she could hide from the specter of death. She and Ash could build their own safe little world. A pleasant dream—even if it could never happen.

She found Ash sitting in the chair before the fire. He wore only his trousers, and his broad naked back gleamed in the firelight as he bent over something, his shoulders and biceps working, flexing and rippling as he labored.

Hugging herself, she approached silently, stopping behind him. A faint scratching sound filled the air.

"Ash?"

He looked swiftly over his shoulder. "Oh. I thought you were sleeping." He glanced to the window. She followed his gaze, noticing the faint purple light of impending morning. "Happy Christmas," he murmured, rising to his feet.

He offered her what he had been working on. A set of crudely carved figures filled his palms. She instantly recognized the three figures. She touched them with a shaking hand.

"I didn't have time to craft all the figures." His voice was rough with apology.

She took them from him, examining them as if they were the finest-crafted crystal. The small Mary, Joseph, and baby Jesus fit snugly into her palms. "You stayed up making these for me?"

He shrugged. "I'll finish the set for you someday. Perhaps next Christmas. If you like them."

Next Christmas.

"I love them," she managed to say, squeezing the words out thickly.

Her eyes burned at the thought of him finishing the set, and the Christmases to come when they could display them in their drawing room on a bed of holly. The children that would surround them, singing carols . . .

She stopped, shaking her head at the fanciful notion.

Before he saw the tears in her eyes and misunderstood, she flung her arms around his neck and hugged him tightly, speaking into the warm flesh of his neck. "I love them." *I love you.*

His arms came up, surrounding her, making her feel safe, protected, *loved.* And she prayed that she would be. That nothing would tear her from what she'd found with him. That this could last.

His hand trailed through her hair, dragging through the dark snarls. "I almost hate to leave this place."

She released a breathy laugh. "Me, too." Resting her cheek on the smooth skin of his shoulder, she added, "But we must." She had much to accomplish.

"Yes, I'm sure your father is worried about you."

She snorted. "I'm certain he's not. And even if he were, I would not care."

"He is your father, Marguerite. He should be told."

She stiffened in his arms. Yes, Ash would want him to know.

"Marguerite?" He pulled back to stare into her face. "What is it?"

She studied him closely. Was it still about *that* for him? Revenging himself on her father? Showing her father that he could be denied nothing?

"You're anxious to see my father?" she asked, her voice halting and suspicious. She could not help herself. "To inform him of our marriage?"

"Marguerite." A touch of exasperation laced his voice. He clearly read her suspicions. "It's not like that."

"Indeed?" She shrugged free of his arms, calling herself ten kinds of fool to let herself be seduced into thinking he actually cared for her. That *this* had become about them.

"Indeed," he echoed crisply, pulling her back into his embrace, indifferent to her stiff and resisting body. "You've come to mean more to me in this short time than any resentment I harbored toward your father. Than any matter of business."

"Such matters bore weight before. Why should I believe they no longer do?"

He slid a hand over her cheek, gripping her face. "You'll come to believe me," he vowed, his eyes glittering down at her. "If keeping you meant I had to turn everything over to Jack, renounce my share of the hells, the mine, the factory, then I would. I was angry before, determined to get as much of the properties as I could for myself, but now I know that I can stand on my own. I don't need Jack Hadley. I need you."

She glanced down at the carved figures in her hand, and realized that perhaps she needed him, too.

He continued, "I've not felt this way—" Stopping, a stark look came into his dark eyes. In a more even voice, he said, "I mean to be a true husband to you, Marguerite. I will make you happy."

He kissed her then. A fortunate circumstance. Closing her eyes, relief stole over her that he could not see the tears gathering. Because she wanted what he promised with every fiber of her being, craved the happiness he spoke of but doubted its possibility.

A sensation seized her then as he deepened the kiss, slanting his mouth against hers. She slid her fingers into his thick hair, kissing him back with equal fervor.

Burning conviction filled her. Determination.

As soon as they reached Town, she would return to St. Giles and confront Madame Foster. Marguerite would glean every bit of information that she could about her demise and do whatever necessary to stay alive. To stay with Ash. It was no longer for herself. It was for the both of them.

Chapter 19

A sh guided Marguerite to a long cushioned bench before a crackling fire at the inn where they stopped to change horses.

Sighing her relief, she slipped her gloved hands from her muff and extended them to the warming flames. It has been a hard day of travel, but they were close to Town.

"I shall see to a repast while we wait," Ash said. "Warm yourself." With a caressing stroke to her cheek, he ventured off to see to her comfort. The journey south had been full of smiles and caresses and decadent kisses, convincing Marguerite that she had made the right decision. She lifted her fingers to her lips, tracing a secret smile there, imagining she could still feel the warm imprint of his mouth.

She looked up at the sound of her name, her hand dropping away. The blood washed from her face at the sight of the man striding toward her, his cloak whipping about him like a dark wind. A coldness swept through her that rivaled the winter winds outside.

She staggered to her feet, then dropped back down at the unsteadiness of her limbs. Her dry and aching eyes swept over the man as though he were a terrible apparition come to life.

"Marguerite, is it truly you?"

"R-Roger." A quick glance beyond his shoulder showed no sight of Ash. Much to her relief.

He grasped her by the arms and pulled her into his embrace. "I feared something ill befell you when you vanished."

"I am well," she murmured, arching away from his arms.

"What happened to you?"

She shook her head, struggling for words.

Roger pushed on, heedless of her explanation. His eyes swept over her hungrily, his voice husky. "Whatever the case, you are a vision. Did I not have my sisters with me, I would claim you now—take a room upstairs and not emerge for days."

She shook her head harder. "Roger, you don't understand—"

"Unfortunately, the girls are stretching their legs out in the yard and I am not free to do so." He cupped her cheek and dared to slide his thumb over her mouth. With a small cry, she pulled her head free from his bold touch and opened her mouth to apprise him of her recent married status.

She did not have the chance.

Roger was ripped from her side and tossed through the air. He crashed into the bench with a horrible gurgled cry, shattering it to splinters. Ash jumped upon him before Marguerite could even move.

She cringed at the first smack of Ash's fist, the terrible crunch of bone on bone reminding her of that day in St. Giles when she first spied him beating another man to an inch of his life.

"Ash! No!" She grasped hold of his arm and hung on, stopping him from striking Roger again.

Ash sent her a quick glare. "He gave you insult."

"You don't understand!" she cried. Aware of the gathering crowd in the public room, she leaned closer, hissing hurriedly in his ear, "He is my protector. Or rather, I had intended for him to be. He's the one I was journeying to Spain with . . ."

Ash's sinewy arm tensed beneath her fingers, turning to stone.

Then, he moved, slamming one final blow that snapped Roger's head back. The viscount fell to the floor. Ash stepped forward, his legs braced wide. Roger stared up at him with unfocused eyes, blood dribbling thickly from a misshapen nose.

Ash reached down and grabbed him by his bloodstained cravat. "She is no longer your concern. Look at her, *touch* her, and I shall kill you. She's mine now."

Roger clasped a hand to his gushing nose and nodded fiercely.

"Ash," Marguerite breathed, making a move toward Roger, concerned only that Ash had not hurt him beyond repair.

Ash grabbed her hand and swung her around before she could attend to the viscount.

"Come," he growled in a voice she had never heard from him before.

"I only seek to see that he is not—"

"You are not to go near him again, Marguerite," he snapped, his voice humming with barely checked violence.

She bristled. "Is that the way of it then? Am I to follow your commands as though I'm mindless chattel?"

"Don't," he spat, pulling her outside and across the yard to their carriage.

"Don't what?" Her feet tripped to keep up. "You promised me a marriage where I would have freedom, independence. This hardly smacks of that!"

He flung her into the carriage ahead of him, following close behind. With a rap on the ceiling, the vehicle lurched into motion.

She stared across the carriage at him and was brought to mind of a deadly coiled snake, ready to spring. "Indeed, you are right," he said in a voice that was clipped and tight. "Thank you for the reminder. I seem to recall ours is a marriage of convenience. I've no call to expect or command anything of you—"

She shook her head, feeling as though everything were unraveling around her. "That's not what I meant—"

"In a reasonable time," he pushed on as if she had not spoken. "In a few months, we shall go our separate ways. I only ask that until then you refrain from making a fool of me. I'll be no cuckold whilst the two of us wait to part ways."

She shook her head, staring at him helplessly. Even as she sat across from him, she felt a gulf rise between them, an ever-yawning chasm that she could not cross.

Eyes burning, she shook her head, bewildered, marveling at what had become of her. Suddenly, the fate she had sought so desperately to avoid was no longer the worst thing that could befall her.

A week later, ensconced in her new home on Cavendish Square, Marguerite sat in the solarium. She'd quickly designated the room her favorite, with its sunny wallpaper and framed landscapes of sunlit Italian orchards. Colorful floral and striped pillows crowded the brightly upholstered sofas and chairs, beckoning her to sit. As a sick nurse she'd worked in many a fine home, but nothing compared to Ash's townhouse. She could almost convince herself that all was perfect in her world. If only her husband were speaking to her. If only a certain diviner had not filled her head with dire prophecies.

On this afternoon she resigned herself to the task of penning a letter to Fallon and Evie. The elusive words were slow to flow from her pen. As she didn't want to particularly worry her friends, she avoided mentioning the particulars involving her marriage to Ash. A skillful bit of subterfuge on her part to avoid mention of her abduction.

She looked up as Mrs. Harkens entered the elegant room pushing a cart laden with more tea and biscuits than Marguerite could possibly eat in a score of days.

Marguerite smiled. The housekeeper had been most solicitous since their arrival. "Mrs. Harkens, you are much too kind, but you needn't wait on me."

The wiry housekeeper batted a hand, stopping the cart near the crackling hearth. "Just happy to have someone here during the day. The master works such long hours. Even with servants to spare, this place feels empty and quiet. This great mausoleum needs children, if you ask me."

Marguerite's cheeks burned at the candid speech.

"Ah, forgive my runaway tongue." The housekeeper rushed to apologize. "I'm just over the moon that the master took a bride . . . only anxious for the next step. You must admit, this place needs a little life in it. Nothing like babes to put life in a house."

Marguerite nodded distractedly, trying not to imagine those babes. Toddlers with dark eyes and gold-kissed hair. It was too painful to consider they may never exist. She did, however, understand the housekeeper's meaning perfectly. The house felt empty. Marguerite had never been buried in such hushed silence. If not for Mrs. Harkens and the occasional servant lurking about, she would have thought herself quite alone here.

She glanced around at the splendid room with its great panels of windows that revealed a rather typical dreary winter day. Nothing inspiring in the sight.

She returned her attention to Mrs. Harkens, still prattling on. "At times, the master doesn't appear for days. Eats and sleeps and works at the hells, he does. It's nice to have someone to feed and dote on for a change."

Marguerite frowned. They'd arrived only two days ago, but Ash had been absent except for a few hours of sleep their first night in Town. She had not seen him since then, when he had pulled her beneath him and treated her to fierce and silent lovemaking. Clearly, he was still angered over the incident with Roger.

He had not appeared yesterday. Not last night. Nor today.

Was she to expect what Mrs. Harkens described? Would he only rarely put in an appearance? Did overseeing his establishments truly require so much of his time? Or was he merely avoiding her?

Already the memory of those idyllic days in Scotland seemed distant, the intimacy and closeness a thing of the past. Deep in thought, she selected a biscuit from the tray. Nibbling on a frosted edge, she watched the housekeeper as she tidied the elegant pillows scattered along the window seat, appearing more than happy to linger.

"Mrs. Harkens, would you mind having a carriage brought around? I should like to pay a call."

The craggy-faced woman nodded agreeably. "Aye, of course. No sense you staying holed up here all alone with the master gone so much."

A smile wobbled on her lips at the less than heartening reply. She had expected to spend *some* time with her new husband. She had counted on the magic they shared in Scotland to continue here. Evidently, he had not formed the same level of attachment. She had believed him when he told her their marriage wasn't about her father. Perhaps that had been foolish on her part given how quickly he'd abandoned her side. Was he simply using his anger at her over Roger as an excuse to push her away? To forget she was even around?

"I'll fetch Roland. He's a crack driver," Mrs. Harkens hastened from the room.

Marguerite rose and smoothed a hand over her skirts, trying to decide whether to change for her visit to Madame Foster. Before she could decide, Mrs. Harkens returned, her face flushed.

"Sorry, Mrs. Courtland."

Marguerite blinked, still unaccustomed to the designation.

"You've a caller. I tried to make him wait, but—"

"I insisted on seeing you at once."

Marguerite's head snapped in the direction of the rough, uncultured voice. Staring into the heavily lined face, she instantly knew she faced her father. The deep-set whiskey eyes resembled her own. Just as her mother had always said. She swallowed the lump rising in her throat. The father who never had time for her now suddenly found her worth his attention.

"Jack," she muttered breathlessly.

Mrs. Harkens sputtered. "You cannot barge in here, no matter who you are. The master would not like—"

"Enough. Don't speak of Courtland to me. Be gone, woman."

Mrs. Harkens's chin jerked to an obstinate angle. She squared herself, settling her feet onto the carpet, clearly determined to stay put.

"It's fine, Mrs. Harkens," Marguerite said softly. "I will be fine. You may go now."

With a last baleful look at Jack, she departed the room. "Just shout if you need me."

Her father crossed his arms over his barrel of a chest and stared down his nose at her. "I suppose it's too much to expect you call me 'Father.' "

She pulled back her shoulders, hot indignation flaming through her chest. "Yes, that would be a bit of a stretch."

"Very well." His gaze flicked her up and down, and she could not help feeling as though she were a bit of horseflesh being examined for market value. "You've the look of your mother about you."

Her hands knotted to fists at her sides. Did he expect an acknowledgment of that observation?

That she resembled the woman he had seques-
tered in the country like some shameful secret?

"Suppose that's a good thing," he grunted. "She
was beautiful."

They stared at each other, father and daughter,
unspeaking for a long moment. Then he blinked,
breaking the standoff, and his voice returned, cold,
flat, like he was discussing business and not par-
taking in a conversation with his once unacknowl-
edged child. "I'm sorry this has happened to you."
He glanced around them, his expression one of
distaste. "Ash can be ruthless. I knew I offended
him and should have realized he would resort to
something like this. But fear not, nothing has happened that cannot be undone."

"Indeed?" She shook her head, prepared to tell
him that nothing required *undoing*.

He continued, "I realize you might think it a
little late for me to play at the protective father."

"A little?"

He stopped and leveled her a cross look. As if
she were a wayward child and he the beleaguered
parent. "Whatever the case, I am your father, your
sole living parent—"

"I'm not a child to be commanded!" She followed this with a single stomp of her foot. The action clearly did little to support her claim.

He arched an eyebrow at her. "You will be coming with me, Marguerite—"

She shook her head, incredulous that he should think to order her anywhere. "No!"

"I have powerful friends and wealth to see that this travesty of a marriage is set aside—"

"No!" she shouted again, beyond outraged now. "I'm not asking you to—"

"You can't mean to stay wedded to Courtland, Marguerite. Are you that daft?" He stared at her, his brown eyes cruelly bright. "Don't tell me he's woven his spell over you. Don't you know how many skirts he's rooted beneath?"

"Surely no more than the great Jack Hadley."

He pressed his mouth into a grim line. "True. He and I are very alike, and that is not to his recommendation. His favorite pastime is diddling the girls in his employ."

She gazed at her father, speechless, his words sinking like heavy rocks. She pressed a hand to her suddenly queasy stomach. Was it true? Did Ash occupy himself with other women? Did he do that even now?

Her father shook his head. "You've no idea what type of man he is. For all his money, he's ruthless, only one step above the gutter, he's—"

"You!" she spat, her voice stinging with defiance.

His face burned red, even purple in some spots. His hands knotted into fists at his sides and she knew she'd hit a nerve. "Indeed I have said as much. If you can move past your hatred of me, you'll see the sense in gathering your things and leaving with me at once before you make a fool of yourself over the blackguard. He's broken countless hearts. I'd have that he not add my daughter to his list of conquered skirts. You will come with me, Marguerite."

She began to shake her head, but his next words cut her off.

"I've two men in the carriage. I can call for them if need be."

"You would drag me by force? Your own daughter?"

He shrugged, his face as hard as granite. "I'll do what I must."

And suddenly she was reminded that her father was every inch the villain who grew his wealth by crushing all in his path. He did not rise to the

designation of "King of St. Giles" through his com-
passionate endeavors.

She nodded, her throat thick, clogged with emotion. "Very well. I'll go." She would leave with him
rather than create a scene and risk Mrs. Harkens's
safety, or that of one of the other servants who had
treated her so kindly and welcomed her with such
warmth. She'd not have them harmed by two of
her father's henchmen.

"Smart girl," he drawled, reaching for her arm.
She steered herself clear of him and swept from
the room, head held high even as she was quivering with rage.

"Shall we have someone fetch your things?" he
asked behind her.

"Unnecessary. I'll return soon." Bold words.
Even as she uttered them, she wondered if they
were true.

Would Ash confront her father and demand her
return? Or had he proved his point, winning his majority share of the business and punishing the great
Jack Hadley by stealing one of his daughters out
from under him and then having his way with her?

Her quivering suddenly had little to do with
rage. Other emotions pressed down on her, making

her throat burn and eyes sting. Did Ash care what happened to her at all?

She would soon find out.

Ash returned home well after nightfall. The townhouse was silent, the footman in the foyer dozing in his chair as Ash ascended the stairs. Cowardly of him, he knew, to stay away so long in order to avoid his bride as if she were some shrew who had been thrust upon him, and not the other way around.

True, he did have business awaiting him after his absence, but nothing so pressing he could not have attended more care to his wife. He could have worked at home, but that would have been close to Marguerite, and he needed distance from her . . . and the dangerous feelings she stirred.

Seeing her in the arms of her *protector* had sent a blind rage knifing through him. In that moment, he'd felt like his father, full of fury and violence whenever Ash's mother returned home with coin in her reticule from the men she'd serviced. Of course, it failed to matter that his father was the one who sent her whoring for their dinner in the first place. The fury was there just the same.

The memory of that man's hands on Marguerite twisted his gut into knots even now. It made Ash recall why he'd never wanted to marry. He did not want the same bitterness that had poisoned his father to contaminate him, and the best way to guarantee that was to return to his original plan of a short-lived marriage of convenience. A wife in name only. Not a wife he craved as desperately as oxygen.

His tread fell whisper-soft, and he shook off the feeling that he'd done something wrong that would make him move about with such stealth. Many husbands and wives lived separate lives, hardly intersecting. What he had with Marguerite was more than that. Better. He'd secured her in *his* bedchamber the moment they returned home, after all. More than what many *ton* gentlemen would do. Of course, his motives were selfish. Ash wasn't about to deny himself access to Marguerite.

The bedchamber was dark when he entered, the fire low, dying embers barely glowing. Frowning, he quickly stoked the logs, shooting sparks into the air. Turning, his gaze fell on the curtained bed. He moved toward the great monstrosity. Marguerite had to use the steps to climb within.

Pulse pounding against his neck, he pulled back the curtain, easing one knee down as he reached for his wife's body, eager for her yielding heat. His arm stretched, finding nothing.

Scowling, he scanned the shadows of the bed for her lithesome shape.

Rising, he stalked across the room and yanked open the door to her dressing room. Finding no sight of her within, he swept back through the bedchamber. Flinging open the door, he called for Mrs. Harkens, heedless that he sounded like a bellowing tyrant or that he likely woke his entire staff.

His temper seethed at a dangerous simmer. Had Marguerite requested a room change? Tired of his absence, did she think to avoid him? He'd quickly remedy her of that notion.

He was frothing by the time Mrs. Harkens appeared, her brow knitted in concern as she belted her dressing gown. "Mr. Courtland?"

"My wife," he gritted. "Where is she?"

The housekeeper blinked. "Did she not send you word? Oh, dear. I thought she would—"

"My wife," he barked.

"She's gone."

Gone. He felt as though he just took a punch to his chest with those words. "Where?"

"Her father fetched her." Mrs. Harkens twisted one shoulder in an awkward shrug. "Thought it a bit odd, but Mrs. Courtland told me not to worry. Though I must say she didn't look too happy to see him."

Bloody hell. Apparently, Jack had gotten wind that he and Marguerite were back in Town—and *married.* No surprise that he hadn't been pleased with the news. With Jack's connections, Ash should have expected something like this. It was his own damn fault he'd left her alone.

Without a word, he stormed past his gaping housekeeper and out of the house, intent on reclaiming his wife, and doing a better job of keeping her.

Chapter 20

Marguerite paced the bedchamber she had been given for the night. A servant had arrived earlier to invite her downstairs to dinner. She had refused, too angry to sit across from her father and abide the sight of him. How had her mother ever loved such an arrogant wretch?

Wearing a night rail she presumed belonged to one of her sisters, she resigned herself to the fact that she would have to stay the night. At least one night. Whether Ash came for her or not, she refused to stay a second night in her father's house. Simply begetting her did not make him her father—did not give him any rights as a parent.

A knock at the door brought her pacing to a halt.

"Who is it?" she called out.

"Grier and Cleo," a voice called.

A feeling of both elation and dread stole over

her. The last visit with her half sisters had been awkward, mostly because she had wanted the encounter to be . . . well, something. *Everything*.

Foolish, she knew. How can a lifetime bond be formed in a first meeting? It was too much to expect. Also, she had rushed from the room with such haste they probably thought she wanted nothing to do with them.

"Come in," she called.

They tumbled into the room, reminding her of a pair of anxious little girls tripping over each other in their haste to reach a table laden with cakes and biscuits.

"The prodigal daughter has returned," Grier exclaimed, stepping forward, larger than life with her hands on her hips. She no doubt stood out in any group. She possessed that sort of presence. She was hard to miss, even without her unfashionably sun-browned freckled skin and deep auburn hair.

"Don't you mean the prodigal son?" Cleo asked.

Grier rolled her eyes. "Have some imagination."

"You've more than enough for all of us," Cleo returned.

Marguerite glanced back and forth. They seemed even better acquainted than before. A situation that only made her feel more distant from them.

As if she read her mind, Cleo stepped forward and hugged Marguerite. "We're so glad you've returned. Forgive us for intruding on your privacy. Jack said you were not feeling quite the thing, but we could not resist checking on you. Our last visit was dreadfully brief. Oh, but I confess I'm thrilled you did not go to Spain. But then what a shame," she clucked. "We could have spent Christmas together."

Grier dropped inelegantly upon the bed as if she planned to remain for a good while. "I hope you plan to stay longer this time." Grier plucked at an invisible thread on the counterpane. "Jack would no doubt appreciate a daughter more accommodating to his matchmaking efforts. We haven't been the most successful."

"Grier," Cleo admonished. "Give it time. He's paraded a score of gentlemen before us."

"Then I suppose he should parade a score more, because thus far, this entire endeavor has been quite the disappointment. Why not toss a real man our way and cease with all these sniveling dandies?"

"I'm certain we shall meet acceptable gentlemen in due time," Cleo assured her. "Jack is determined, if nothing else."

Marguerite glanced around the elegant bedchamber that served as her prison. Indeed, they possessed no notion how determined their father could be.

Grier pulled a face. "Yes, well, we aren't all as young as you. And this city air is making me itch." She rubbed her arm. "I can't stay here forever."

Cleo rolled her eyes. "I suppose we must yet again narrow your excessive criteria. Shall you now require a gentleman in possession of a country estate?"

"Not a bad idea, that," Grier muttered, still chafing her arm, either missing or ignoring Cleo's derision. "Wouldn't hurt you to raise your standards a bit, too. Don't you want more than to simply escape that overcrowded nest you call home? As unpleasant as it is to share your bed with two little sisters, don't forget you'll be sharing your bed with some man . . . best take care he's someone you can tolerate for the next fifty years."

Marguerite watched the pair, listening raptly, fascinated with the notion that they had turned their lives over so readily to Jack Hadley. And yet it made sense. From their remarks, she gathered that their lives fell short on opportunities.

Cleo caught her looking and lifted one slim shoulder in a fatalistic shrug.

A loud commotion from somewhere within the house drew their attention. Marguerite cocked her head to the side, straining to listen to the distant voices.

"What's that?" Grier asked, moving to the door.

Feet pounded up the stairs like stampeding horses.

"Holy hellfire!" Grier sputtered, peering out into the corridor.

Almost in answer to this, a masculine voice shouted, "Marguerite! Marguerite, where are you?"

Her heart tripped at the familiar voice.

"Ash," she murmured, her chest seizing.

Grier swung her incredulous gaze to Marguerite. "You know him?" she demanded. "Who's Ash?"

"My husband," Marguerite volunteered, the words easier to say than she had ever imagined. Especially now that she knew he had not forgotten her.

"Your husband?" Cleo shook her head. "Since when?"

"Since he abducted me on my last visit here." She refrained from adding that it could have been any one of them he snatched that evening.

Cleo gasped, eyes rounding in horror.

"The wretch! Shall I dispatch him for you?" Grier's hands curled into fists at her sides as if she would pummel the offending man herself. And somehow, Marguerite didn't doubt she would. There was something very *capable* about the woman.

"Fetch the Guard!" Cleo exclaimed, looking prepared to bolt from the room to do that very thing.

Jack's voice rang out then, loud and intractable, booming at the end of the corridor as he commanded his men to remove Ash from the house.

"Marguerite!" Ash bellowed yet again, and this time there was a desperate quality to his voice.

Marguerite squeezed past Grier in the doorway, her breath falling fast and hard, anxious to reach her husband. He had come. *Ash had come for her.*

Her stomach plummeted at the sight of him. He thrashed in the arms of several of her father's men. Jack stood near, face mottled red with fury.

Ash surged with unsuppressed violence in the arms of his captors. Eyes locked Jack, he growled, spitting the words, "Marguerite is mine. You'll have to bury me to stop me from coming for her." One corner of his mouth curled with wicked threat. "And even then I may come for her."

A shiver raced through Marguerite at that heated avowal.

Jack only looked more enraged at this. He swung a finger back in the direction of the stairs. "Get him out of here!"

Ash's eyes found her, bright and alive, glittering darkly in his harshly handsome face. He brought to mind an avenging angel, fearsome and deadly in his beauty.

His lips moved, mouthing her name so quietly, appealing to her alone.

Her chest squeezed, an aching, twisting mass at its center. She stumbled forward, rushed into her fate with full awareness that she might be rushing to her doom. And not caring. She had to have him, craved him like a woman denied air for far too long. "Ash, wait!"

"Marguerite, get back in your room!" Jack barked.

She turned on her father, snarling. "You mistake yourself to think you have any authority over me."

He blinked at her hissed words and waved roughly at Ash. "You can't think he cares for you."

"He's here, is he not?" she retorted, thinking that meant something. To her, at that moment, it meant everything.

Jack laughed harshly, his eyes cold and pitying as they swept over her. "This isn't about you. This is about me. About him and me. He's here to protect his interests, to secure only a greater share of our business. You play no part, stupid girl."

Ash broke from his captors then, charged Jack with a roar, connecting his fist to her father's face with a sickening crack.

Marguerite jumped from the force of the blow, wincing.

Her sisters yelped behind her.

She blinked, frozen to stone, shocked at the image of her father crashing against the wall. A painting rattled loose, tumbling with a bang alongside him.

Even Jack's henchmen didn't move, gaping at their employer, the great King of St. Giles a broken pile upon the floor. Jack glared up at Ash, gingerly touching his bloodied lip.

Ash stood over her father. "You'll not speak to her like that again," Ash gasped, broad chest heaving with serrated breaths. Somehow in the scuffle his cheek had been scratched. A thin line of blood oozed just beneath his eye, making him look all the more feral, dangerous.

"What?" he bit. "The truth?"

"You're the one who knows nothing. This isn't about you anymore. Marguerite's my wife now. Forever. You can't undo that."

Jack stared unblinkingly, as if he were seeing Ash for the first time. In some ways, *she* felt she was seeing him for the first time. Seeing and believing that this man cared for her. Needed her. Not because he wanted to prove something to her father, not because he wished to protect his assets, but because he needed her for himself.

Marguerite moved to Ash's side. He wrapped a strong arm around her and pulled her closer, leading her away. She sent a small wave to her gawking sisters. They waved back, both wearing similar expressions of astonishment.

Marguerite and Ash walked down the corridor, descending the stairs side by side. She shivered when they stepped out into the chill night. Only then did she recall she wore a night rail.

Ash pulled her close and folded her within his greatcoat. At the door to his waiting carriage, he swept her inside.

Sinking onto the comfortable squabs, she permitted him to bundle her up in a blanket. She was shaking, but it had little to do with the cold and everything to do with him.

He came for me.

She opened her mouth to speak, mutter some flippant remark about overprotective fathers, something to bring levity to the tension that weighed the air between them, but she didn't get the chance. He finished tucking the blanket around her and lifted his hands to her face in one smooth movement, hauling her toward his mouth for a kiss that robbed her of words, breath, thought.

He slanted his lips over hers again and again, his tongue slipping inside her mouth, tasting of spicy drink and all that was him.

His kiss burned, consumed her, desperate and

hungry like it was the first time, the last time they would ever kiss each other.

She arched against him with a restless mewl, sliding her fingers through his hair, drinking desire from the hot melding of their lips.

He groaned, deepening the kiss, lips fusing. Their teeth clanged with violent need. Pleasure raced through her, scalding her blood when he bit down on her lip. She bit him back. A shudder racked him, rippling through her. Their fingers moved over each other, roving, touching, groping with ungentle hands.

Her fingers flew to his breeches, moving feverishly, her need a desperate, hungry thing. Dark and feral, coppery-rich in her mouth. She closed around the silken length of him. They shuddered together, unified in their desire, their need for each other.

Her blanket fell to the side as he swung her around, planting her on his lap. Her night rail billowed out around her as her thighs slipped down on each side of his hips. He found her heat and she felt the bare tip of him prodding, seeking, pushing up inside her.

And then he was there. Filling her.

She surged at the sudden thrust of him inside her, clutching his shoulders as if he was her lifeline, as if she would never let go.

And she wouldn't, she realized.

Not if she could help it. Not as long as she drew breath.

Gasping, sated, still shuddering from the power of his release, Ash flexed his hands over her sleek hips, loving the sensation of her satiny skin in his hands. He buried his face in her neck, inhaling her honey and milk scent, knowing this was the aroma he wanted to wake to every morning.

"Sorry," he murmured. "A bed would have been more comfortable, I know. With you, I just can't help myself."

"Don't apologize. I'm just as guilty."

He lifted his head and stared at the dim shadow of her face. "Why did you leave with him?" His chest clenched as he recalled his feelings when he first found Marguerite gone from their bed. In that moment, his sense of loss had outweighed any fears he'd ever had of turning into his father, of losing all he'd built with Jack.

"He was insistent, and I didn't want to drag

Mrs. Harkens or any of the other servants into harm's way—"

"It's their duty to protect you, Marguerite." He winced. *It was his duty.* He'd do better by her from now on. "You must believe you're worth that protection." *Worth everything.* He held her tighter. "Say I'll never come home to find you gone. Never leave me," he murmured. He would never again thrust her from him because he was too afraid of turning into his father.

When she said nothing, he lowered his forehead to hers. tasting her warm breath on his lips. He closed his eyes as a slight tremor passed through her and bled into him. Still, she said nothing.

Chapter 21

Marguerite woke the following morning to find Ash still in their bed. A first, to be certain. He had not crept from their bed like a thief in the night while she slept. He'd stayed. Warmth suffused her chest, spreading through her.

Her mind drifted to last night and his whispered request that she promise never to leave him. She had tried to speak, but could not summon the words. Not when she couldn't yet believe them herself.

She glanced around the curtained bed, letting it sink in that this was her life. With him. No more genteel servitude, holding the hands of the dying as they faded from earth. This was her life for however long it lasted. A month or half a century.

Her hand crossed the space that separated them, covering his fingers where they curled on the bed beside her. She lay still for several moments, perfectly content, sated at this simple connection. She watched him in sleep, the dark gold of his hair tossed wildly about his head. She loved to run her fingers through the silken strands. His face appeared relaxed, the angles and hollows unguarded, less severe.

He'd carried her inside the house carriage as if she were fragile and treasured. *Loved*.

She wanted that. Wanted his love. Wanted to love him with no fearful specter hanging over her. She bit her bottom lip and eased up on one elbow, lightly stroking the back of his hand, trailing up his arm, tracing the corded muscle.

Before being dragged off to her father's house, she had been in the process of venturing to see Madame Foster. She would not delay another day. She could not. She must see the diviner, must find hope that all she'd found with Ash would not vanish in an instant.

She could put it off no longer. How could she look at Ash, her heart full yet aching, without having done all she could? Without having done everything in her power? She could not be with him in earnest, with all freedom of heart, knowing she had not tried to safeguard her survival for as long as possible.

Slipping her hand from Ash, she eased from the bed, moving quietly about the room, dressing herself with one eye on her sleeping husband.

No matter what she learned from Madame Foster, she would have peace knowing she'd exhausted every avenue available. Following that, come what may, she would live each day to the fullest. Loving life. Loving Ash.

Dressed, she snatched a fistful of pins from her dressing table and took a final lingering glance at him before departing the room, hope brimming in her heart.

She'd found something with Ash. Something she'd never had before. Something she never knew to hope for. For the first time, her life was about more than caring for the needs of others. Her life was about . . . *living*. He woke her, made her feel alive. Ironic, considering she might soon be dead.

Her pace quickened down the corridor. She squeezed her eyes in a tight blink, fighting the burn at the backs of her eyes. God would not be so unkind to take her from him. Not now. Not yet.

Dawn scarcely tinged the air, filtering through the windows she passed. Her shadow stretched long before as she strode ahead, her hands lifted to her head, working the pins into her hair. Her clumsy efforts would have to suffice. She could not risk ringing for a maid. She'd never needed a maid to assist her before, after all. Calling for a carriage was out of the question, too. She could not leave a trail for Ash. Later, she would fabricate an excuse. Anything but the truth.

"Mrs. Courtland?" She practically jumped free of her skin at the voice.

Marguerite donned a falsely cheerful smile for the housekeeper. "Mrs. Harkens," she breathed.

The craggy-faced woman looked Marguerite over, her thick brows lifting. Clearly, the sight of her walking boots peeping beneath her skirts and the cloak draped over her shoulders signified that she was venturing out.

Marguerite held her breath, convinced the housekeeper was on the verge of inquiring where she was going at this early hour. Instead, she said, "You've a caller. A lady awaits you in the drawing room. I told her it was too early, but she's quite determined."

"I'll see her," Marguerite quickly said, beyond curious who had called upon her.

Upon entering the drawing room, she located Grier's willowy figure standing near the window.

"Marguerite," she greeted, striding forward. "You are well? I slept not a wink last night for worry. Jack is quite convinced this Ash fellow has seduced your thinking—"

"I'm unharmed and here quite willingly. Didn't you notice that I left of my own accord yesterday?"

She waved a hand. "I said as much to Jack, but he claims you are too frightened—"

Marguerite snorted. "He merely wishes so. Do I appear frightened? Jack simply cannot abide that I've chosen a man he doesn't approve."

Grier nodded. "Oh, he simply can't abide anyone marrying a daughter he seeks to sell off like chattel to an earl or a duke . . . or even a bloody prince," this last she uttered with such heat that Marguerite wondered if there was not one such odious prince in Grier's life, however far-fetched the notion.

The brown freckles on Grier's cheeks stood out more than customary. She inhaled through her nose as though groping for composure. "Forgive me for calling so early, I merely wanted to assure myself that you are not being mistreated and sincerely here of your own will. Cleo will be greatly relieved, too. She thought your husband a veritable brute yesterday."

Marguerite smiled. "She's not too far off the mark."

"Well," Grier said a bit gruffly, "I hope he makes you happy."

Marguerite smiled, then frowned, her thoughts drifting as ever to her uncertain future.

"Did I say something to offend you?" Grier touched her hand, her warm eyes full of concern.

And that was all it took to completely undo her.

Marguerite crumbled, sank down on the sofa, hot tears dripping down her cheeks. Grier followed her down and wrapped her in her arms. Mortifying as it was to lose her composure to tears, the embrace comforted her. Her sister was warm and yielding and smelled of chocolate. "There now." Grier's hand smoothed slow circles on Marguerite's shuddering back. "Don't cry."

"You don't understand."

"Then tell me."

Releasing a deep breath, Marguerite did.

Like a dam opened, everything poured out,

the words a burning rush. Even as incredible as it sounded to her ears, she told her wide-eyed half sister all. She didn't stop once or come up for air until she had unburdened herself.

"Holy hellfire," Grier breathed at the end of it all.

Marguerite swiped at her sniffling nose and nodded grimly. "And now you think I'm mad— straight for Bedlam."

Grier shook her head long and slow. "No. In your shoes, I'm sure I would find myself quite convinced as well." She gazed at Marguerite, her eyes intense beneath her fine, dark brows. With a decisive nod, she announced, "You must go back to this Madame Foster."

Marguerite gave a wobbly smile. "I was on my way to do that very thing this morning."

Grier rose swiftly. "Then I shan't stop you. Go, Marguerite, at once. Press this woman for more information, for every detail about this accident. Glean any clues that you may—"

"I know, I know." Nodding, Marguerite moved toward the door, heartened to know she'd decided on the right course.

"I shall call again tomorrow." Grier followed her, taking Marguerite's hand in her own. "I will help you in any way I can. You need only ask."

"Thank you." Marguerite inhaled, her chest lighter, less tight now that she had told someone. "I think I shall enjoy this."

"What?" Grier shook her head faintly.

"Having a sister."

"Oh." Grier's face flushed warmly beneath her tanned skin. "Me, too."

They walked arm in arm through the grand foyer out into the sleeting morning. Tucking her face inside her hood to avoid the icy wet, Marguerite issued a brief prayer, grateful that Grier had paid call, grateful that Ash had not yet woken and investigated her disappearance from their bed.

With luck, she would be back home before he even noticed she'd left the house. Home and armed with the information to ensure her future.

Ash pounded up the steps of Jack's Mayfair home. He hadn't expected to be back so soon, to be sure, but waking to an empty bed, his wife nowhere in sight, he'd reached only one furious conclusion. Jack had stolen his wife again.

Without bothering to knock, he charged into the house. Storming through the foyer, he grasped the bottom balustrade, and bellowed Marguerite's name, much in the manner of yesterday.

She didn't appear, but several footmen did. He struggled against their grasping hands as they tried to drag him back out the front door. A bitter sense of déjà vu washed over him. "Marguerite!" Did Jack have her locked in some room? He'd tear apart this mausoleum in his search for her.

Jack appeared, the color riding high in his already ruddy face. "You again?"

"I warned you yesterday . . . Marguerite is mine!"

"Lost her already, have you?" His father-in-law sneered. "Can't say I'm surprised."

"Where is she?" he ground out.

"I don't know," Jack snapped, waving a hand angrily. "Why don't you keep better tabs on your wife?"

"Don't lie to me. I know you sent one of your other daughters for her." He recalled the housekeeper's description. "The tall freckled one."

"Grier?" Jack scowled. "What's she got to do with this?"

"Grier came to my house this morning. Marguerite was seen leaving with her. *Hours* ago."

"Grier's here, upstairs having a fitting with the modiste, but I haven't seen Marguerite."

Ash ignored him, not about to believe him when it came to Marguerite. He'd underestimated Jack once. Not again. When it came to marrying off his daughters, the ambitions of Jack Hadley knew no limit. He'd steal Marguerite away—

Ash grimaced, abruptly realizing he knew this because he was the same way. At least he *had* been.

Jack had taught him to be relentless, selfish, hungry for success above all else. *Seize what you want, no matter the cost.* That had been Ash, and it shamed him.

With this cold realization settling over him, he felt raw and exposed, a stranger inside himself, a man he didn't like, didn't want to be.

He'd abducted Marguerite simply to further his own goals. To win greater control over his business assets and force Jack to receive him as a son-in-law. As if marrying one of his daughters would make him whole, complete. As if that approval would rub out all the insecurities of his youth and erase from memory the boy he had once been.

Staring at the ruddy face of the man he'd looked to as a father for so many years, Ash shook his head. He no longer craved or needed the approval of Jack Hadley to validate him. He no longer cared about his past.

The only thing he craved now was Marguerite. In his arms. In his bed. Throwing back his head, he shouted her name again.

"Cease your shouting!" Grier scolded, advancing down the stairs, holding her amber-gold skirts as she descended. "You're scaring the maids, and your wife is not here."

"My housekeeper saw you leave together."

Grier shook her head. "We went separate ways. Marguerite is not here."

He shook off the footmen's hold. They still hovered close, breathing thickly against his back.

Ash studied Grier closely, seeking the truth in her eyes. She had trouble holding his stare. She may not be lying, but she was certainly not telling him everything.

"But you know where she is," he declared, tugging at the cuffs of his jacket.

Her gaze swung to the floor, to her father, to the wall beyond. Anywhere but at his face. Her voice emerged, brittle with falseness, "She didn't mention—"

"Grier," he said sharply. "Tell me where she is."

She lifted her gaze to his face, her brown eyes beseeching. "I can't."

He took several careful steps toward her, cautioning himself not to grab her by the shoulders and give her a good shake. "Yes, you can."

She shook her head doggedly, "She would not want you to know. And what kind of sister would I be if I couldn't keep the first secret she entrusted to me?"

"A terrible one," Jack inserted with undisguised relish. "Don't tell him, Grier. Make him suffer. It's his own bloody fault he lost her."

She scowled at her father. "He didn't lose her, so enough of that nonsense from you. You're being cruel. Can't you see they love each other?"

Ash blinked, and opened his mouth to deny that outrageous claim. But no words fell. His mouth and throat felt parchment dry, incapable of speech.

Grier angled her head to the side, smiling broadly at him. "What's the matter? Did you not know that?"

He shook his head, dragging a hand roughly through his hair. "Know . . . what?"

She nodded with annoying confidence, clarifying again in succinct tones, "That you love your wife."

He snapped shut his sagging mouth, absorbing her words, letting them sink deep, settle in his gut . . . trying to decide whether there was any truth to them. And he found his answer.

Yes. He loved his wife. And no, until that moment he had not realized it.

Shaking his head, he clenched his hands into fists at his sides. "You have to tell me, Grier. She's my wife."

"*And . . .*" she stressed, clearly requiring he admit his love, "you love her."

He pressed his lips together, staring at her in silent mutiny. It was one thing to admit it to himself, another to confess his love before others.

Jack snorted. "Ash? In love?"

Ash turned on him, practically snarling.

"Jack," Grier admonished.

"I've a right to know where my wife has—"

"And. You. Love. Her." Grier glared at him, a most vexed expression on her face. A dog with a bone, she wasn't going to stop. Suddenly, he felt sorry for whatever aristocrat Jack paired up with her. The fellow didn't stand a chance.

He released a ragged sigh. "Very well," he growled, casting a resentful glance toward Jack who watched on avidly. "And," Ash admitted, "I love her."

The words were not as difficult to say as he'd imagined. Not that he ever imagined uttering them. He shook his head once, marveling over himself. He was in love. With the woman he'd married, no less. The very thing he had vowed to never let happen had happened.

She nodded in seeming approval. "She's gone to visit a seer. Madame Foster is her name."

"In St. Giles?" he snapped, frowning.

He'd heard of Madame Foster. Many of the girls who worked for him spoke of her. Mary visited her regularly.

Pieces slowly clicked together. That would be what she'd been doing the day they first met on the street. Marguerite had never said what she was doing there, but what else could be the reason?

His frown deepened into a scowl at the thought of his wife alone in the stew. He'd told Marguerite to never visit that part of Town again. Course, he'd been nothing to her then, no better than street trash, but now he was her husband. Did that not count for something?

"Don't be angry," Grier admonished, clearly reading his expression. "She had to go."

"Why?"

Grier's gaze turned so bleak that a trickle of unease crept beneath his skin. Still, even with that foreboding sensation, nothing could have prepared him for her next words.

"She's going to die."

He pulled his head back, a hissing breath stinging past his lips.

"What do you mean?" he demanded, stepping forward to seize her by the arms. She winced and he immediately softened his grasp. "Please," he whispered hoarsely, a terrible burn eating up his throat.

"She's known for some time—"

"Is she ill?" he demanded, thinking of how he had dragged her across the country in the cold of winter. She was small, such a slight female, but he had thought her hearty enough.

"No. Nothing like that. Madame Foster told her."

"Madame Foster?" He shook his head and released Grier with a curse. Pressing a hand to his temples, he asked quietly in a voice that remarkably reflected none of his impatience or frustration. "What exactly did Madame Foster tell her?"

"That Marguerite would die. Before the year is out . . ." her voice faded in such a way that he knew there was more. She averted her eyes, stared down at her fingers.

"And?" he prompted.

"She'll have an accident of some sort . . . some time following her marriage to you."

He pulled his head back as if he'd been dealt a blow. That would explain her contrary nature—wanting to marry him one moment and not the next. This is what she had been so afraid of.

This shed light on everything. The day they had wed, there'd been something in her eyes. A dimness, the light fading in the amber depths. She had considered her vows to him tantamount to death. The knowledge infuriated him.

"Madame Foster predicted her marriage to me?" He snorted with disbelief.

Grier nodded. "Yes."

"Rubbish," he hissed.

Something snapped inside him, a wire cracking in two. A feeling grew, built inside him, expanding his chest, tightening the skin of his face.

Rage. Prickly hot and smoldering through him. His hands curled and uncurled at his sides, craving violence. He wanted to punch a wall. Or the swindler stuffing Marguerite's head with such nonsense. He even felt rage at Grier for accepting the nonsense so simply. And yet the most dangerous of his emotions were directed at Marguerite for believing. For letting superstitious rot drive a wedge between them.

He whirled on his heels, ignoring Grier's urgent voice. "Ash, please, understand! Don't be angry, don't do anything you'll regret."

Regret? He'd do nothing *he* would regret. He simply intended to shake some sense into his seriously foolish wife, and make *her* regret the day she ever decided to believe the prophecies of an artful con. Marguerite was not going to die. At least no time in the near future.

She wasn't. He inhaled thickly through a chest that suddenly felt too tight, his lungs too constricted. *She was not*.

Against his bidding, his sister's body, so sickly small, frail and broken at the end, flashed before his mind. The memory of his grief, his utter helplessness, swept over him in a bitter tide.

He would not endure that again. He blinked, cursing himself. Of course not. Madame Foster was nothing more than a clever actress.

Body rigid, he strode from the house, fighting the dark, unfamiliar emotions that stewed deep inside him. Beneath the rage a sliver of doubt sank into his heart. Remote and impossible, it still found its way inside him. *What if he was wrong? What if this diviner was right?*

At that notion, an emotion similar to the way he'd felt standing over his sister's small casket pierced his heart. And yet even then, that feeling had been milder somehow. Bearable in a way that this was not. He'd known he would go on after Charlotte, fight to survive somehow after her death.

But this . . .

Marguerite . . .

At once he knew. The emotion that lurked beneath his rage was one thing only. *Fear.*

Chapter 22

Marguerite was finally admitted into Madame Foster's parlor after sitting for several hours in one of several hardback chairs lining the wall of a cramped corridor.

Apparently, she'd chosen a busy day to call. Half a dozen females took their turns before her. A strange experience. On one side of Marguerite had been a maidservant in a soiled gown, her hems badly frayed and far too short. On her other side sat a girl dressed in pink muslin, a fine velvet cloak draped over her shoulders, her hands buried in an ermine muff. Marguerite felt certain the chit had escaped her governess for the afternoon.

She tried not to think about the minutes slipping past or that she had been absent half the day as she took her seat.

"So," Madame Foster said, settling in her chair across from Marguerite. She lifted a steaming cup of tea to her lips and sighed as if her throat ached and was in dire need of relief. "You're back."

Marguerite's lips curved ever so slightly. "You mean you didn't know I would return?"

Madame Foster narrowed her gaze on Marguerite, her expression thoughtful. "Something's different about you."

Marguerite lifted her chin, holding silent. This was the last person who should have to be *told* anything.

Madame leaned forward, sliding a pudgy hand across the tablecloth and seizing hold of Marguerite's hand. Marguerite willingly gave up her hand to Madame's warmer grip.

Turning her fingers over, she studied the lines of Marguerite's hand carefully before flicking her gaze to her face. "You've married," she announced at last. "Just as I foretold."

Marguerite nodded. "Inevitable, I suppose." She smiled tremulously.

Madame Foster snorted, still clinging to her hand. "You say that with such acceptance. *Now.*"

"My marriage, I accept." Marguerite leaned

across the table drilling her gaze into the woman. "But the rest I do not. I'm not ready to leave this world."

Madame snorted again. "We never are, my dear. We never are."

"There must be something I can do. Some way . . ." Marguerite shook her head fiercely, feeling the dangerous burn of tears in her eyes. She flattened her free hand on the top of the table. "I can't go. Not yet. Can't you give me more information about this accident so that I might prevent it?"

Madame bowed her head over her hand yet again. "Let me have another look."

Marguerite held her breath while she looked her fill, Madame's thumbs exerting the slightest pressure into the base of her palm. "It's misty, but I see a carriage, wheels turning, rolling so fast . . . horses scream. It's raining. Thundering." She nodded her head gravely, her brow creasing. "Yes. I can see you there." Madame flicked her gaze up to Marguerite's. "Dead."

She shivered almost like it was the first time she ever heard the news of her death. "Can you see where I am?"

"No," she said with a sharp shake of her head.

"But you're filthy. I see mud. You're lying in mud. Covered in it."

"Brilliant," Marguerite muttered. "I need only stay indoors when it rains and after it rains. This is England." She shook her head. "I shall never step outside again."

Madame chuckled.

Marguerite scooted to the edge of her chair. "Can you not see anything else? Please. A hint of where I am?"

Madame went back to examining her hand. Closing her eyes, she dropped her head with a great exhale and pressed their hands together, palm to palm.

Her voice washed over Marguerite. "There's someone with you. Over you, shaking you, holding you. A man with gold hair." Her lips twitched. "Your splendid specimen of a husband, I gather."

"Ash," Marguerite sighed. She shouldn't have felt relieved, but she did. She wouldn't be alone. No matter what happened, it wouldn't be so bad if he was there. "Can you see no more? A carriage accident? In the rain. That is all?"

"Marguerite," Madame said, shaking her head, the tone of her voice unsettling, like she was about to impart something grave. "You're happy now, aren't you? Unlike the last time I saw you? You have a lightness. A glow."

Marguerite thought of Ash and nodded. "I am happy. Yes."

"Then be happy." Madame fluttered a hand as though she spoke of a mere nuisance and not her life. Her death. "Stop worrying about what I see. Perhaps it will come to pass, perhaps not."

"Yes." Marguerite nodded slowly. Hadn't she thought that same thing before? That she should live like each day was her last. With no regrets? Shaking her head, she rose to her feet, that single-minded purpose filling her, consuming her. She looked around at the shabby little parlor overflowing with knickknacks as if she didn't know what she was doing here. "I must go." To Ash. To the life awaiting her.

Madame smiled approvingly. "Good girl."

"Good-bye." She hastened to the door, calling over her shoulder, "And thank you."

Leaving Madame Foster's shop, Marguerite no longer felt a burning conviction to escape the specter of death. Everyone died. If she happened to die sooner rather than later, so be it. She would be certain she lived a lifetime in the time left to her, however many days that numbered.

Descending the steps of Madame's stoop, she buried her hands deep into her muff. A lone female, dressed like Quality, she earned several stares and tried not to fidget beneath the scrutiny.

She spotted the hack across the street, glad to see the driver had waited as she asked. He leaned against the side smoking a cheroot. Nodded in her direction, he put out his cheroot, moving toward the carriage door. Looking both ways, she proceeded across the street, mindful of the puddles.

And that's when she saw him.

Ash, riding hell-bent down the middle of the street for her. He held her transfixed, a prisoner of his black-eyed gaze. A chill rippled over her. She had never seen him look quite like this. Not even when he chased her down in that field. Satan himself couldn't look so wicked.

Dear heavens, how would she explain her presence here, outside Madame Foster's shop? She sent a guilty glance over her shoulder, eyeing the narrow shop squeezed between two buildings, its crude wood sign swinging over the door.

He'd think her mad if she confessed the truth to him. Declaring everything to the understanding Grier was one thing, but her jaded, rough-edged husband was another. Even worse, what if he truly believed her? Could she abide to see pity, perhaps even fear, in his gaze when he looked at her? She shuddered. Absolutely not.

She couldn't tell him the truth.

He was closer now. She could see the light glittering off his dark pupils. The hard press of his mouth. The tiny tick near the corner of his eye. The stark whiteness of his crescent-shaped scar.

Her breath froze, her heart stilling at the cold fury in his face. He *knew*. Of course. How else did he come to be here? Grier had told him. She had told him everything.

Dread sank in her belly, as heavy as stone. Her heart wasn't the only thing frozen. Her legs were locked immobile. Her feet didn't move, didn't budge, had become great leaden weights where she stood. She opened her mouth, but no words fell. She didn't know what to say that could make him understand . . . to make any of this seem less absurd.

Then his face changed. Altered in a flash. Became something terrible and fierce. Harsh-cut lines, his mouth open, gaping.

"Marguerite!" Her name tore through the misty air, a horrible broken sound. He wasn't looking at her, but somewhere beyond her.

She turned.

It seemed she moved slowly, but she was sure she did not. She was sure she whipped her head around on her shoulders swiftly—in perfect time to see the phaeton bearing down on her.

A thought skittered across her mind, irrational, dim.

Not a carriage. It was a phaeton.

Madame Foster had been wrong about that.

The phaeton's driver was laughing, his ruddy, jovial face turned on his companion beside him. Glancing ahead, he saw her. His eyes flew wide and he jerked on the reins with both hands, dropping a bottle from one hand. It seemed to bounce, skip in the air, its amber contents spraying out into the rain.

Rain. It had begun to rain some time during the last few moments. The pound of rainfall filled the air, like the steady distant roar of a faraway beast.

Only it wasn't far. It was on top of her, soaking her to the bone.

The driver fought to bring the speeding horses under control. Their eyes rolled wildly in their heads. They screamed, clawing air with their hooves high above her.

Bile rose high in her throat. She lunged to the side. Her heel caught. She fell, splashed in a puddle with a jar hard enough to rattle her teeth.

Wet, cold, *covered in mud*—Marguerite suddenly felt removed from everything, outside herself looking in.

She threw her hands before her in a feeble effort to protect herself, scooting backward, using a rut for leverage. Hooves crashed down beside her, shaking the ground, vibrating up her body. She rolled, shrank away, trying to avoid those glinting hooves dancing violently around her, crashing in every direction.

She cried out when one hoof grazed her shoulder. She didn't have time to recover from the pain before she was struck again. Agony exploded in the side of her head. Darkness sucked her down, pulling her in, under . . .

Then there were hands. On her, over her. Beneath her arms, hauling her from the tangled fray of horseflesh and cutting hooves. She blinked past the black, emerging through the gray and breaking into misty-hued reality.

Voices clamored around her, congesting the air and adding to the buzzing pain in her head. An incessant clacking noise filled her ears—her chattering teeth, she realized. The more she tried to still her jaw, the harder her teeth chattered.

"Marguerite, can you hear me?"

She winced. "I'd hear you in China," she muttered, her speech slurred.

She tried to touch her head where it throbbed, but she couldn't. The effort to lift her arm was too great.

The rain had abated to a slow, freezing drizzle that penetrated her clothes, sank into her with a bone-deep chill so cold it burned.

"Marguerite!" Ash loomed above her, the sound of her name an angry bite on the air.

She lifted her head sharply, pain hissing past her teeth. She fought it, swallowed down the discomfort, the bile that rose up in her throat as she glanced down at herself. Cold and shaking on the ground. Wet. Muddy.

Just as Madame Foster predicted.

"Marguerite? Do you know where you are?"

"I haven't had the sense knocked out of me, if that's what you mean."

"No, just trampled by horses," he replied dryly.

"You'd think you'd sound a bit happier and not so cross with me. I'm not dead," she snapped. And she realized with a start that she wasn't. She wasn't dead.

A jolt of energy shot through her. She forced one elbow down in the cold sludge, propping herself up. Ash quickly moved to help her. Sliding an arm beneath her, he pulled her to her feet. When her legs gave out, he swept her up into his arms, his face stark, a tangled blend of concern and anger.

"I'm fine," she said with a breathy gasp. Better than fine. She was wonderful, even with her body battered and broken and aching. *She was alive* . . . and going to stay that way for a good while.

He adjusted her in his arms, his movements gentle. "We'll see about that."

He strode toward the hack, his every step jarring, shooting pain through her body, but even that could not stop the smile from curving her lips. Her fingers smoothed over his shoulder, relishing the strength there, the rippling power beneath the fine fabric of his greatcoat. At their approach, the driver scurried to attach Ash's mount to the back of his conveyance.

Calling out directions to the driver, Ash settled and arranged her on the squabs like she was an invalid he must treat with care for fear of breaking. Missing his arms around her—the strength and comfort—and loathing the way his dark eyes skimmed over her, like she was something broken, she straightened on the seat, inadvertently bumping her tender head into the carriage wall. A cry slipped past her lips.

She could cope with his anger, preferred it even. Let him be mad. His solicitous pity she could do without.

He didn't miss the sound. With a curse, he glared back over his shoulder as if he would vault from the hack. "I've a mind to take a whip to that bloody driver. Was he blind—?"

She reached for his hand. "But I need you here. With me."

He dragged his gaze back to her. "You could have gotten yourself killed," he growled.

"But I didn't," she said, her voice gaining strength. "I won't."

He looked at her intently, his gaze drifting from her face, scanning the length of her shivering body. She could well surmise his thoughts. He was thinking about why she'd come here . . . wondering if she might not have been correct to believe the predictions of a diviner.

"It's over," she said, happy relief swelling her chest. For nothing else mattered. It was over and they could be together without fear of tomorrow.

He shook his head, clearly not understanding.

She clasped his warm hand, not realizing until that moment how cold she was, her fingers wet icicles. "You know why I came here . . ."

He nodded tightly, his dark eyes intense, accusing. The hard cut of his lips sent an uneasy trickle down her back. "Madame Foster, yes, I know. Grier told me."

"Madame Foster saw me like this." Marguerite waved a hand over her body. "In the rain, covered in mud." Her words rushed loose in a babble. He had to see, had to believe . . . "There was a carriage, and rain and thunder and then *you* over me." She gestured between them for emphasis. "*This*. This is what she saw happening. She didn't read the situation correctly. She thought I died. Don't you see? It's happened. And I'm still alive."

Ash dragged a hand through his hair, pulling at the long ends. "*If* I'm inclined to believe some fortune-teller—"

"I didn't believe her at first either, but everything she says always comes to pass."

"So," he said slowly, air exhaling from his nose as though he was grappling for control. "You think this woman can truly see into the future? That she foresaw what happened just now—" he cut himself off, his beautifully carved lips twisting.

"You have to admit it's more than coincidence. How else could she relate so many details?" She nodded, then stopped, hissing at the fresh pain it produced in her head. She pressed a trembling hand there, fingering the goose egg.

He scooted closer, removing her hand and gently testing the knot with his warm fingers, his voice distracted as he muttered, "I only care that you no longer believe you are going to die."

Disappointment surged through her. "You think I'm mad then. That I can't be right about this?"

"Sweetheart, I'll believe anything you want right now."

"I am not a little girl with fanciful notions that must be indulged." Bristling, she glared up at him through her lashes. "I'm not daft, Ash. I'm quite serious—"

"I know you are," he snapped, "as much as I'd like to pretend otherwise. I can't fathom why you've let some charlatan's tales guide you in your dealings with me, Marguerite. I credited you with far more sense."

She sucked in a breath, glaring at him, unaccountably hurt. "I'm not foolish," she whispered, her voice low and wounded. "And you needn't scold me like a child. I'm full-grown."

He rubbed a hand over his forehead, looking suddenly weary, but still angry. She marked that at once in the flexing of his jaw. As though he ground his teeth together to cling to his composure.

"I don't want to argue with you. I'm still trying to rid my head of the image of you falling beneath those horses . . ." His voice faded and he sighed deeply, raggedly, pausing as if words were elusive, beyond him.

Her chest felt tight and prickly, watching him.

She'd never seen him so . . . *affected*. He swallowed, his throat working. "When I thought I lost you . . . I don't want to ever feel that way again," he said thickly.

Is that what worried him? She reached for his cheek, hoping to reassure him. He turned his face away and her fingers only grazed his jaw. "You won't. I promise."

He busied himself removing his greatcoat and draping it over her shivering form, and in that moment, in that carriage with him, it didn't matter that he was unable to look her in the eyes, that his face looked carved from granite, that a foreboding quiet hung about him. She told herself it was just because he cared about her. Perhaps he even loved her.

He just didn't know it. Yet.

Chapter 23

He was a bloody fool.

All this time he'd thought his parents' marriage would be the worst fate imaginable. The type of marriage where love soured and turned twisted, descending into a state of constant hostility. The kind of poisonous union that had killed his sister and left him scavenging the streets of St. Giles at an early age.

But even worse than that fate, there loomed another.

Loving and then losing someone to death . . . well, that was a pain he wouldn't face. Not if he could help it.

And he could.

Evidently, falling in love was not something one chose, but *embracing* that love was. As the choice was his, he chose not to embrace what he felt for Marguerite. He knew it would hurt to let her go. Just the thought made his throat squeeze. Yet nothing could hurt him as much as those moments when he watched Marguerite fall beneath slashing hooves.

He'd miss her, long for the yielding heat of her in his bed, the way her eyes softened when she looked at him, but the ache would ebb. Eventually, he'd grow numb. Perhaps even forget her. His chest clenched suddenly at that thought.

Marguerite slept, snoring lightly beside him. She'd scarcely moved since nodding off after the physician Ash had called for examined her and treated her with a small dose of laudanum.

Lying beside her on the bed, he trailed his hand through the cascade of her ink-black hair. Rubbing the tendrils between his fingers, he watched her, memorized every delicate line of her heart-shaped face until a faint blue-gray of dawn tinged the air, seeping into the room beneath the damask drapes.

He knew she believed the risk to herself over, but he didn't believe in fortune-tellers. He didn't believe that one's fate was decided in the dregs left in a teacup. One's fate could not be foreseen. He brushed an ebony strand off her forehead, wincing at the sight of the nasty scrape edging her hairline, so stark against her fair skin. Life was dangerous, full of loss and pain. A diviner didn't need to tell him that.

He'd died inside when those horses reared over Marguerite. The sound of her cries ripped through him, playing through his head still. He doubted he could ever close his eyes and not hear her screams . . . not live in a state of constant unease that he would one day suffer that again. Only worse because the next time she might not survive.

He took her hand and raised it to his lips, marveling at how entangled he'd become with her in so short a time. The slow clatter of carriage wheels sounded below.

Lowering her hand back to the bed, he rose and moved toward the window. He recognized Jack's carriage. A groom helped two women. He recognized Grier at the lead. The other one—smaller and younger—was vaguely familiar from the night he'd stormed Jack's house looking for Marguerite. He slipped quietly from the room, sparing one last glance at Marguerite, still sleeping soundly.

He met the women as they entered the foyer.

Grier fixed her steel-eyed gaze on him. "We came as soon as we heard."

Ash snorted. "Indeed. Ash Courtland rescuing a woman from beneath a carriage. I'm certain it was all over St. Giles."

"Jack wouldn't permit us to call on you last night," Grier complained. "He made plans for us to attend the opera with the Duke of Colbourne. Bloody ass," she muttered.

Ash wasn't certain she referred to her father or the duke, but he didn't inquire. "Marguerite is resting," he informed them. "The doctor assured me she'll be fine."

"Madame Foster was right then," Grier said.

He angled his head dangerously at Grier. "Not you, too," he warned.

"Come now. Don't you find it a coincidence—"

"Yes," he snapped, cutting her off. She sounded too much like Marguerite. "A coincidence. Nothing more."

"Cheerful fellow, aren't you?" Grier asked with a wry twist of her lips.

He swept his gaze over the pair of them. "You're

welcome to wait in the drawing room, but it could be a while."

"We would not wish to overwhelm Marguerite the moment she wakes," the sister who had yet to speak murmured. "We'll call again when she's better. Please let her know we were here."

"You may not find her here," he announced.

Grier blinked. "You've just arrived in Town and you're departing again?"

"I've an estate outside Town that I've paid little mind over the years. The place needs a proper mistress to care for it—"

"You're moving then—"

"No. I'm staying. I still have the gaming hells to oversee here. God knows your father won't see to their operation."

"But you're dumping her in the country?" The younger sister crossed her arms over her chest, dragging them back to the subject of Marguerite. The very subject he wished to avoid.

He stared at the two females. They'd only just met Marguerite, but they behaved like the fiercest of protectors. "It would seem the safest place for her. She'll enjoy it there, away from the dreary City."

"What nonsense is this?" Grier held up a hand in supplication. "You said you love her."

"That bears no significance," he snapped, his face heating with the reminder of his confession. "This is the best thing for Marguerite."

Grier shook her head. "Marguerite is asleep. I wager she has no notion you've made this decision for her. Why don't you ask her when she wakes if she wants to be discarded—"

"Because I know what she wants!" he shouted, tossing his arms wide. "And I can't give her that. I won't go through yesterday all over again. I can't."

The sisters looked alike in that moment. With brown eyes similar to Jack's, they gawked at him in wide-eyed wonder.

Grier looked him up and down with ill-concealed disgust and sneered, "Coward."

"You know nothing of me," he spat. "Or Marguerite for that matter. Sharing blood doesn't make you an instant family, it doesn't make love just magically emerge." He swept his hand toward them in an angry wave.

The young one spoke quietly. "You're absolutely right." She stepped forward, undaunted by his glare or that he towered over her. "Love is something that doesn't happen instantly or easily. But for whatever reason it's happened between you and Marguerite. And you're a fool to throw it away." With a slow exhale, she swept Grier a glance. "I'll wait in the carriage."

Feeling as though she'd taken her reticule and beaten him about the head with it, Ash watched the female he had dismissed as unassuming take her leave. With a weak smile that looked damnably close to pity, Grier followed her.

Ash stared at the door for some moments with a scowl on his face before marching away to his study to write a missive for his housekeeper in the country, informing her of his wife's impending arrival.

"What do you mean I'm going to spend some time in the country? By myself?" Marguerite lowered her fork to her plate, the breakfast she had thus far consumed suddenly rebelling in her stomach. The rasher of bacon that she had so looked forward to sinking her teeth into no longer looked appetizing.

"It's a lovely estate," was Ash's only reply.

He stared at her, so cold-faced and distant where

he stood at the window. She could scarcely stomach to look at him from where she sat propped against pillows, a bed tray over her lap. The damask drapes had been pulled back. He turned away and looked down at the street, his hands clasped behind his back, as if something was occurring below of vast interest.

He looked stark, officious. Every inch the gentleman. Nothing like the scoundrel she'd met on the streets of St. Giles. Nothing like the man who had swept her up into his arms yesterday and looked down at her with such longing and anguish. As though her pain were his own.

Where had that man gone? The man whose face had been the first sight she sought when she woke this morning?

"Where are you going to be while I'm buried in the country?" she asked, unable to mask the quaver in her voice.

He finally looked at her. "I've business to attend here." He must have read something in her face, for he added, "I shall visit, of course."

Was that the way it was to be then? She had escaped death, emerging ready to seize her life with him only to find he had no wish for her presence.

"The house is magnificent, the grounds vast, but it needs a woman's touch. I've neglected it appallingly ever since I won it off some baron two years ago."

She shook her head, bewildered. "Did I do something . . . are you still angry that I visited with Madame Foster—"

"It is not that, Marguerite. I'm not angry with you." He gazed at her with dull eyes. "This is simply the way it has to be."

They way it has to be. He, here, and she in the country.

"I don't understand—"

"I never wanted this."

"What? Me?" She made a low sound in her throat, tossing her head. "Hard to fathom when you abducted me and chased me across England you didn't want this."

"I wanted to marry you, wanted you in my bed, I simply never wanted . . ." His voice faded and he tore his gaze from her.

What?

"It's become complicated, Marguerite. These feelings . . . I never expected them."

He had feelings for her? Her heart raced, beating a mad rhythm against her throat. Hope surged inside her. She propped herself up on the bed. "I have feelings for you, too," she began.

"And that's just it," he said abruptly. "I don't want you to. I can't, I *won't*—" he stopped, shaking his head, and her heart dropped heavily in her chest. She heard everything he wasn't saying, sensed, *felt* his unspoken words like a penetrating wound deep in her bones. He *wouldn't* love her.

Finally, he looked at her again, and the last of her hope withered. His eyes looked empty. Dead.

"Well," she said with a rushed exhale, quickly grasping the tattered remnants of her pride and storing them inside her. "I will strive to be a dutiful wife and please you." Tearing her gaze from his handsome face, she resumed eating. Or at least pretending to eat. She scooted her kipper around her plate. "When shall I leave?"

"Tomorrow. If you feel fit for travel and can pack in that time."

She stabbed the kipper with her fork, hoping he

did not notice the amount of force she used. "I'm fit," she said, her voice tight. "Tomorrow is fine."

"Good," he murmured, moving from the window and striding swiftly from the room.

She stared after him, her heart lodged in her throat, wondering where the Ash she had come to love had gone. Had he ever existed at all?

Chapter 24

Ash stood staring out the window in his dressing room the following morning. A dark sky hung and it felt more like evening than morning. A perfect backdrop to his mood.

Today, he banished his wife to the country, an action certain to earn him her eternal enmity. For the best, he supposed. Hard to love someone who reviled you, and he knew from the hurt in her eyes yesterday that she would soon hate him. A few weeks in isolation at his estate, and it would be a certainty.

With a fist squeezing his heart, he watched as one of the grooms loaded the final trunk, waiting for her to appear. He hadn't seen her since yesterday, burying himself in his office at the Devil's Palace, fearing that if he spent another moment in her company he would relent—break from his purpose and keep her with him forever. However fleeting that may be.

At the sound of the door, he turned, a sinking sensation in his chest telling him who he would find there.

"Marguerite," he murmured as she strolled toward him, something akin to dread beating a staccato in his pulse. Her red cloak swished about her slim ankles, and that simple sight made his mouth water.

He opened his mouth to speak, but she pressed cool fingers to his lips, shaking her head sternly at him.

He held silent, watching her. It was easier to say nothing. Everything had been said between them. Eyes locked with his, she pushed him back onto a chaise at the center of the narrow room with a roughness he had never seen in her.

Ash fell back. She dropped down on her knees before him. Hands sure and fast on his trousers, she freed him, her silken fingers closing around the length of him. He was already hard. He had been since the moment she stepped into the room.

She stroked him up and down with deep, slow pulls.

He groaned. "What are you doing?"

She looked up at him through the dark fan of her lashes. "Making sure you remember me."

Then her head lowered and she took him in her mouth, her soft lips sucking first at the head of him, then all of him, drawing him deep into the warm wet of her mouth. She licked and tasted him until he was bucking, desperately seeking more. He ran his hand over her head, scattering her pins. Her dark hair tumbled over him. Her mouth increased its pressure, working faster until he was begging, grinding his teeth against the incredible sensation.

Then she stopped.

He blinked, his desire-clouded vision watching her as she rose to her feet before him. For a panicked moment, he thought she was leaving. Her hands flattened on his chest and sent him backward on the chaise. Lifting her cloak and skirts, she climbed atop him. Her fingers found his cock and guided him to her sweet heat. She glided the tip of him against her folds, back and forth, back and forth, teasing him at her opening until he was pleading and groaning again, his hands digging into her hips through layers of clothing.

At last, she seated herself fully on him, sinking down with a breathy sigh. Her slick flesh surrounded him, clenching and wringing him in blissful agony.

She took his hands and placed them on her breasts. Her own hands fell to his chest and she leveraged herself, working her hips over him, setting a steady pace, pumping slow and deep over him.

Fondling her breasts through her dress, he tried to rouse her into quickening her pace, desperate to end his torment.

"Marguerite," he begged.

If anything, she slowed her movements, the tight, dragging sensation of her body on his too much. A hissing breath escaped him as she ground down on him and then held herself still, unmoving save for the flexing of her inner muscles around his cock.

He tightened his hold on her hips, prepared to toss her on her back and finish what she had begun.

Her voice stopped him, hard and firm in a way he had never heard. "No. This is my game."

She stared down at him, her delicate jaw locked

hard, determined, the fire glowing in her whiskey eyes more than passion . . . more than lust.

With a nod, he loosened his hands on her hips and thrust his hips up. Her hands pressed harder on his chest, stopping even that effort on his part. She angled her head in warning at him and tormented him with another delicious squeeze around his cock.

He stroked her breasts, found her nipples through the fabric and circled them. Her breath hitched. Gratified, hoping to rouse her into losing control, he tweaked the tips until they were hard points prodding her bodice.

With a slow moan, she released herself, gave herself to him, pushing her body over his again and again, building to a furious, violent pace. His body burned, every nerve stretched, bordering on pleasure and pain.

He clenched his teeth, fighting the need pounding through him, begging to burst free.

Her scream undid him, followed by the sudden drop of her body, sinking deep, quivering all around him.

He pushed up into her sucking warmth, claiming her one last time, bursting from the inside out until he saw spots.

She draped over him, her milk and honey fragrance heady and intoxicating. He smoothed a hand over her jet tresses, silk through his fingers. He was still smiling, dazed, enjoying the aftermath when she pulled herself free of him.

Standing, she straightened her clothing with cool efficiency. He watched, marveling that this composed creature was the woman of moments ago who had made love to him with such abandon. She scooped up a few pins scattered upon the chaise, not even looking at him. It was as if he were no longer in the room at all.

"Marguerite," he began, having no idea what he wanted to say.

She looked at him then, her eyes dull and vacant, more brown than gleaming whiskey. "Yes?" she asked, hardly pausing before adding with a ring of finality, "I have a carriage waiting."

For a moment he thought he saw a flicker of some emotion, something, cross her eyes. But then she was gone, without a farewell, her tread a parting whisper across the carpet.

Moving to the window, he waited for her to

emerge. When she did, he waited for her to look up, toward the room where she knew she had left him. Every fiber of his body pulsed, leaning forward as though he would dive through the glass to reach her. If she would only look at him, mouth his name . . .

His will was insignificant right now. His body weak and broken from her use of him. But that had been her purpose. His mouth pressed into a grim line. She had wanted to ruin him, punish him, leave a mark on him, a permanent imprint.

Foolish female. A corner of his lip curled. Didn't she know she already had?

With a grim heart, he turned from the window, no longer willing to see if she turned and looked for him or not. It didn't matter.

The rain broke free from the skies. Not that its arrival came as any surprise. The winds had been howling for some time, and the air rumbled dark and foreboding outside the carriage. She had ceased peeking out the window, unwilling to let the cold and wet inside with her.

Marguerite felt a twinge of pity for the driver and groom suffering outside in the cold downpour. If

Ash had not been in such a hurry to be rid of her, he might have waited for a more promising day.

She smoothed a hand over her skirts and inhaled a deep breath, instantly detecting *his* familiar scent on her. She doubted she would ever be rid of it, even after she'd changed garments and bathed. He'd always be there, in her head, her blood, her skin.

The carriage picked up speed and she guessed London had fallen behind. She reached for the strap to steady herself on the seat. In this weather, she wished the driver would take more care, even if they were now on less-crowded roads.

A crack of thunder shook the earth and Marguerite jumped, her heart skipping to her throat at the sudden crash of sound. She shivered, unable to recall the last time she'd been caught in a thunderstorm . . . especially the likes of the one that raged outside the walls of her carriage.

She scooted to the center of her seat and settled more snugly into the squabs, desperate to warm herself. As if she would find some sort of reassurance in being warm and cozy in her carriage whilst a storm raged inches away. Unbidden, a voice floated across her mind. *I see a carriage, wheels*

turning, rolling so fast . . . horses scream. It's raining.
Thundering.

Thunder. How had she forgotten Madame Foster's mention of thunder? There had been no thunder the day the carriage nearly ran her down in St. Giles.

Her heart pounded hard in her chest, making it difficult to breathe.

She replayed the rest of Madame Foster's prophecy, searching for an inconsistency, proof that she was wrong to suspect . . .

Ash! Ash was not here. He had sent her away. Madame Foster said Ash was with her at the end. There was no chance of having the accident Madame Foster described. Not now. Not with her husband safe and sound, miles away in London.

Chapter 25

Not one hour after Marguerite's departure, Ash saddled his mount and fell in hard pursuit of his wife.

As he rode out, thunder cracked in the distance and he winced, pulling the collar of his great coat up around his face.

Hopefully, she would forgive him. He hadn't needed much time with his thoughts or solitude to realize he had made a colossal mistake. Putting Marguerite away from him only drove home how desperately he loved her. Distance and time between them wouldn't change that.

Hopefully, the fact that she wouldn't even sleep one night alone at his estate might absolve him in her eyes.

Whatever the case, he would not let fear keep them apart another day. He would make amends and show her his love. In time, perhaps she would grow to love him, too.

At the driver's shout, Marguerite scrambled to the window. Heedless of the rain and wind lashing like needles into her face, she peered outside.

"What is it?" she called up, fearing her voice was lost in the storm.

Fortunately, the driver's voice was not. His loud bellow rang out with terrible clarity. "Highwayman!"

Marguerite whipped her head to look behind them. Dread tightened her chest. Through the hazy rain, she made out the lone horseman. Much of him was indistinguishable. She could only identify a dark-swathed shape crouched low over a mount. He rode hell-bent after them, shouting something, but the words were lost in the roar of rain and wind. Just the same, she imagined she heard his ominous threats. *Stand and deliver? Your money or your life?*

A terrible chill chased down her spine. The carriage lurched forward, increasing its already furious speed. She dropped back inside the carriage, swiping a gloved hand at her dripping face as she was tossed about like a marble inside a box.

She glanced around wildly as though a weapon languished in the confines of the carriage, waiting to be snatched up for just such an event.

Then her world turned over. The carriage rolled. Her shoulder struck a wall, then her back smacked the ceiling. She screamed, her hands groping, clawing for something, anything to hold on to. She rolled, spun like a child's toy inside the constantly spinning space. Bile rose in her throat. She bit it back, swallowed. Fought the hot swell of panic.

Then, everything stilled. The carriage stopped, seemed to hang on the edge of a precipice. Horses screamed, whinnied wildly over the clap of thunder.

Adrenaline pumped through her blood, numbing her to the cold. She panted heavily, her knuckles white and bloodless where they clutched the wall. Several wet strands of hair hung in her face. The dark pieces of hair fluttered with her every exhalation. She swiped at them to better see and take measure of her situation.

It wasn't good. The conveyance had somehow turned on its side. She was sprawled on the inside wall of the carriage, the door above her head. The carriage wobbled suddenly, moaning like the storming winds, and she sobbed a gaspy breath, fingers clinging tighter, knowing it wasn't over. She wasn't safe yet.

Wood creaked, groaned as the carriage tottered. Deciding she couldn't remain inside, she sucked in a breath and stretched a trembling hand for the door above her head. Her thin, wet fingers stretched long as she tentatively rose to her feet, afraid to upset the carriage's precarious balance.

The horses' screams had quieted to panicked whinnies. Where was the driver? The groom? The *highwayman*?

Her thoughts for them all abruptly fled. She screamed as the carriage shifted, plunged down with a shattering force that sent her crashing into the wall.

At impact, her vision grayed, edges blurring to black. Stunned, her body ached. She shook her head to stay awake, to move, to act.

The roaring in her ears altered. Became something else. Not the storm. Not the crush of adrenaline. Blinking, she shrieked as water rushed inside the carriage, penetrating every crack, seen and unseen.

Tears, burning-hot at the back of her throat, choked her as she struggled to rise. The water, black and thick as the pond she used to throw rocks in as a child, overcame her, sucking her down, eating up her body with a speed that she could not fight.

She tilted her face to the ceiling above her. The door seemed so far staring down at her. She reached a hand for it, a single cry reverberating through her heart.

Ash.

Ash vaulted off his mount before the horse ever came to a full stop. His boots sank ankle deep into the mire that was once a road.

"Mr. Courtland!" His driver shouted from the side of the road where he had been thrown, waving an arm weakly for him. "I thought you were a highwayman!"

Ash didn't bother to comment that facing a highwayman would have been a less dangerous prospect than crashing the carriage.

His groom was already to the bridge where the carriage went over. *With Marguerite in it.* He sprinted to join him, his heart in his throat, two words a mantra rolling through his head. *Not her. Not her.* The screaming horses thrashed in the water, fighting to keep their heads up, fighting to pull the carriage from the depths of the stream.

"Should I cut their reins?" the groom cried.

And let the carriage sink deeper? "No!" he shouted the instant before jumping over the small brick wall.

The shock of icy-cold affected him little, didn't stop or slow him from diving beneath the opaque water. The carriage was easy enough to locate. Every second seemed to crawl until he located the door, however. Until his fingers closed around the latch and wrested it open.

Lungs afire, he reached within, his arm sweeping wide, fingers clawing through lightless water, brushing something soft. The silkiest of seaweed grazed his fingertips.

Exulted, he kicked himself closer and pulled Marguerite up by a fistful of hair. Her limp body tumbled into his arms. The seconds stretched, felt like forever before he broke the surface and dragged freezing air deep into his constricted lungs.

He swam to the water's edge, shouting at his servants for their clothes—anything to warm her.

Emerging, he carried Marguerite a few feet before dropping down and lowering her to the ground. The sight of her gray face, her lips a chalky blue, struck terror to his heart.

"Don't be dead. Don't be dead. Don't be dead." Air blew from his lips like hot steam as he choked out this new mantra.

He rolled her to her side and pounded her back with fierce whacks. Water dribbled past her lips, but he had no idea if that was enough. He flipped her to her back again and pressed an ear to her chest. Nothing. Not a sound. Not a movement.

"Marguerite, no!" He pushed on her chest, not really knowing what he was doing, but knowing he had to get her slight chest to rise and fall with breaths. "Sweetheart, breathe! Breathe!" he shouted, pumping his hands over her chest again and again, willing it to move, to rise. Willing her to live!

Still, no sign of life. She didn't stir.

A great sob built in his chest as he grabbed

her icy-slick cheeks in his hands. Holding her face close to his, he pressed his lips to hers, half-kissing, half-blowing his breath into her parted mouth. Willing her to take his own air, willing her to live, to *be* again.

"Please, Marguerite." His voice broke against her frozen lips, tore and twisted into a sound he had never heard from himself. Not even when his sister died. Raw, ugly sobs burst from his lips, pulled from some place deep and forgotten, never touched before. "Please, Marguerite. I love you."

The sound of her name on Ash's lips washed through her, tugging, pulling in a strange way. Consciousness returned gradually.

Marguerite looked down and knew the sight should have confused her, panicked her, but a great calmness filled her. A lightness. A peace she had never known.

It was done.

It had come to pass as Madame Foster said. Ash had somehow found her. He was over her, holding her . . . with her at the end. Only it wasn't *her* anymore.

She hovered above herself, above Ash. Floating

weightless, free. No longer cold. No longer afraid. A great warmth suffused her. And yet even in her warm, tranquil state, she could not fight her sadness as she stared down at Ash clutching her sodden, mud-soaked body.

His whispered words reached her. "Marguerite, I love you."

How she longed for those words in life.

He wept, his great shoulders shuddering. His sobs scraped the air, the sound raw and ugly. She never thought Ash capable of tears. Tears for her.

She wished she could tell him to stop, reassure him. She wished she could whisper her love for him in his ear, but it was too late.

The light grew, swelled in a warming puddle all around her, lifting her, floating her higher . . . moving her away.

Marguerite. She heard her name. Not from Ash but another source. It wasn't spoken. Not like sound passing over lips. The voice spoke her name again, a stroking caress to her soul.

She wasn't alone on whatever unearthly plane she found herself. In the bright light, her mother stood, as young and beautiful as she remembered.

Mama?

They embraced. Held in her mother's arms, Marguerite felt like a small child again. Safe and happy in a way that only innocent youth can feel. Contentment swelled through her. And yet there was still that clinging sadness: pervasive and deep, it filled her heart. She couldn't help but pull away, drift back down from the light, from the love she felt in that glow—in her mother's arms.

Marguerite's gaze sought Ash again. He still hadn't given up. Clutching her shell of a body, he tried to blow his own breath into her, revive her, bring her back to him.

Love for him coursed through her, eclipsing everything else, every blissful emotion she felt in the wondrous light.

Ash continued his plea, calling her name. Each cry tugged at her, pulled her spirit back toward him . . . toward life.

Unable to resist, she faced her mother again. *Mama, I have to go back.*

Her mother's beatific face smiled down at her. *I know, Marguerite. His love is strong—it pulls you. And you want to go.*

She already felt herself slipping away, returning, the warm glow veiling her ebbing and fading like smoke.

We'll be together someday, Marguerite. Go now. He's calling you.

Her mother's face vanished with the light then, her words ringing through Marguerite as she was sucked back into herself. Into the burning cold, into the pain of her battered body.

Back to the living—to Ash's arms.

Marguerite's body jerked to life in his arms. She released a choked breath, murky water sputtering from her colorless lips.

"Marguerite!" Ash shouted, hauling her into his arms and hugging her as though he would never let her go. And he wouldn't. Not again.

"Easy, love," she chided, her voice a dry croak in his ear.

He loosened his arms, pulling her back so that he could stare into her face and assure himself that she lived and breathed and spoke. That she was not in fact lost from him and he had not recreated her in his mind as a result of his grief.

"Marguerite, I'm so sorry."

He grasped her chilled hand, guiding it to his face. She pressed a palm to his raspy cheek, curving her fingers to his face, her look achingly tender.

"You came back," he choked.

"Of course." A tremulous smile shook her lips. "You brought me back."

Epilogue

The following Christmas . . .

Long after everyone had retired to their rooms for the evening, Marguerite left her husband naked in their bed, pausing to admire the taut curve of his backside before she skulked downstairs. Slipping on her dressing gown, she crept silently from the room, Ash's gift wrapped prettily in her hands. She'd visited every watchmaker in Town to find Ash the perfect timepiece, and she couldn't wait to see his face when he unwrapped it in the morning.

Entering the drawing room, she approached the nativity scene she'd arranged upon a bed of holly near the hearth. Presents were already grouped around the little scene. The sight of all the lovely packages warmed her heart, made her think of all the blessings she had in her life beneath this very roof. A husband who adored her. Fallon and Evie and their families asleep upstairs. This Christmas, she had everything she ever wanted. A loving husband, a splendid home, her closest friends together with her. *Life*.

Squatting to position her gift among the others, she froze. The nativity no longer consisted of the three figures Ash had crafted for her a year ago in Scotland. Indeed not. A full set of figurines spread out over her bed of holly. Three wise men, a shepherd—even several barn animals. Nothing was forgotten. All matched the original Mary, Joseph, and baby Jesus—clearly fashioned from the same hand. Most beautiful of all was the angel with its delicate fan of wings. Tears clogged her throat as she touched a fingertip to one wing.

"I promised you I would finish them for you before our next Christmas."

Marguerite whirled around at the deep voice.

Ash approached, his dressing robe belted loosely, revealing the broad expanse of his muscular chest. The sight still tied her up in knots.

She glanced back at the nativity. "My next Christmas," she whispered, remembering how she had not thought to be here. Elation swelled in her chest . . . and love. A love for him that, incredibly, was even greater tonight than on that day he pulled her from the submerged carriage. *When his love pulled her from death.*

"I heard you sneak down here. I had to follow you. I wanted to see your face."

"Ash, they're beautiful. When did you find the time . . . without me catching you?" They spent so much time together. When he visited his gaming hells—something he didn't do nearly as much anymore—he often brought her with him, appreciating her input and inviting her involvement in the business.

His lips twisted wryly as he pulled her flush against him. "I had to do something while you were visiting all those watchmakers."

She gasped. "You knew!"

He grinned wickedly. "I know *everything*."

She knocked a fist against his shoulder. "Not everything."

His grin faded and he dipped his head, his mouth brushing her lips. "I know you're the best thing that ever happened to me. I know I couldn't have stolen a better bride." He kissed her so hard her knees grew weak. "And," he murmured against her lips, "I know I love you."

She fanned her fingers against his cheek. "I love you, too."

A slow smile spread out over his face. "I know that, too."

Taking his hand, she watched his face as she pressed it to her belly. "But you didn't know about this."

Next month, don't miss these exciting new love stories only from Avon Books

Wedding of the Season by Laura Lee Guhrke

Lady Beatrix Danbury always knew she'd marry William Mallory. So when he left England for the chance of a lifetime mere days before their wedding, Beatrix was heartbroken. Six years later, she's finally forgotten the wretch and is poised to make a splendid new match. Then William suddenly returns, and all the old feelings come rushing back...but is it too late?

Whisper Falls by Toni Blake

Following a failed career as an interior designer, Tessa Sheridan is forced to return home to make ends meet. A sexy bad boy neighbor who makes her feel weak and breathless is the last thing she needs...

Eternal Prey by Nina Bangs

Seeking vengeance for his brother's murder, Utah plans to vanquish all of his immortal enemies. Now that the beast within him is unleashed, he won't stop until every vampire is destroyed. But when he meets their beautiful, bewitching and mortal leader, Lia, they fall into a love that could prove dangerous for the both of them...

Sin and Surrender by Julia Latham

Paul Hilliard wants nothing to do with the League of the Blade—the secret, elite organization that raised him. But when he's offered a mission to save king and country, he can't refuse. Paul just never imagined his greatest challenge would be Juliana, the stunning warrior assigned as his partner for this task...

Visit www.AuthorTracker.com for exclusive information on your favorite HarperCollins authors.

REL 1210

Available wherever books are sold or please call 1-800-331-3761 to order.

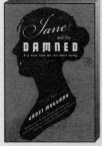

*At Avon Books, we know your passion
for romance—once you finish one of our
novels, you find yourself wanting more.*

May we tempt you with . . .

- **Excerpts** from our upcoming releases.

- Entertaining **extras**, including authors'
  personal photo albums and book lists.

- Behind-the-scenes **scoop** on your favorite
  characters and series.

- **Sweepstakes** for the chance to win free books,
  romantic getaways, and other fun prizes.

- Writing **tips** from our authors and editors.

- **Blog** with our authors and find out why they
  love to write romance.

- **Exclusive content** that's not contained
  within the pages of our novels.

Join us at
www.avonbooks.com

An Imprint of HarperCollins*Publishers*
www.avonromance.com

Available wherever books are sold or please call 1-800-331-3761 to order.

FTH 0708